Silent Crusade

By Richard Cozicar

Silent Crusade

Richard Cozicar

Calgary, Alberta, Canada

www.Richardcozicar.com

Copyright © – 2016 Richard Cozicar

First Edition - 2016

ISBN

978-0-9950946-2-8 (Hardcover)

978-0-9950946-1-1 (Paperback)

978-0-9950946-0-4 (eBook)

1. Mystery, Thriller

Richard Cozicar

Richard Cozicar

Author

Contact Information:

Twitter: @RichardCozicar

www.facebook.com/RichardCozicar

richardcozicar@gmail.com

www.richardcozicar.com

Silent Crusade

To my wife Laura

For over thirty-five years you have stood by
my side with words of encouragement.

Thank You

Chapter 1

The sidewalks in downtown Toronto were streaming with people as the business day in Canada's largest city came to an end. Office workers fled their cubicles and corner offices, rode elevators and escalators away from the daily grind and flooded out of the concrete towers to join in the afternoon rush outside.

Thousands of men and women thankful for the end of the workday were now working their way toward their ride home so they could enjoy the beautiful spring evening. It was the middle of May in Southern Ontario, and the daytime temperature was already hovering around the mid-twenties. Outdoor patios quickly filled as workers exchanged spreadsheets and desk chairs for menus and a seat at a patio table where they could relax and enjoy their favourite beverages.

Those who longed for the sanctity of their suburban homes joined the torrent of sidewalk traffic and drained down the concrete steps into the subway station where they fought against the rising tides of fellow commuters then patiently waited for the next available train to take them far from downtown. The platforms in the tunnels filled to overflowing with every passing minute. The trains scheduled one after the other with five or six cars to a unit. As fast as one pulled out the next would arrive, and people wedged themselves in for the ride home.

A young couple with their two small children stood near the front of the queue poised to climb on a train that slowly eased up to the loading area. The train had just arrived but was already near capacity with people from previous stops. With the small children's hands held securely, the young couple playfully avoided departing commuters as they squeezed through the open doors. The little family still exuberant from their big trip into the teeming city, the children excitedly talking about all the sites they had visited that day.

Jostling the young family from behind came a group of sharply dressed businessmen, Bay Street types. The group of mid twenty something financial interns had only enough room to enter the car behind the family and were forced to huddle together tight against the train doors while some of their co-workers lagged behind shoving and bumping other commuters aside trying to board the same train.

Silent Crusade

The Bay Street workers moved with arrogance and lack of respect that depicted convoluted thoughts of self-entitlement to be placed ahead of others because of their important jobs on Bay Street. The ticker watchers were unable to fathom the unyielding response from the other commuters who refused to move aside for them, the egos of these young up and coming financial gurus bolstered their attitudes in a skewed self-justification about the rudeness they displayed to the other subway commuters.

The second set of suits hesitated at the open car doors long enough for a burka-clad woman to slide around them and stuff herself into the last crevice of room remaining before the cars doors slid shut. The men stood at the front of an ever-growing crush of people that pooled outside the doors, forced to wait for the next train.

The packed rail car doors slid shut, and the train started its slow crawl away from the platform. A short blast of the train's whistle served as the only warning followed by the grind of steel wheels on an iron track.

A couple of feet into its journey the side of the train car erupted in a massive explosion. In an instant, the people packed tight against the inside doors, and closest to the epicentre of the bombing perished, long before their brains had a chance to register the bright flash and searing pain brought on by the blast. They were the lucky ones.

The passengers packed deeper in the car were not as fortunate. The outward force of the explosion intensified by the heat and shrapnel moved like a wave radiating from the doors and through the unsuspecting passengers. The train car rocked violently on the tracks. Simultaneously the side of the car facing the platform exploded outward in a tsunami of flames, scorched air and flying debris both metal and human. The shock wave from the bomb tossed the stacked throngs of commuters backward in a domino-like action.

Before the deafening reverberations of the blast had died down screams of pain and fear started gradually then reached a loud crescendo adding a bizarre soundtrack to the ethereal scene happening underground. There were only a few seconds of suspended disbelief before the chaos spread throughout the long subway tunnel.

The commuters crowded on the platform closest to the epicentre of the explosion that were able to move rushed from area of the smoking wreckage and stampeded over fellow passengers as they scrambled for the stairs leading out of the tunnel. Hundreds of disoriented and frightened travellers stumbled around in

2

the now flickering emergency lights and met a wall of arriving patrons blocking their escape.

As the realization of what had happened started to make its way throughout the subway tunnel, countless numbers of other commuters joined in the crush of people. Human carnage marked a bloody trail of retreat across the platform first by pieces of the fragmented train car driven into the bodies by the explosion and then by the stampeding hoards of commuters racing for the exit.

The adjoining subway cars laid as twisted wrecks on the tracks. A chorus of wailing and frightened screams joined the smoke and flames rising in the air. The passengers closest to the explosion died instantly, but they were a small percentage of the impacted people.

The solid wall of people packed on the subway platform immediately in front of the exploding car and in the two adjacent cars received the brunt of the damage by the outward force as broken glass, and other debris hurled their way.

A thick, black, toxic cloud of smoke followed on the heals of the river of commuters rushing up the stairs leading out of the tunnel to the street above. Pedestrians on the sidewalks stopped to gawk at the scene that was unfolding, cell phone cameras by the hundreds appeared to document every minute of the calamity.

The people in the patios and on the streets above the subway station thought that an earthquake had struck Toronto. Drinks shook and sloshed over the tops of glasses onto the packed patio tables while the workers who remained in the surrounding office towers ducked under their desks for protection as their offices swayed and trembled.

Within minutes of the explosion the emergency lines at the 911 call centers were inundated with hysterical people phoning in about the blast. The switchboards quickly started to overload as operators tried to piece together what the rash of excited callers was reporting: some callers were crying, others yelling in panic.

Soon cooler heads with years of training at the call centre prevailed, notifying first responders. The police were called to shut down the streets; the fire departments and EMS were dispatched to help the wounded and on their heels came the news cameras. An attack of this sort had never happened in Canada before...BREAKING NEWS...Stop the presses...

The arrival of the local police was heralded with the wailing of sirens as they fought to clear the busy street of traffic and dazed commuters to allow the fire department and the paramedics' access to the area. Fire trucks arrived seconds after the police, the magnitude of the catastrophe demanded all departments from across the city be sent to help with the evacuation of the tunnel. Emergency responders from outlying suburbs made their way through the town toward the train station, the sounds of sirens and honking horns filled the air. Every hospital in the Greater Toronto area was put on standby and told to prepare for the onslaught of wounded.

*****

John Beener, a twenty-five year veteran with the fire department was one of the first to arrive on the scene and enter the damaged train tunnel. In all his years of service, he figured he had seen every kind of human tragedy there was to witness, many of the memories remaining with him would always steal sleep from him at night. He had grown as acclimated as one could be in this line of work so as to not go crazy.

Without hesitation, he rushed into the tunnel swimming against the tide of commuters desperately struggling to make their way out. He paused at the bottom of the stairs to survey the damage; the flickering lights, horrifying screams, and clouds of thick smoke greeted him as he got his bearings. The lights in the tunnel flickered off and on adding a strobe effect, the macabre scene flashing before his eyes. Thankful for the mask on his face he slowly made his way through the dense black smoke, his head swinging left and right as he took in the horror of the whole scene.

He fought his way to the train car closest to the entrance and pried open the bent doors freeing the trapped commuters. As other emergency crews caught up with him and offered their help, John continued to work his way to the centre car. There was a huge hole blown in the side of this car. Several dead bodies lay stacked on the floor inside, small fires still burning on the clothing on some of the bodies. He was once again thankful for the mask he was wearing; the smell of burnt flesh would be atrocious.

John carefully stepped among the bodies in his search for the injured. He waded farther into the carnage slowly checking for survivors amongst the

4

jumble of limbs and debris. Noticing a movement Beener stopped and reached down to grab the hand of a young woman. Just as his hand gripped her arm, he lost his balance and started to stumble. Catching himself, he quickly straightened up then on steady feet he looked down at his hand. In it was a ladies arm, her hand still gripping the hand of a small child.

Twenty-five years on the force and he figured he had seen it all...well not entirely...John's brain shut down...he was frozen on the spot...he was barely breathing. When he was finally able to move, he opened his hand letting the arm fall, left the damaged car and walked down the platform past the other train cars.

With trembling hands he pulled his breathing mask and helmet off and leaned over the side of the platform. The lunch he had enjoyed a short time ago came gushing out of his mouth as his stomach heaved again and again. Without even bothering to wipe his face he sat down, a vacant look in his eyes and proceeded to cry. Twenty-five years of faithful service...ended.

*****

Help poured into the area all through the afternoon well into the night and into next day. Cities close to the disaster area sent all the available responders they could spare to help out. It was late the next day before all the bodies were removed either to the hospitals or makeshift morgues. While the emergency workers were attending to the wounded, investigators from the R.C.M.P. and CSIS roamed the wreckage and worked alongside the local police in search of clues.

In the city attending a business conference the Canadian Prime Minister, Darren Reynolds was notified of the subway bombing. With little in the way of an apology he left the meeting and rushed to the site of the tragedy. Surrounded by his protection detail, he exited his car and stood amongst the responders and the wounded, mesmerized by the unthinkable act of terror.

The Prime Minister ignored the advice from his protection detail and rolled up his sleeves to assist the first responders as the wounded were evacuated from the tunnel. Through words of comfort, he consoled and reassured the victims. His job as Prime Minister was to ensure the safety of the citizens of this country, they had elected him to the job, and he had let them down. Now it would be up to him to right this wrong.

Deeply saddened by the leagues of wounded and terrified commuters he remained among the victims and the emergency workers supporting the victims and praising the rescuers. Time and again he paused and surveyed the carnage...each time his anger rose...he became furious...mad as hell... He wanted every law enforcement agency in the country working on this; he wanted answers, and he wanted them fast.

There would be no rest for the agencies working this tragedy and there would be no hiding for the terrorist cowards who caused this. By God, he would find them. The investigators would have every tool at their disposal; Parliament would bring in new bills allowing the police services greater access to information to aid the investigation and no law enforcement agency in this country would rest or be allowed to forget this heinous, cowardly act until all the perpetrators faced justice.

His next step he decided was to gather together his defence advisors and military leaders to discuss and formulate a plan for preparing and securing the country against any further attacks. He didn't care how many law enforcement officers it took, all the usual suspects would be watched that much closer, and he dared the opposition to question the money needed for such an enormous task. He would tear them apart on the Parliament floor if he had to!

One of the first things he meant to do when he was back at his office was to call his close ally south of the border, the President of the United States. It was the time they had another serious talk about ending this rabble coming out of the Middle East, the constant threats, the attacks on other allied countries and now this. The cowards want to hide behind masks and women and children while they spread their terror around the globe, it was about time they got their due. The conversation would include the use of bombs, not building or city-destroying bombs; country-destroying bombs would be the only way to send a clear enough message.

He had already been in heated discussions with leaders from other allied countries that had suffered the same fate he was now witnessing. Several of the allied leaders were currently pressuring the U.S. President to up the size and scale of the defensive the Western World was deploying against terrorism in the Middle East. The States led the fight and had the kind of bombs that were needed, the rest of the countries didn't.

*****

The terrorist attack on Toronto was the third such attack of its kind in as many months. Two months prior England suffered an attack of the same magnitude and only a month before that France reeled after a deadly series of bombings that had crippled the country leaving the French people mourning for their dead and wounded. The whole western world was furious at the escalated attacks that had taken place, and now Canada was added to that list.

The Prime Minister was now more resolute than ever to add his voice and the full support of the nation to back Canada's allies, determined to stop the spread of this terrorist plague by taking the fight back to the terrorist's front door and stomping it out at its source.

The bombing missions and the other feeble attempts by the allied forces that were used to try and stem the spread of terrorism had so far failed; the time had come to drop bombs that catch the terrorist's attention, bombs starting in the N-class. Time to get serious and end the threat once and for all. The American weapons were designed to solve problems like this, and past events proved that they weren't afraid to pull the big boys out and use them.

Silent Crusade

Chapter 2

Before Brand walked onto the airplane in Saskatoon, he dialled Sara's phone number. He had been out of phone service for a week now and was looking forward to hearing her voice. They hadn't gone this long without speaking since she moved to Calgary the previous fall and although he would never admit it to anyone, he missed her and was eager to talk to her.

His phone rang several times then went to her voice mail. He decided against leaving a message. He would be back in Calgary in a couple of hours, and he could talk to her then.

He boarded the plane and found his seat, fastened his seatbelt and stared out the window. He was looking forward to sleeping in his bed once again, but the first thing he wanted on arrival was a quick shave and shower and hopefully a late supper date with Sara. After spending the past week in the remote fishing camp, he realized he was now ready to get back to the city life. He nestled in his seat while the airplane taxied down the runway.

As a retired CSIS officer turned fishing guide, Brand took advantage of the opportunity to visit new locations in Canada and check out the fishing. When some of the other guides he had befriended throughout the years suggested he join them on a fly-in trip to a remote lodge on Lake Athabasca, he jumped at the chance. It was early June, and the ice was just coming off the massive lake. The lodge the group stayed at was located on the Saskatchewan side of the lake and that far north in that province always had excellent fishing.

Brand enjoyed these types of exploration trips largely because of the contrast to what he considered his previous life. The chance to relax in guest cabins constructed of canvas and heated by wood stoves, to fall asleep every night exhausted from reeling in the vast numbers of fish made the rigours of city life disappear. The winter-starved fish driven into a feeding frenzy by the spring runoff were not shy about biting the hand tied flies they were offered.

During this trip, three fly rods were broken bringing the huge fish to the boats. Fly reels had spun out of control as the large Lakers ran for the depths whenever they were hooked, battering knuckles. No fishing stories were needed, the fish here exceeded even the most colourful storytellers expectations. In all his years of fishing, Brand had never seen fish of this size or the numbers the group caught. What could be a better way to spend your days? If there was something else, Brand didn't know what it was.

The only thing more pleasing than the fishing were the gourmet meals served at the lodge. The food was plentiful, the service top rate. The guys that accompanied Brand to the camp combined with the guides and the staff from the lodge made the trip one he would remember for years to come. It was the complete opposite life from what he lived as a CSIS agent; the main reason Brand had taken the trip.

Now the trip back to civilization seemed to take forever. In retracing the flights from the lodge time appeared to drag. The departing band of fishermen had to wait at Stony Rapids after returning on the floatplane. The charter back to Saskatoon wouldn't arrive for a couple more hours. The plane schedule into the remote parts of the country was more limited than in the bigger cities.

Once in Saskatoon, he had to wait again for a connecting flight to Calgary. Deep-rooted instincts made him anticipate every move, never resting, always ready for action. That wasn't his life anymore he had to keep reminding himself, just have to sit back and relax.

He leaned deep into the seat and reflected on the trip. On the way to the lodge, he was full of the wonder of the stories he had heard from the other guides of the size and numbers of fish. Now that the trip was almost over he felt a certain sense of loss. As much as he wanted to get home he still hated having to leave, and this was a trip he would have to do again.

He smirked. For a second, he thought about asking Sara to join him, but then he remembered whom he was talking about knowing full well Sara hated the outdoors. She would not enjoy the pristine surroundings, and besides, the Wi-Fi was horrible, she'd never make it.

With his head resting against the back of his seat, he found his mind traveling between the two thoughts. He closed his eyes and made himself comfortable for the flight home.

*****

The plane's tires touching down on the tarmac in Calgary jarred Brand awake. Rubbing the sleep from his eyes, he gazed out the small window at the sky dark with clouds, a light rain giving the runway a wet glossy sheen. Turning his cell phone on, Brand readied himself for deplaning while the aircraft taxied to a stop at the terminal and the stewardess opened the cabin door, welcoming everyone to Calgary.

The temperature was currently fifteen degrees with rain; the flight attendant announced over the intercom as the passengers stood up to collect their luggage from the overhead compartments. Brand stood up to join the fray grabbing the two fly rods he had stored overhead then held them by his side as he stood in line with the other passengers waiting to exit.

The airport concourse was crowded as he walked through the terminal to the luggage carousel. Brand stepped away from the other passengers while he pulled his phone out of his pocket and checked its messages to see if Sara had returned his calls while he was in flight. Nothing. He'd call her again when he reached his truck.

Outside the terminal, Brand walked over to wait for the shuttle bus that would return him to the lot where he had left his truck. He stepped off the bus and stood beside his truck, dug out his phone and tried Sara again, straight to voice mail.

That's odd he thought to himself as he threw his fishing gear into the cab of the truck and climbed in after it. He had never known Sara not to have her phone close. He would try calling her again once he reached his house.

The trip from the airport to his house was a good thirty minutes if traffic cooperated. He merged onto the Deerfoot and drove straight south finding that rush hour traffic had nearly ended. At Southland, it bottlenecked briefly but continued at a rapid crawl, and then the rest of the way to the house the traffic remained light.

Pulling into the back alley, Brand pulled slightly past his garage, stuck the truck in reverse and backed into the garage. He removed the fishing gear from the back seat and set it on a shelf in the garage before he walked into the house.

Brand sauntered around the interior of his house and opened the windows to let a breeze blow through. The air smelled stale, the result of the house being sealed tight for the past week. The rush of air stirring up dust as it chased out the stale air.

He took his phone in hand and dialed Sara's number again. Still no answer as his call went straight to voicemail. He stared at the phone for a second. Shower first he decided as he climbed the stairs and then he'd drive over to Sara's.

Chapter 3

Freshly showered, Brand wiped the fogged mirror clear and stared at his reflection. His brown hair bleached by the early June sun and the shadows under his eyes were a little more prominent than the week before caused by the late nights drinking and talking and the early mornings on the lake with a rod in his hand.

The skin on his thin face was darker now from the sun that had reflected off the water, his face sporting a week's growth of beard. His spirits lifted as he applied the shaving cream and then carefully guided the razor blade as the grizzled facial hair fell away.

He whistled as he buttoned his shirt and climbed back down the stairs to call Sara one more time. Again, straight to voice mail. His refreshed feeling now interrupted by a tinge of concern. She's just busy he told himself as he picked up his truck keys, grabbed a coat and walked out the door.

The traffic seemed heavier now than it had been when he was driving home. He merged onto the busy Deerfoot driving north to the Sara's house in Fairview, a little north, and west of where Brand lived. Frustration was starting to build inside him; he had never known Sara to ignore her phone like this before.

While changing lanes to get onto the off-ramp for Southland Drive a man driving a Beamer cut him off and came within inches of hitting the front of his truck. Brand rammed his palm against the truck's horn, his frustration, and concern getting the better of him. He blasted the inconsiderate driver and instantly followed that up with a few colourful adjectives shouted in the sanctity of the trucks cab. The driver of the car barely glanced in his rear-view mirror and didn't seem too concerned with Brand's warning but at least, Brand released a little frustration although it didn't make him feel a whole lot better.

Turning onto Sara's street, he pulled his truck up to the curb in front of her house and peered through the windshield at her car parked on the street out front. Puzzled by her lack of response to his repeated calls he sat in the truck and watched the early evening rain mix with a layer of dust that had collected on her vehicle. Small rivulets of mud streamed off the top of the car, ran down the sides and joined with the rainwater on the pavement.

Where would she go without her car? As far as he knew she hadn't made many friends during her brief time in town but he supposed that it was possible that she left the house with someone else. He didn't for a second believe she was sitting at home and out of contact with her phone; that was definitely not like her. But with that line of thought he knew if she were out she would surely have taken her phone with her. Warning bells rang in his head as he climbed out of his truck and walked up to the front door.

The instincts he developed and used back in his CSIS days started to push to the surface again. Something was off. Even still he held onto hope that she may have just been up researching all night and was now fast asleep through his calls this whole time.

Brand pulled his coat tight against the chilly drizzle and reached for the doorbell. He listened as the chimes resonated through the house. Time passed without hearing any movement in the house so he reached down and pressed the bell again. The drizzle was starting to give him a chill as he stood on the front step. He waited patiently for a few more minutes then pulled his keys out of his pocket locating the one for Sara's house.

Reaching to insert the key into the lock his hand brushed the knob and the front door moved slightly. Brand froze. Sara wasn't answering her phone and now he finds the front door unlocked...what the hell was going on he wondered?

Careful not to touch the doorknob he placed his hand on the door and slowly pushed it out of his way stepping into the house while calling Sara's name. He waited as her name echoed around the bungalow. No answer. He continued standing in the doorway, confusion momentarily making him advance with caution. The uncertainty quickly receded when the investigative side of him started taking over.

He took another step into the house to allow the front door to be closed. Although it was light outside, inside the house late day shadows started their daily journey to slowly consume the remaining light. Standing completely immobile, Brand let his eyes roam over the interior of the house. Everything appeared to be fine. The furniture in its place...not disrupted...a bit of clutter, a half full cup of coffee on the table as per usual...nothing out of the ordinary... but Brand couldn't get past the unsettled feeling in his stomach.

His eyes continued their search past the front entrance deeper into Sara's house. Still everything seemed fine. Satisfied that what he saw was completely natural, Brand slipped off his shoes and started walking slowly through the house searching. The house consisted of a main floor and basement, the initial search taking little time.

Passing through the dining room nothing seemed out of place. He left the dining room with a niggling feeling in the back of his head. The contents of the room seemed untouched but the feeling that he was missing something troubled him. He couldn't put his finger on it at the moment so he carried on his search and then returned to the dining room.

Standing in the doorway, he remained motionless letting his eyes and his brain slowly go over the place. He couldn't shake the thought that he might be missing some important detail. His eyes traveled over the counters, passed the fridge, across the table and around the other side of the room.

That was it. He turned his head back to the table. Sara kept her computer on the table; the computers power cord lay off to the side. Sara's computer was her life, whenever she took her computer with her the power cord was an added necessity. The computer's power source sat resting on the table…the computer was nowhere in sight.

Brand reached for his phone and tried calling Sara's phone. Again his call went directly to voice mail. The tinge of worry he was feeling before increased to a full on assault of concern. Where the hell could she be that she would take her computer but not answer her phone and how had she gotten there? Her car was parked out front.

Brand set out to search the house again. This time, he wasn't looking for her; he was hunting for clues that might reveal what had happened to her. He very methodically checked every square inch of her house. Nothing.

Remembering that the door was unlocked when he arrived, he made his way back to the door and glanced down at the exterior part of the lock for signs of forced entry. Leaning closer, he studied the metal around the keyhole. He found no markings that would have been made by someone trying to force the lock. With the same close inspection, he studied the doorjamb. The lock showed no signs of being tampered with.

His concern deepened. Brand walked into the living room and tried Sara's number once again. Voice mail. Frustration forced Brand to tightly squeeze the phone in his hand. Standing in the middle of the floor he was immobilized by indecision and the frustration continued to build.

Unable to contain himself any longer he raised the phone in his hand and violently threw it at a wall, the force of his throw hard enough that it made a hole in the drywall. The phone smashed into the wall falling to the carpet in pieces instantly rendering it useless compounding Brand's already maxed frustration levels. He gulped down a couple of large breaths trying to get his mixed feelings under control. Wrecking things wasn't going to help accomplish much and it certainly wasn't going to help him find Sara.

This time Brand started looking for evidence of abduction. That was where his mind was as he slowly surveyed the floor for marks of struggle. He walked over to the chair and was about to sit down realizing he never checked the furniture in this room. Instead of sitting on the cushion he raised it combing for any clues that may be hidden.

The chair was clean so he turned his attention to the couch. Tucked in behind the second cushion he found Sara's cell phone. He tried to turn it on but the battery was dead forcing him to take the phone with him into the kitchen where he knew she kept the phone charger. He knew she had one, he just wasn't sure where.

It wasn't in the drawers. Passing by the fridge, he noticed a picture of the two of them Sara had stuck to the door. Gazing fondly at the picture taken on their trip to Bali he was struck again by the color of her emerald green eyes and soft brown hair that lay nestled on her shoulders. Hair several shades darker than his that framed her pale white Irish skin with a tinge of red added from the hot Bali sun during their last holiday. Passing a finger over the picture he could almost feel the softness of her skin.

He turned away from the picture and next to the microwave he found the cord rolled in a ball. Carrying the phone and its cord over to the dining room table Brand plugged the phone in. Once the screen on the phone lit up, Brand punched in Sara's code and waited for the next screen to appear. A recording app filled the screen. The phone must have been left on record mode and over time killed the battery.

Fumbling with the phone Brand played the recording. The message lasted only a few seconds ...long enough for him to hear a male voice.

"...Take the computer, I'll bring her along...hurry, let's go..." In the background Brand could hear sounds of Sara struggling.

Chapter 4

Somehow Sara had managed to hit the record button on her phone and stash it in the cushions. Brand didn't know what to make of the recording. When he had left for his trip a week ago, Sara had been screening footage of the Toronto subway explosion for her employer, Gallows Security.

The Canadian Security Intelligence Service, CSIS, had employed both the owner of Gallows Security, Brent Gallows and Brand. During that time, the two had become close friends, both serving on the same special ops unit for the Canadian Intelligence Agency. It was through this connection that Brand and Sara had first met.

Shortly after Brand's retirement from the agency Brent had gone on to start his own security company. Currently, Gallows Security along with several other law enforcement agencies across the country had been requested to work on the investigation of the worst terrorist attack on Canadian soil. This fact along with Sara's disappearance left Brand wondering if the two weren't somehow connected.

Suddenly memories of a darker period in his life came rushing back flooding his thoughts and momentarily paralyzing him. These were the kind of horrible, dark memories that he had spent years suppressing to retain his sanity.

The year was two thousand and three. A fellow CSIS agent in his covert unit and his love interest, Rebecca Stone, had at that time been kidnapped while vacationing in Morocco. Her abduction took place shortly after their special ops unit had successfully completed a sanctioned mission in Sudan involving modern day pirates. The new age cyber Pirates were at home sailing and pillaging on the vast seas of information available through the Internet instead of the open seas like their ancestors, both groups were learned to be equally feared and ruthless.

Rebecca had separated from the group at the end of the mission and had flown to Morocco for a short holiday while Brand and the rest of the unit flew back to Canada.

By the time, he was able to track the kidnappers to the Moroccan city of Casablanca the Sudanese captors had fled. Brand discovered Rebecca in a hotel room, dead, lying in a pool of her own blood. Her body was still warm when he arrived but her life had ended.

In the weeks that followed, he had hunted down every man involved in her death and swore to himself to never let anyone get close to him again. A promise he kept faithfully until a year earlier when he found himself on the wrong end of a Russian ploy to manipulate power from within the Canadian government. During that time, he had met Sarah while the two worked together in revealing the Russian deception.

As he found himself falling for the timid computer geek he had justified that it had been twelve years since Rebecca's death and he was no longer in "the business. Now standing in the middle of Sara's empty house with her phone in his hand he found that once again the girl that he loved had disappeared.

Not again he swore to himself. Not again.

Pushing Rebecca's memory away he forced his body to move and willed his mind to concentrate on the here and now. He checked the date the recording was made. The digital stamp was from three days ago.

Anger replaced the heart-wrenching despair that always accompanied thoughts of Rebecca's death. He should have been with Sara, protecting her, not stuck in some faraway fishing camp. DAMN IT! He was sitting in a goddamn boat fishing while she was being abducted, no one around to help her. He swore at himself for letting it happen, then just as quickly he pulled his emotions back in. He'd have plenty of time to punish himself once he found her…right now he needed to focus.

Dialling Sara's phone, Brand called 911, explained where he was and what he thought had taken place and then got busy searching the house one more time…the search, this time, was done with a different purpose. He wanted to make sure he hadn't missed anything of importance before the police arrived and asked him to leave while they investigated.

Finding nothing else of use, he walked out of the house and stood on the front lawn. There he remained for several minutes plotting his next move. He looked up and down the street with a flicker of hope that maybe one of Sara's neighbours may have witnessed her leaving. Brand cut across the lawn to the house next door and knocked.

An elderly gentleman answered. Brand explained to the man that he was looking for the lady who lived next door and if anybody in the house had noticed anything peculiar three days ago. With the shake of his head, the man explained that he and his wife were the only two in the house and they had been away for the past week.

Brand continued this same line of questioning up and down the block for several houses. Similar responses met him at all the other doors. No one had seen anything. His ray of hope was dimming as he walked across the street and continued his door knocking. At a house almost directly across the street from the one Sara rented he climbed the step and rapped his knuckles against the wooden door.

He knocked on the door a couple more times before a lady from the house next-door stepped outside to talk to him. He was told that the woman who lived there was away visiting…she wouldn't be back for another day or two…yes, she believed that her friend was home at that time and if anyone knew the comings and goings on the street her neighbour certainly would.

Brand crossed the rain-soaked lawn and explained once again about Sara's mysterious disappearance. Before thanking the elderly woman he pulled a business card out of his wallet and asked if she could pass it along to her friend.

Brand continued crossing wet lawns and canvassing the street with the same lack of success. By this time, he noticed the police pull up in front of Sara's house. A single squad car appeared, two officers climbed out. Brand crossed the street to meet them. One of the officers remained with Brand and recorded his statement, the other officer walked into the house, the front door left open by Brand. The officer taking Brand's statement asked to see his I.D. questioning whom he was and why he was at the house. Brand explained and then told the police that he had spoken with a few of the other homeowners on the street.

The police officer looked at Brand with a slightly annoyed look on his face, "Are you a cop he asked?"

"No!" Brand answered just as curtly.

"Well, then how about you leave the police work to us. Can't have every Joe on the street playing detective now can we?" The officer berated him in a condescending tone. At this, Brand thought about telling the officer where he could stick it, then thought better of it.

He'd spent a good part of his life doing a job much like theirs. He had started out working for the RCMP when he was young and then advanced his career working for the Canadian Security Intelligence Services. Throughout his law enforcement career, he'd been involved in some very major, very dangerous investigations in the service of this country all while these two uniforms were probably still playing marbles in elementary.

Brand felt a flash of anger start to rise but quickly pushed it away. Not here…not now…these guys were just trying to do their job he reminded himself. Getting mad at them would just be a waste of everybody's time so instead; he left his phone number with the uniform in case they found anything.

Memories of the first time he had seen Sara crept into his mind. He had only known her since the previous fall when the two had met while he was investigating a conspiracy involving a disloyal MP and his Russian backers and their misguided attempt to derail the Canadian government. During that time, three of Brand's friends and former CSIS colleagues had been killed in that insane plot and an attempt had been made on his life.

Nothing like a traumatic experience to bring two people closer together he mused. The two had really hit it off and Sara must have thought so too or she wouldn't have moved to Calgary to be closer to him. Her line of work was mostly online so she could be located anywhere in the country whereas he had made a name for himself in the fishing community of Southern Alberta and B.C. so he was sort of tied down for now.

Pushing these thoughts out of his mind Brand climbed back into his truck and headed for a mall, his first order of business was to buy a new phone. Throwing his into the wall and destroying it hadn't been the smartest thing to do. It did help relieve some frustration but in the long term being an idiot like that always cost him money and time. He would quickly stop by the mall; purchase a new phone and then beeline for his house.

He had to call Brent Gallows, Sara's employer and let him know the situation. Brand was hopeful Brent could shed some light on what exactly Sara had been researching. Maybe, and it was a big maybe, especially after hearing the phone recording, he was wrong… maybe Sara wasn't abducted after all… maybe he was jumping to conclusions…maybe Brent knew where she was.

Chapter 5

National days before Brand's return from his fishing trip, Sara had been at home sitting cross-legged in front of her computer as usual. That morning she had woken up early and excited to continue her work from the night before. She rushed her shower, dressed in a pair of comfortable jeans and an oversized sweater, brewed a pot of coffee, skipped breakfast and parked herself in front of her computer.

Late the previous night she had been reviewing scores of uploaded videos and still pictures that had flooded the net from the Toronto subway bombing. After hours of relentless searching, she stumbled upon footage of the suicide bomber before they had entered the subway tunnel.

A lot of the images she found were from the subway's security cameras seconds before the explosion. The law enforcement community now had a general description of the bomber's features and a reasonably accurate timeline to go on. From there all Sara had to do was sort through the thousands of video feeds that were uploaded online and correlate the video's timestamps to the date of the bombing.

A tourist in Toronto had unwittingly filmed the bomber while taking video of some friends on a street across from the subway station and had proceeded to upload the video to the web. The video was shot minutes before the explosion and had captured footage of the supposed bomber hiding in an alley while pulling on a burka and then wrapping their head in a niqab. Before the niqab was fully in place the person had turned around and the video captured a few seconds of the bomber's exposed face.

Sara wasn't entirely sure that this was the bomber but the video feed and the general appearance matched closely with the descriptions handed out to the law enforcement agencies in the country.

Still she was eighty-five percent certain that the video was of the actual bomber. In the slightly out of focus video, she watched as the suspect changed into the same type of clothing that had been reported in several witness statements and the timeline and location worked.

Captured in the video along with the bomber were a couple of other men who appeared to talk with the suspect. The brief video showed the three men involved in a rather heated conversation and in Sara's opinion what she conceived to be the trio looking and pointing down the alley toward the subway entrance.

She methodically searched through every CCTV camera she could find in the area surrounding the tunnel opening and methodically backtracked the suspect's movements. With the excitement of finding the video, she had placed a call to her boss, Brent Gallows, in Ottawa.

Sara was recruited by Gallows Security, a firm that was internationally renowned for providing security to companies that often operated in hostile countries or under threatening conditions. In addition to being classified as a first notch firewall against both physical and cyber threats, the company carried a dark secret.

She soon learned that Gallows Security was a front for the Canadian government's clandestine operations. This is where Sara's skill as a computer hacker was mostly utilized. While the firm's day-to-day operations remained focused on the interest of their private client's worldwide, the company's international dealings provided a screen for the group to move about the world undetected while carrying out the shadow operations. Covert ops that often required a computer savvy tech to evade and at times enter securely protected sites for Intel prevalent to the cases. Sara had both the skills and tenacity the company required for their operations.

The shadow task force was overseen by Canadian Senator Audrey Meadows and run directly out of the Prime Minister's office, a secret service that remained hidden from Canada's other intelligent agencies.

Many of the employees at Gallows Security were, in fact, ex-CSIS operatives that had either been recruited, or joined the firm after being disbanded from different federal agencies. These lucrative employees were extremely dedicated to the protection of Canada and its people with a drive to follow through on an operation no matter the consequences.

In her late night phone call, Sara explained that she had discovered something of interest about the bomber and she would forward the pictures as soon as she had a chance to further verify her suspicions. Give her a couple hours in the morning Sara had told her boss. She needed to do some more digging to check the video and would call back the next day if she could prove her theory.

Sitting at her table frantically looking through the cameras in the subway area her heart was pounding. She had traced the bombers route from the tunnel entrance all the way back to the alley. The phone video was the only source she was so far able to find that showed the lane at that time. She carefully reviewed the video. The other men in the alley left the picture and as the bomber turned to exit the alley, the camera had recorded what she was sure was the suspect adjusting the hijab over their face.

Sara manipulated the video, playing it back and forth, slowing it down frame-by-frame paying careful attention as she watched the person adjust the hijab. The video was grainy and out of focus and as best as she could tell the person in the video had what looked like facial hair, light brown facial hair? To the best of Sara's knowledge, she wasn't aware of Muslim women wearing a niqab because they grew beards, especially light coloured beards.

The video was still too grainy for Sara to make a positive I.D. so she stubbornly manipulated the feed searching for a crisper picture. This is what she had been stuck on the previous evening and she bullishly continued adjusting the pictures with the realization that if she were unsuccessful in improving the clarity of the images, she would forward it the way it was. The technology at Gallow's Security was much better than the computer she was using and maybe someone in his office would have better luck but it wasn't in her nature to admit defeat so easily.

Desperately needing a break to stretch her legs she left her computer poured a fresh cup of coffee and leaned against the kitchen counter trying to think of a different approach she could use to enhance the video. A couple of sips into her coffee, the doorbell rang. Irritated at the unwanted distraction she walked from the kitchen, setting her coffee cup down on the living room table on her way to the door.

Parting the blind on the front door she saw two men in suits standing on the front step. The man closest to the door was the taller of the two. Short trimmed hair, dark glasses in place and dressed in a dark navy suit. The second man was a shorter, stockier version of the first, same glasses, same blue suit. Sara chuckled. The two men looked like they were auditioning for a "Men in Black" movie.

Sara was still relatively new to Calgary and she didn't have many visitors so the two men standing on her front step put her on edge a bit. Her closest companion was normally her computer and Brand was out of town. Who else would be calling on her this time of day? Probably well meaning religious people she mused. She had become used to them coming to her door at all hours of the day.

Too early in the day for salesmen, she supposed, although these men were dressed the part. She also considered the possibility that they were officers of some sort. She had worked closely with several different police agencies lately and that's what these two reminded her of. Sara relaxed…maybe Brent had sent them to her house because of her phone call last night, on that thought, she opened the door widely. She smiled and bid the two welcome from her doorway.

"Sara Monahan?" the man in front inquired.

"Yes," Sara replied.

"May we come in Miss Monahan?" the man quickly asked.

"Yes. Sure," she turned and led the two of them inside. "Did Brent send you?" she asked. She wasn't even sure about what she had found yet, she didn't want these two wasting their time for nothing. Brent's really on the ball sending these two here already, she thought as she heard the door close. At the sound of the closing door, she turned back around to face the men who had followed her inside. The smile on her face disappeared as she found herself staring into the barrel of a gun.

The man holding the gun put his hand on her shoulder and gently pushed her backward until her legs touched the couch stopping her movement.

"Sit down." She was instructed. Addressing the second man he stated. "Search the house, I'll keep an eye on Miss Monahan."

"What's this about?" Sara blurted out.

"Sit still and be quiet," the gunman told her. "My friend here is going to have a quick look around and then you will have to come with us."

Fighting against a rising panic Sara forced herself to think quickly. Her cell phone was in her back pocket and she needed to work it out of her pocket somehow. If she could dial 911 unobserved…maybe, just maybe the police would be able to get to her house in time and stop the two men she was now facing. Despite her makeshift plan, Sara was nervous. What did they want with her and what did they intend to do with her?

Very carefully Sara eased her phone free from the pocket of her jeans. The gunman's eyes roamed around the front room while he held his gun pointed at her. Holding her breath she ever so slowly maneuvered the phone behind her, careful not to be noticed by the gun-toting intruder, daring not to risk a look at it.

She managed to turn it out of sleep mode and thanked the developers for installing fingerprint recognition security. When she judged she was on the home screen, she tried to steal a glance at the phone and allow her to notify the police but the ever-roaming eyes of the intruder made looking too risky…instead, she decided to rely on repetition. She had dialed her phone almost blindly several times. She was very practiced with it. She prayed she was making progress.

The second man called from the kitchen. The house is clear he said. He told the gunman that he found her computer on the table in the kitchen.

"Good…bring the computer, I'll take her…hurry, let's go…"

The gunman motioned for Sara to stand up and briefly turned his attention to his partner coming out of the kitchen with Sara's computer in his hands. While the gunman's attention wavered, Sara slid her phone into a slot between the cushion and the back of the couch away from the eyes of her unwelcomed guests. Uncertain if she had successfully dialed out Sara had to believe that the call went thru.

Before exiting the house, the gunman spoke to Sara.

"My gun will remain pointed at your back. Walk casually to the car and climb in, I will have no need to shoot you if you do as you're told… do you comprehend what I'm saying?" he ended.

Sara was too afraid to do anything but nod her head in acknowledgement. She walked in front of the two men toward their car. As the three made their way down the sidewalk, Sara noticed one of her neighbours watching from across the street. An older retired lady that Sara had talked to briefly a few times. She tried desperately with her eyes to communicate with her about the trouble she was facing; just wishing her neighbour would understand and call for help.

When the trio reached the car, the man carrying her computer opened the back door, threw her computer on the seat and then moved aside allowing her to climb in. Sara sat sullenly in the back seat while the two men climbed into the front. Sara fixated on the back door handle and wondered what her chances would be of jumping out of the car and making a run for freedom.

"The door handles back there are disabled if that's what you're thinking," the gunman said. Sara raised her eyes to the front and saw the driver's eyes staring right back at her in the rear-view mirror.

"Best for you to sit back and enjoy the ride. We're not here to kill you…those aren't our instructions. We were only ordered to grab you and your computer," he continued.

"Where are you taking me, who ordered you to apprehend me?" she demanded with more bravado than she was feeling.

"Don't ask any questions. Sit back, be quiet and enjoy the ride," came the response from the front seat.

Chapter 6

Sara cowered in the back seat, her mouth was dry and her heart was pounding. Every time she risked a question, she was given the same reply. She hung her head and occasionally brushed away a stray tear; panic wasn't starting to overcome her...it already had her firm in its grip. The next time she lifted her eyes and looked out the window she noticed that they were on McLeod Trail driving south.

The driver pulled the car off the busy road and stopped alongside a bank of pumps. The gunman caught Sara's eye in the mirror. With a smirk he told her to remain still and not to try to attract any attention, he would have his gun aimed at her until they left the station. Sara nodded her compliance. She wanted to say something else but was scared she'd provoke her captor in the front seat. Putting the back of her hand up to her face Sara wiped away a stray tear fighting to gain her composer. She had no choice at the moment but to do as she was told.

"I have to use the washroom," she finally found the courage to say, willing to try anything to get away from the two men.

The man glanced back up at the mirror to look at her, a smile on his face. "I'm afraid you are just going to have to cross your legs and wait until we get somewhere a little less crowded."

Disappointed, she turned her head and looked wistfully toward the gas station, the driver was already on his way back to the car, a bag hung in his hand. Climbing into the driver's seat he passed Sara a pop and a couple of bars before starting the car and re-entering the flow of traffic continuing south.

Sara set the pop and bars on the seat. Her thoughts conflicted between the man's thoughtfulness even while she was held captive in their car. She watched out the window as the people she saw went about their everyday lives. How could everybody carry on like nothing was happening while she was being held a prisoner in this car? It wasn't fair...

With a vacant look in her eyes, she watched the city as they rolled through it. When she finally came out of her reverie, she noticed that they had already passed the last set of lights on McLeod and were now on the highway. The thought of leaving the city raised the panic level in her body once again. Nobody was going to be able to find or help her now.

The gunman turned to her and told her to get comfortable, they still had a long drive ahead of them. She reminded the gunman of her need to go to the bathroom. Hold on a while longer he said. They would stop somewhere so she could go as soon as they found a remote spot away from the city. Her mind fought against another attack of panic. Her imagination furnished her with all sorts of dreadful possibilities that would await her once the three of them were far away from the crowded city.

Sara didn't know if she wanted to cry or scream. The farther away from the city, the speeding car traveled, the greater the feeling of helplessness settled upon her. She started to accept the inevitability of her situation. There wasn't much she was able to do at the moment and certainly no one to rescue her. She would have to wait until an opportunity presented itself.

Several miles south of Nanton, the gunman pointed to a rest area on the side of the highway. When the car had coasted to a standstill, the gunman got out and opened the back passenger door motioning Sara out.

"You needed to stop didn't you?" he told her. Sara looked around. The rest stop consisted of a pull out lane with a single garbage can.

"You've got to be kidding!" she exclaimed.

The man looked at her and shrugged. "I'll turn my back," he said to her. "It's either this or you wait until we get to where we're going, but we won't be there for quite a few hours, the choice is yours."

Not seeing any other option, Sara did what she had to. Once she climbed back into the car, the gunman climbed back into the front seat and the drive continued. Hours later Highway Two South merged onto Highway Three. The driver turned right and headed west toward the mountains. Panic once again built up inside of her.

Highway two had at least been busy with midday traffic. She had started to feel relaxed comforted by the other traffic. In her mind, she reasoned that these men wouldn't try to kill her with so much activity around but now

Richard Cozicar

they were headed into an area less traveled, a much sparser population with lots of back roads into the surrounding foothills. There was no way this was going to be good for her.

Sara's emotions fluctuated between thoughts of what could happen to her and moments of relief as the driver stuck to the main highway where she reasoned she would be unharmed for the time being. The three continued driving, through the Crowsnest Pass, through Sparwood and Fernie. Where were they going she wondered? This was crazy and only getting crazier. Looking between her two captors in the front seat, Sara noticed the time on the dashboard clock. One thirty-seven. It had been about four hours since she was abducted. Only four hours and they were well into another province.

Out the front window, she could see buildings starting to appear. The Roosville/Grasmere border crossing was the next occupied place on the road according to the sign they just passed. What the hell were these guys up to, surely the guards at the border crossing would figure out that Sara was being kidnapped. Suddenly Sara's spirits started to rise although the new situation didn't make much sense to her. Why would they abduct her and then drive up to a place like this where they must know that the car and passengers would be checked.

Sara waited apprehensively, her hand on the door handle, ready to try and throw the door open and escape once the border guard started questioning the men in the front seat. It wasn't conceivable to think that these men would try to drive or shoot their way through a border crossing. Not with all the security around. Sara found she was holding her breath as the car pulled up even with the guardhouse.

The car inched closer to the window and the driver lowered his window. The guard took his time looking into the front seat. Before he said anything to the driver, the man in the passenger seat pulled his wallet out of his pocket, opened it and handed the wallet to the guard. Sara's heart sank with what she saw next. A badge and police ID. She thought about signalling for help when the gunman turned to face her shaking his head in warning.

The guard handed back the ID and motioned the car on. Passing the booth, the gunman turned and looked Sara in the eye. He winked at her as his face lit up with a smile.

"You didn't think we were that stupid, did you?" he said with a laugh. "We haven't got much further to go. There's a beautiful room reserved for you."

The ID and badge made Sara wonder what she had done to be detained by the American law. She rarely left the house and had not been to the States in years. Lately, all she had been doing was searching and reviewing the net for clues to the Toronto bombing, all sanctioned by her government. Something about this whole situation didn't make sense to her.

The gunman's cavalier attitude and the smile on his face sent shivers of dread shooting through her body. For a moment, she had allowed herself to think that the ordeal might be over soon but now, as a result, further feelings of despair flooded through her. Sara let out a small-disheartened gasp and settled back into her seat.

Her head was swimming as she tried to figure out why some government agency from the States would need or want to kidnap her. If these two were with some American law enforcement division why would they come to her house and remove her as they did, why wouldn't they go through the proper channels to talk to her?

She relaxed a bit; the two had apparently not wanted her dead. They had had ample opportunity along the way to do just that and they had treated her fine so far if you called being abducted and transported out of the country proper treatment. Go along for the ride and see where it takes you she told herself to ward off deepening feelings of dread that were threatening to overcome all of her other thoughts.

While conflicting thoughts circled Sara's mind, her eyes fell upon a highway sign as the car raced passed it. The name of a river they had crossed before they entered the town of Eureka, Montana. The Tobacco River. Funny. This made her think of Brand and his cigarettes.

The thought made her eyes well up with tears again. If only he would have been in town then maybe she would have been with him and not held against her will in the back of a car heading to who knows where. Would he be able to find her? Would she ever see him again? These questions settled over her forcing her thoughts back into a deep dark abyss and forcing tears to appear on her cheeks. Despite her best efforts to remain composed, she couldn't help but fear the worst. She had watched too many crime dramas to expect her predicament to get any better.

The gunman turned in his seat and angrily snapped, "Dry your eyes, quit your damn hysterics… you'll be okay for now," annoyance creeping into his voice. Sara fought to get her emotions in check; she didn't want to risk angering her abductors.

Wiping her face with her sleeve she once again turned her attention to the countryside as it rolled past. Whitefish...fifty-one miles she read on the highway sign. The beauty of the landscape helped to settle her nerves. She had never been to this part of the country and the magnificent surroundings shone a brief light into the darkness she was feeling.

The trio traveled into Whitefish, Montana, stopped briefly at the drive-thru of a local burger joint before crossing the city and exiting the northeast corner. Minutes later they turned onto a rarely used road that wound through thick trees up the side of a mountain. The car slowly wove its way around numerous switchbacks as the car ascended the mountain.

Mid afternoon, the sun high in the sky by the time the car rolled through a treed entrance onto a gravel driveway. Through the windshield, Sara watched as a cabin, albeit a huge cabin, appeared built in an opening of the forest at the end of this deserted country road. The rustic dwelling was bigger than most houses Sara had ever seen and came complete with an enormous garage attached to the side, adding to the bulk of the building.

Several luxury cars were lined up on the driveway. Men dressed in jeans and buttoned shirts milled about the yard, rifles held by their sides. The gunman stepped out of the car and opened the back door letting Sara out; she stretched and took in the surroundings. From where she stood, she could see a huge lake back down the valley they had driven through earlier, the water sparkling in the sunshine. The view was breathtaking. Trees, mountains and lots of blue skies, momentarily making her forget the situation she faced.

"Inside," the gunman demanded as he motioned toward the house.

Silent Crusade

Chapter 7

Michael Johnson rose up from the cot he had been relaxing on, opened the flap to his tent and wondered out into the frigid evening air. He had been in Afghanistan for the past six months now, living and working among the Pashtun tribes of this remote region. These tribes have roamed and ruled this section of the border between the Khost Province and Pakistan for centuries.

Accompanying Johnson was a small band of ex-militants. Their mission: use the remoteness of the desolate area to discreetly carry out their assignment while using the tribe's connections to gain favours with the Taliban.

Johnson and his crew ventured into Afghanistan to seek a deal with the Taliban. The gist of the deal was that his backers would supply money and weapons to the Taliban in return for help in the bombing a few prominent western cities, cities of his choosing. No western government sanctioned this deal; Michael Johnson was a freelance soldier for hire and worked privately for a wealthy organization.

The other men in Johnson's group consisted of soldiers who had also left the army life behind them for the private sector, men who had been handpicked for both their military talents and their devout loyalty to the Christian faith. Men who would do whatever it took to protect and advance their belief in God.

Dean Adams had retired from the American Special Forces. Barret Hammond and Dexter Tranter were both former British SAS members. George Williams had joined the group after years of serving as a Marine in the United States Military. While they all shared extensive combat training and an extreme Christian devotion, the primary connection between the men was through the group that had brought them all together.

At one time or another, the members of this group had all been stationed in Afghanistan while on deployment by their respected governments. This had aided the small band of soldier's journey into this remote and dangerous part of the world.

While serving in Afghanistan, Michael Johnson had come to know several Afghan soldiers and when he was asked to return to the country he had used this to his advantage. One of the Afghanis who had assisted Michael's voyage back into Afghanistan, Wasim Zawar, now acted as his liaison to the Pashtun tribe that sheltered the men.

The group's trip to Pakistan and then through the mountainous terrain into the Khost Province was filled with anxiety. Each and every one of these former soldiers was well aware that the locals they now found themselves allied with could lead them into a trap and surrender them to the same hostiles they had once faced across the battlefields. Along with the chance of capture or certain death, the trip had to be carried out without detection by any form of western government.

Five Western militants crossing into these territories without being captured or detected was a hard enough task in itself. The fact that these mercenaries were highly trained and had little fear made the crossing possible. Once they met up with the tribal group in Khost, their safety was in the hands of the tribal leaders. As long as they remained with the tribe they had assured protection.

From within the safety net of the Pashtun tribe, Michael Johnson and his associates set about earning the trust of the Taliban leaders. The largest obstacle the Westerners faced was the distrust of the Taliban. Years of being enemies made the Taliban wonder what brought these soldiers to Afghanistan with promises of money and guns? Were their promises real or was this some kind of plot against them?

When Michael Johnson explained what part he needed his hosts to play, the Taliban leaders were again skeptical. Why would these westerners want to bomb their own countries? But after the second bomb exploded in France the Taliban leaders grew less suspicious. Johnson and his crew handled the planning of the operations with the Taliban providing ground support and happily laying claim to the strikes against the common enemies. For this, the Taliban continued to hide and work with the mercenaries. The deal had so far worked out well for both sides.

The actual reason that Johnson had sought out, the help of the Taliban, was not one he shared with his new allies. The forming of the unusual partnership and all the backroom antics was known only to a very few people, Johnson and his small group included.

As Johnson wondered around the makeshift tent village, he dwelled on the irony of the deal he had brokered. If this far-fetched plan succeeded, the

Taliban itself would be to blame for bringing about the demise of their own country and its people.

He kicked at some dust covered rocks, his mind elsewhere. In reality, he loathed these people and their backwards country. He sat in their council because he had a job to do and as far as he was concerned, the sooner they were destroyed, the better. His disdain for his hosts was hard to keep in check; however, years in the military had taught him how to keep an unrevealing poker face, helping him keep his thoughts to himself.

Walking around the compound he searched for Nabi Hussoini, one of the Taliban leaders who had been very helpful with this mission so far. He needed the leaders help once more, time for another terrorist attack against the west.

Aware that many of the leaders of the western countries were putting enormous pressure on the American President to now bomb this region of the Middle East he was also aware that the President continued to resist. That wasn't what the group that employed Johnson wanted. His latest instructions were to come up with a new assault that would further convince the President. Maybe a major attack on a U.S. city with thousands of American's killed he thought as he walked, that should make the President more compliant.

Johnson needed to find Hussoini and start planning the attack. He felt a pang of grief for the innocent people he knew would die, but in every war casualties were unavoidable. Sacrifice the few for the greater good. After an attack on American soil, he could envision that the only other people who would die would be the population of several of these Mid Eastern countries harbouring the terrorists.

Johnson's command of the Pashto language had become more fluent with every day that passed. Pashto was the primary language spoken in these parts and even though he had Wasim to translate he spent a lot of time talking with the locals, this way he would be certain that nothing got lost in the translation. He would only trust these people so far, his life and the lives of his team depended on it.

Michael stopped and talked to a few of the local tribesmen in his search for Nabi Hussoini. No one had seen the man recently so Michael decided to find his translator Wasim. A short time later Michael was quizzing Wasim about Nabi's location.

"Hussoini is across the border in Pakistan," Wasim bragged. "He has taken another shipment of opium to sell."

Johnson was not surprised at this. Opium was the main cash crop for the Taliban and provided much-needed money to pay for their war.

The money the Taliban received from Johnson's backer's for their assistance was a pittance compared to money from the illicit drug business. Afghanistan was the leading supplier of opium to the Middle East and Europe. Caravans continually crossed the border into Pakistan with their products and then returned with much-needed cash. Cash to buy loyalty from the locals. Nabi wouldn't be back until the next day Wasim informed him.

Leaving Wasim, Johnson went in search of the rest of his unit. He and his men would start the planning of the next attack in America and he would fill Nabi in later.

Gathering his men far away from the people of the village the mercenaries huddled together. This attack had to be planned very carefully. The time had come to choose a site in the good ole U.S.A. that would create such an impact that the American President was left with no choice but to authorize the use of the atomic bombs at his command.

Chicago…possibly while a baseball game was being played…large crowds in attendance… An attack in the middle of America during a game involving America's favourite pastime… this should be the shove that even the President could not avoid.

The group started with an idea and then worked with their combined years of military experience to iron out the details. Michael would talk to Nabi about the plan tomorrow but the details would already be worked out and he didn't really care what Nabi thought. He would share just enough information to feed the man's ego and to keep him compliant until the mission was completed. Once the mercenaries no longer needed his support, they would gladly take leave of their host and this wretched part of the world.

When the initial planning started, Johnson knew he would have to broach this idea with his employers. The concept was good; the bombing of an American landmark filled with large crowds should cause the catalyst they'd been searching for. The downside, this one hit close to home, too close.

Chapter 8

Sara was ushered into the house by her captors, the taller of the men still brandishing his gun. Leading the trio into the house, the gunman stopped to speak to the men stationed in the foyer.

"Why the show of force in the yard?" He asked a man they approached in the hallway then glanced back at his partner. "Are you expecting an attack?"

In reply to his question the trio was told that the founding members of the group had been gathered for an urgent meeting. The tall man shrugged and the trio moved deeper into the massive house. "Something big must be up" He wondered out loud.

More armed men were positioned throughout the inside of the house and nodded to Sara's detainers. The lead man called one of the guards over and pulled him aside for a talk. Sara watched the two as they talked and when the conversation was over she was motioned to follow once more, the guard falling in behind her.

Without a word, she was led through the center of the house to a large ornate staircase in the back. At the top of the stairs, Sara noticed some closed doors that she presumed led to bedrooms contained in this great house. She continued trailing down the hall toward the back of the house. At the end of the hallway her escort stopped, opened the door and directed her inside.

"Make yourself comfortable, somebody will be up to check in on you shortly," He told her before leaving the room. "There will be a guard posted outside the door so behave yourself."

Sara stood and stared at the door listening to the lock on the door clicking into place. She remained motionless for several minutes coming to grasp with the fact that she was being held prisoner and still had absolutely no idea why. Moving in a dreamlike trance with the hopelessness of the situation weighing on her, she walked over to the bed and sat down as the intense fear of the unknown seeped into her mind.

Fighting against another overwhelming bout of panic, she breathed deeply to relax and clear her mind. Her thoughts drifted back to the morning and how she had woken up filled with enthusiasm about her discovery and now several hours later she was a prisoner in a bedroom who knows where being held captive in a different country by what she had to believe were American federal agents. She had no idea what she had done to cause the American's to cross the border and abduct her but yet here she was.

To ease her mind wondered around and occupied her time by studying the contents of the room that were now her prison. The bedroom was large but thoughtfully decorated and included a huge closet and a very accommodating en suite bathroom.

The journey around the room brought her to a set of double windows hidden behind dark curtains. Pulling aside the drapes she checked the windows to see if they opened. Her heart sank. Metal bars drilled into the windowsill blocked her access to the glass itself and indeed stopped her from leaving the room that way.

She stood beside the bars and stared through the glass. The view directly out the window was the side of a tree-covered mountain. By craning her neck, she discovered that she was able to see part of the driveway at the front of the house. Glancing down she watched several men entered her line of vision while walking towards the cars parked out front.

Some of the armed men were opening car doors and assisting a group of older, elegantly dressed gentlemen into the vehicles. Of the men climbing into the cars that she could see, the average age had to be at least seventy if not older. While she continued staring, one of the departing men raised his head in the direction of her window as he was climbing into his town car. Sarah felt a shiver go down her spine. The man hesitated and for some weird reason it appeared to Sarah the man had been looking right at her.

"What is this, some kind of Elks club or something?" she mumbled under her breath. What would force a group of old men to meet in a remote cabin hidden in the mountains of Montana? And what was with all the guns.

Then the stress of her situation kicked her imagination into overdrive. Scenes from old gangster movies played in her mind. Sara hoped against hope that she hadn't been dragged into a mafia hideaway. If they put cement shoes on her and dropped her in the river, there was no hope at all that anyone would ever find her.

She remained glued to the window her attention focused on the buzz of activity that took place at the front of the house. She continued to stare at the driveway until all the cars in her line of sight had driven away. When the last one disappeared, she secretly wished that her presence in the house would be forgotten about. Her overactive imagination had her starting to dread the time when someone would come to fetch her.

*****

On the main floor of the cabin, a group of wealthy international businessmen attended the meeting called by the owner of the house, American billionaire August Jackson. The cabin was built on land that he had purchased decades before as a retreat for his family. Born and raised on the east coast of the United States and in his forties had inherited a coal empire from his grandfather.

The inheritance from his grandfather was very significant in itself, but with unbridled determination, August had parlayed the inheritance into an unparalleled fortune making him one of the richest men in the world. August's grandfather was one of the original robber barons at the turn of the twentieth century but August took a different approach building his portion of the empire; where his grandfather made his money on the backs of disadvantaged workers, August preached fairness. He had nearly unrealistic expectations and demanded hard work from everyone in his employ, but he also treated his employees with respect.

The other men at his mountain retreat this day were peers of his. Not many men in the world could come close to what August had done, but these gentlemen had. All of them in their own right were his equals but it wasn't their vast fortunes or success that linked the influential men attending this secret meeting.

The men gathered in the dark paneled room on the main floor of the cabin were bound together by more than their success and power by a calling much higher than money, unwavering faith in the Christian religion and God Almighty. Each of these men had been raised devout Christians and not in the sense of occasionally going to church or donating funds.

Dedicated lives that revolved around the word of God and as a group fought a relentless war to protect the dying religion. For nearly eight decades their lives were lived according to their beliefs. They financed the building of Churches around the world, contributed large sums of money to various organizations so they could go forward and spread the word of God.

While their fortunes increased the dedication to God and church was further fortified. For the last four decades, they toiled tirelessly only to witness the desecration of the Christian faith, the slow decline of parishioners and a rapidly multiplying population of non-believers. Some of the changes they had come to accept. If God were okay with homosexuals or men and women living together without the blessing of marriage, then they would have to live with that...times change, and not always for the better. They didn't agree but they were only mere followers.

But in the last two decades, the war against their beloved religion had fuelled their ire and finally made them fight back at the ever-increasing spread of the Muslims. The last decade and a half were rife with increased terrorist activities that these men associated with the hated religion always reminding them of the growing war between the two religions. The nightly news was filled with stories of the impending war as the Islamic terrorists waged an all out attack on innocent people with their bombs and beheadings.

Chapter 9

There was a consensus among the seven men in the room. The war against Christianity had to be stopped. At first, they were overwhelmed by the massive scope of fighting back against the advancing Muslim religion and its leagues of followers. How would it be possible for a small group of men to fight the rising tide of Islam?

Undaunted, they slowly began amassing an army of faithful followers of their own. It was a painstaking task to find the dedicated numbers of trained personnel the religious war would require. But with the same persistence applied throughout their lives to build their vast fortunes, the group progressed and their Christian army grew.

Despite years of recruiting and privately financing their own religious crusade, the end of the last decade still found them losing ground to the Muslim extremists. What they decided they needed was a game changer. The idea of fighting fire with bigger fire became their ideal going forward. But all together a few old men and a growing army of faithful followers stood a small chance of accomplishing the goal they deemed necessary.

What they needed was a way to attack the extremists where they lived. What they needed were weapons of mass destruction to aid in their fight against the barbaric religion. The American government had such devices and they made it their duty to persuade the powers that be to use those tools of destruction to rid the world of their common enemy by any means necessary.

One of the problems the "Cabal" kept returning to were how to convince the American President and the other leaders of the Western world that it was in everyone's favour to eradicate the Muslim countries that were harbouring the terrorists and spreading the word of the Quran around the world at alarming rates. If Christianity were to survive, a divine intervention of nuclear proportion might be what was called for. This was more than a war on terror; this was a crusade to remove those that posed the largest threat to the spread of Christianity. The word of God needed to be dissipated over the globe, and the Muslim religion stood in the way.

With great trepidation, the Cabal decided that the only way to convince the Allied leaders of the free Christian countries to annihilate the enemy was by fuelling the fear that all Muslims and the religion of Islam was synonymous with terrorism.

The initial plan was to bomb select Western targets causing scores of casualties and directing the blame at the feet of an already existing group of extremists centered in the godless Middle East. The group now had had a strategy and the capabilities to win a war they perceived to be between Muslims and Christians.

The manipulation by their group was easy to hide because they firmly believed that people in the West had the built in ignorance that the Muslim population were out to convert the world to Islam. The vast majority of people already had the bias that to be a Muslim meant one was a terrorist.

Years had been spent in recruiting people to help with this mission and now that they had built a network of secret soldiers the last phase of their plan was set in place. Funding had to be set up to cover the project, contacts had to be made, a way of tracking and communicating had to be devised. The moves were executed with caution because they knew they had to be extremely careful not to have their secret war discovered before the final blow was delivered.

Each of the men accepted the fact that they would be pariahs in the eyes of the world's population if their mission were discovered but it was a risk they were willing to take. They were dedicated to the cause and to have their plan disrupted before the final blow was delivered would be unacceptable

They had hand picked a loyal crew and laid the groundwork to establish the team of Christian soldiers deep in the heart of Afghanistan, part of their mortal enemies territory. To get this far in their mission was a blessing in itself. Now the planning for the last stage of the secret war had arrived. They had proceeded with the bombings of allied countries but still the American President had refused to assist in ending the war. How else could they convince him to bomb these miscreants back into the dark ages?

While the group wanted to inspire fear and loathing of Muslims among the Western superpowers, they hoped to avoid needless destruction on American soil. They felt the U.S.A. had suffered enough with the high losses of 9/11 and they wanted to spare the American people any additional loss. Strategically they attacked London, and then France finally followed by Canada, but still the American President hesitated. He stood up to the other leaders stating that he was not entirely convinced that nuking Middle Eastern countries were the best solution to this problem.

The attacks on the other countries had proven relatively ineffective. The outrage shown by the leaders of these countries failed to convince the President of the necessity to use the weapons only he had access to.

Now the Cabal huddled at this hastily called meeting at August Jackson's family retreat. He came to realize that some type of attack deep within the United States in a place where the American people thought they were safe and far removed from the reality of terrorism was inevitable. The cries of the American public after again being targeted in their own country would inevitably leave the country's leader and fellow members of Congress no choice but to act.

August Jackson looked around the large table in his meeting room. The men his eyes rested upon were besieged with the signs of the long battle they fought in the name of Christianity. To his right at the table was Sir Richard Brown, a Media baron from England. Next to the Englishman was Davis Walker, another American. Davis Walker's holdings between the large Wall Street firm he owned, along with his diverse portfolio of mainly American companies made him the second richest man in the room next to August.

Nelson Bakker was next, the only Canadian at this secretive meeting. While these men forged their empires through industry the Swiss financier, Alain Berlinger stuck to what his family did best and had done since the late eighteen hundreds. His family owned one of the oldest banks in Switzerland.

The last man August looked at was Ramesh Banerjee, born in India and schooled in London. Ramesh ran the family textile business in Bombay, India. For Ramesh, as well as the other members in attendance, their money and power allowed them the means to further spread the word of the Lord. Christianity was served by this group of modern day knights who had sworn to the protection of the church and the advancing of the word of God in the face of the onslaught of Islam.

"Once again gentlemen we are forced to play the hand of the devil to make the light of our Lord shine through. This great Muslim scourge has not been slain by our actions thus far. President Monroe still refuses to see what is plainly evident. Regretfully we must again try to force the President's hand. To leave him no option but to do what he should have done years ago when this plague first started spreading.

"The time has come to force the American people to rise up and demand action. The combined appeals from America's allies have not achieved the goal we have worked for. Unfortunately, it is time for a terrorist bombing to be unleashed…" August paused staring at his clasped hands as he collected his thoughts. "I have been in contact with our asset in Afghanistan. The next attack will… take place here within the borders of America. The President will be unable to ignore the anger of the American people once their voices join the chorus of demands from our allies. Anger brought on by the fear of escalating terrorism. More precisely the action we have worked for all along."

"Haven't we caused enough death and carnage in our war against the Muslim faith?" the Canadian, Nelson Bakker asked. "If we have to keep killing innocent people to save our religion are we really any better than the Islamic extremists?" he questioned.

"We are in a fight to save Christianity," August replied with conviction. "Unfortunately, more of the Lords children will go to join him earlier than they should have, but what choice is there? We can not stand by while the Muslim religion continues spreading driving Christianity from this earth."

The Englishman, Sir Richard Brown joined the conversation. A brief flash of annoyance crossed his face as he addressed the Canadian. "We all knew going into this battle that there would have to be innocent casualties, that won't change until we eradicate the Muslim religion and send it back to the dark ages where it won't be a threat to the Lord or his followers again!" The now angered Englishman slammed his fist on the table.

"I know you're right," Nelson cowed. "It's necessary, I realize, I accept that, but I don't know how much more my faith can take."

"It's hard on all of us Nelson," Ramesh Banerjee cut in. "None of us agreed to this without a bit of soul searching, but we have an obligation to take the fight to those devils. The good Lord blessed all of us here with immense wealth and power, for that we must fight this battle for him."

"What's the next step we need to take?" Ramesh turned the conversation back to August.

"We've decided on a site in Chicago to be the target. Our men in Afghanistan are going to smuggle some volunteer Jihadist's into the country to complete what is hopefully the last leg of our fight. You all know that we've had to change our plans. The use of westerners disguised as Muslim women for the bombings almost backfired on us. We were lucky that we found the Canadian woman in time. If she were able to share her discovery of the you-tube video of our bomber the results would have been disastrous," the old man stated as he rubbed his temple.

"Having a tourist accidently record our man changing in the alley and then posting the video online was an unforeseen complication. Thanks to the computer program Ramesh designed to ghost the Internet we were able to discover the video and the young lady.

Ramesh has assured me that the image has been scrubbed from the Internet preventing any more accidental discoveries. The world must not falter in the belief that Muslims are the ones carrying out these bombings for our plan to succeed," August halted his speech and looked down at his hands. Raising his head, he glanced at each man in turn as he continued. "Gentlemen, I am hopeful that our 'Silent Crusade' is nearing its conclusion."

August outlined the strategy for the attack in the city of Chicago. Young Afghanistan men would be smuggled into the country to complete the mission. The men would be kept out of sight until they were needed and passage into the baseball stadium for the young Jihadists would be handled by the second group of followers. It was decided that multiple bombers would be required to maximize the destruction.

August reassured his audience that this would undoubtedly be enough to force the hand of the reluctant President. The final details still remained but the attack had to happen soon.

"The only thing left for us to do," August said as he looked at each of the individuals gathered at the table, "is to beg God for forgiveness for the deeds we've been forced to do and are yet about to do."

Silent Crusade

Chapter 10

Brand wasted a valuable hour in the mall purchasing a new phone. New phone in hand he left the mall and sped home. The hour was late by the time he walked into his house. He still had to track Brent down and let him know that Sara was missing.

The salesman at the phone store was able to transfer Brand's contact numbers off his wrecked phone onto his new one. Thankful for technological advances, Brand was relieved that he was saved the immeasurable grief of finding the information on his own, considering that a lot of the numbers on his phone would be hard to replace. These are the things he didn't think about until after the phone had left his hand. Glad he was getting better at managing his anger, it was still a pain in the ass to deal with the consequences.

Brand grabbed a beer out of the fridge and took a seat at the kitchen table. Scrolling through the contact list on his phone, he found Brent's personal number and made the call. A few rings had passed before Brent answered.

"Brand, you're back from your fishing trip are you? Well, tell me all about the monster fish that got away," said Brent, chuckling at his own joke.

"I'll tell you about it later Brent. Did you call Sara to Ottawa or have you sent her on another assignment?" Brand quizzed his friend.

"No," came the quick reply. "Last time I talked to her she was, let's see…three, no four evenings ago. She left me a message late Tuesday night. Something about a video on the Toronto bombing and by the sounds of her voice it had her excited. Sara said that once she had a chance to verify the video she would contact me. I haven't heard from her since that call so I presume that the video wasn't what she thought it was…why?"

"I'd been calling her through the day on my way back to town, but her phone kept going to voicemail so I drove to her place once I hit town." Brand went on to describe what he had found at Sara's house.

"I canvased the neighborhood while I waited for the cops," Brand added. "There were a couple of people not home so I left my number with their neighbors."

"Shit! What are you telling me? You don't figure that she might have disappeared before she had a chance to call me, do you?" Brent's voice grew louder with concern. "I should have sent someone there to assist her but...honestly...she was only doing some routine searches...I would never have imagined...this," He paused. "What do you have planned?" He finished and waited for Brand's answer. He knew Brand well enough to assume that a game plan was already being worked on. Then he added, "I'll be on the next flight to Calgary. Do you need me to bring anything along with me?"

"Maybe drag one of your tech geniuses along. If her vanishing is tied to something she found online than we might have to try and track her that way."

"Gotcha...I should hit town early tomorrow morning. I'll grab a car at the airport and meet you at your house bright and early." Brent ended the call, leaving Brand with nothing to do but think about Sara.

Brand spent what remained of the evening and several hours the next morning reviewing the limited facts he had gathered from Sara's house. With the worry of Sara missing and the troubling thoughts of what he had found, Brand fell into an uneasy sleep sitting up on his couch.

The chiming of the doorbell eventually seeped into his subconscious and woke him up. Taking a moment to gather his senses, he stood up and walked to the door. Brent's sorry face greeted him as he pulled the door open. His friend wore an expensive, tailored suit that Brand assumed had cost more than the truck he drove. The man's thin face was clean-shaven with a mouth locked in a perpetual boyish smirk. His facial features sharp with a high forehead that was topped by a mat of medium long reddish brown hair. The head propped up by a long reedy neck. The concern hidden behind Brent's dark eyes underlined the reason for the visit.

The man standing beside Brent was a study in contrast to Brand's friend. Darcy Fields, one of the best computer techs in the country stared back at Brand through a pair of thick glasses poised on a short flat nose. The computer geeks hair was sticking in all directions and a bushy unkempt beard rounded his features, his clothes hung listlessly off his chubby frame, wrinkled and stained. Clutched in Darcy's stubby hands was a pair of hard computer cases.

Brand stepped aside and motioned the two men into his house.

"Grab yourselves some coffee, I've got to have a quick shower while you set your computers up. Then we can get started," Brand told the men as he led the way into the kitchen.

Brent assisted his tech as he set up his computers on the table in Brand's kitchen. The two men were seated and drinking coffee by the time Brand walked back down the stairs.

Brent waved his cup at Brand. "Darcy's hooked up and ready to go. He needs a few more minutes to link into the mainframes back at my office. Once he has the connection established, we could start scouring the net for video from the bombing."

"Sounds good," Brand answered. "The sooner we sort through the pictures, the quicker we can find the video that Sara had called about."

"It's a long shot," Brent reminded his friend. "There must be thousands upon thousands of pictures and videos downloaded to the net since the explosions. No way that she didn't just leave with some friends of hers and left her phone at her house?"

"Sara hasn't really been in town long enough to make many friends and the recording on her phone..." Brand stopped, "the front door of her house being unlocked... yeah, I'm pretty confident."

Brent nodded his head in affirmation. "You're right. From what you have told me, her sudden disappearance is looking more like abduction. What could she have possibly have found and why take her? Also, how would anyone know what she found, it's not like her to broadcast this sort of information?"

"I have a hard time believing that the same terrorist cell who planned the subway bombing would be tech savvied enough to blanket the net. That's pretty high tech." Brent stopped lost in thought. "Hell, I can't even imagine any factions that would have that kind of technology.

Sitting at the table, his jaw resting in his hands Brand thought about Brent's statement.

"You're right," he said. "It doesn't seem likely that a bunch of guys willing to blow themselves up would be overly concerned about being discovered even if they do have the technology. Hell, they're constantly online boasting about their deeds. This whole computer thing doesn't smell right, that's not how terrorists operate."

Darcy interrupted the conversation when the computers were connected and the three men sat in front of the lit screens and slowly plodded through the endless videos from the bombing.

Brand sat in front of his own computer; it was nowhere near as powerful as the ones Brent had brought along, but it still served the purpose. Several hours later in need of a break, Brand stood up to stretch and left the kitchen for his front deck to have a cigarette. He had almost reached the door when his phone rang. The number was one he didn't recognize, he pressed the receive button connecting the call on his way out the door.

Brand answered and waited, a female voice spoke.

"Mr. Coldstream?" asked the woman on the other end.

"Yes. This is Brand Coldstream, may I ask who's calling?"

"My name is Betty Anderson, I live across the street from Sara Monahan. Sally from next-door came over when I arrived home and told me you had been by. She gave me your card and asked that I call you. I did watch Miss Monahan leave her house with two gentlemen the other day. I don't know if that helps you much?" she finished.

"Are you at home now Mrs. Anderson?" asked Brand as he rushed back into the house.

"I plan to be home for the rest of the evening, Mr. Coldstream."

With his heart racing, Brand continued, "Brand...you can call me Brand. Would you mind if I came to your house right away? I'd like to ask you some questions about Miss Monahan and the men she left with if you can spare the time?"

"I'll expect you soon then, do you think Miss Monahan's alright? She asked.

"I hope so," Brand choked out. Brand confirmed the address and ended the call.

Brand stared at the phone in his hand for a second and took a few deep breaths. Finally, he had some proof of what he had been suspicious of since his return home. He allowed himself to hope that Mrs. Anderson could shed some light on the situation and help him piece together what had happened to Sarah.

Silent Crusade

Chapter 11

"Grab your coat Brent," Brand almost shouted as he rushed back into the house. "I think we might have a lead on Sara's abductors. I just talked to a lady who lives across the street from Sara. She witnessed Sara leaving her house with a couple of men. She'll be at home the rest of the day so I told her we'd be right over."

The two men climbed into Brand's truck. Gravel flew down the back alley as Brand sped away from his house. Numerous traffic laws were broken as he raced toward Betty Anderson's house. More than once Brent had to put his hand on the dash to keep from being thrown out of his seat. He thought of ribbing his friend about his driving habits but the look on Brand's face made him hold his tongue.

Brand slammed on the brakes in front of the Anderson house, the truck coming to a stop with one wheel on the sidewalk. Brand flung open the drivers door and sprinted for the house leaving Brent to catch up with him as he sprinted up the sidewalk and knocked on the front door.

"Mrs. Anderson, I'm Brand Coldstream. This is my friend Brent Gallows," Brand spit out the words motioning behind him. "He's assisting in the search for Sara Monahan."

"Come on in and have a seat Mr. Coldstream, Mr. Gallows. Can I get you two something to drink?" She asked leading them into the living room.

"No thanks, we're good," Brand remained standing. "You told me on the phone that you saw Sara leave with a couple of men the other day. Is there any chance you remember what they looked like?" Brand asked impatiently.

"Well...they looked kind of like salesmen, you know...they both wore nice suits like Mr. Gallows, but the suits were a little more lived in, like the men had been wearing them for a long time. When I first noticed the men that was the first thing that came to mind, what kind of salesmen drive to a person's house and picks them up."

"How about their car, anything particular you could tell us about that?" Brand prompted.

"Blue…at least I'm pretty sure it was blue…or black maybe. Big car, four doors, kind of low to the ground, nice looking car if the color wasn't so dark," she said, speaking slowly while searching her memory for the details from that day.

"Anything else about the car you can remember, anything that stands out would be helpful," Brent joined the conversation trying to coax out details. "How about the licence plate, any chance you saw the plate number?"

"Oh, well…there was a number on the trunk of the car…Three Hundred…I think…with a letter after it, a letter…" Mrs. Anderson paused, trying to picture the back of the car. "…C, yes the letter C after the number Three Hundred and the licence plate wasn't an Alberta plate, that's what got me wondering about the salesmen. They must have driven a long way to pick Miss Monahan up. The plate was grey, lighter grey. The writing on the plate was hard to see but I am certain the first letter of the name on the plate was an M."

"So the car had a customized plate," Brand interjected, trying to picture the plate that was being described to him.

"No, no the plate had regular numbers on it, the M was the name above the numbers, just like Alberta is above the numbers on our plates. The car was across the street, I couldn't make the name out very clearly from here," she corrected Brand. "Give me one minute, I wrote the plate number down, I was suspicious of the salesmen and we've had some trouble in the neighbourhood lately. I may not be in the neighbourhood watch, but I still like to keep an eye on things. With the kids these days, you just never know when something might be helpful," she rambled on then stood up and shuffled into the kitchen. Brand could hear her rummaging through papers. Brent gave Brand a weak smile and a half-hearted thumbs up.

"Here it is!" Brand heard her call from the kitchen then she shuffled back into the living room. Walking over to where Brand stood she passed him a piece of paper. Removing his phone from his pocket he recorded the plate number. "Anything else at all you can remember. The men, do you recall what they looked like."

"Average, I'd have to say," Mrs. Anderson replied. "One was close to your height I guess and probably about your build. They both had short hair, brown or black hair. Both looked kind of the same. You know, same suits, same build, even pretty much the same hair color. And glasses, they both had sunglasses on," she finished. "I hope this helps you two, I sure hope Miss Monahan is alright, maybe I should have called the police when they first left."

"You've been a big help. Thank you," Brand consoled her. Bidding her farewell, the two climbed back into Brand's truck.

"Well that's a start," Brent said, interrupting Brand's thoughts. "I'll give Darcy a call and ask him to start looking for cars with the number three hundred on the back, the licence plate, starting with an M, Manitoba perhaps."

"All the Manitoba plates I've noticed are white, but it could be a custom plate from there," Brand added. "The Three Hundred, I wonder if that wouldn't be a Chrysler Three Hundred. That's a bigger car isn't it?"

"I'll have Darcy check through Chrysler models for the 300, and then run the plates to see if they are registered to something that matches the vehicle she described. Just try not to kill us on the way back would you," Brent ribbed his friend.

Brand paid more attention to the other cars on his way back to his house, his mind processing the information he'd just received. When the truck was back in the garage, the two of them walked back into his house.

Darcy looked up from his computer as they entered. "The good news is you were right, the Three Hundred is on the back of the Chrysler sedans."

"One down," exclaimed Brent. "Now if we can get lucky with the licence plate, we'll have something solid to go on."

Brand went straight for his computer searched for a Manitoba government page and checked plate styles from that province. "Nope. The plate doesn't match any of the ones they show here."

"Well, what about...Missouri, Maine." Brent volunteered.

Brand stopped his friend. "You're thinking of states from the other side of the country. Montana...Montana's right below us," he stated.

"That would make sense, how far of a drive is it?" Brent asked.

"It's only a few hours to the border, I guess, depending where you cross…but how would you get through the border crossing with an unwilling passenger. The guards at the border are pretty thorough in checking vehicles; so even hiding someone in the trunk wouldn't work, too risky," Brand continued typing on the computer. "It doesn't mean it can't be done, besides we have no idea who we're dealing with so I suppose anything is possible."

Brand asked Darcy to check with the Montana DMV for a possible plate match. If that doesn't work he told him to then check all the states with names starting with M. Brand got up from the table, walked to counter to grab a cup of coffee. With a coffee in hand he leaned back against the counter, his mind racing ahead for the next step to take.

His first thought was to call the police and notify them about the blue Chrysler Three Hundred and that it might possibly have American plates, but why would they bother with that, there are probably hundreds if not thousands of blue Chryslers from the states in town. He could tell them that he had a hunch that she was kidnapped and taken across the border, but again, they would tell him to stay out of their way and quit wasting their time.

Until he had some solid proof, calling the police would be a waste of everyone's time. He was just anxious to enlist more people in the search. Sara had been gone for three days already meaning she could be just about anywhere. Even if they found a match for the plates, a car isn't stationary. He would just have to hope the tech was good enough to track it once they discovered more about it.

"I'm heading out onto the deck for a smoke," he said to no one in particular as he made his way to the front door. Taking a seat on the deck he lit a cigarette and cleared his mind before sifting through the small amount of information he had so far. With so little concrete evidence, all he could do was theorize possible scenarios.

What had Sara found that made her a target? And why would her abductors drive all the way from the States to grab her? Every thread he followed in his head ended in the same result, a dead end. Frustrated he stopped, he accepted the fact that without more details he could speculate endlessly and still be no closer to an answer.

Brand was still sitting on the deck when Brent opened the door and joined him.

"Darcy hacked into the Montana DMV. No luck finding that plate number so far. How certain do you suppose Sara's neighbour is about the plate number, she's old and her eyesight might not be the best?" Brent asked. "None the less, I placed a call to a friend south of the border. He works for the state department so I called in a favour and asked him to run the plate number."

"We have to remember that with the amount of states and the millions of registered vehicles down south this is going to be a long shot. Darcy's working on hacking into the camera feeds at the nearest border crossings between here and the States. Maybe we can get lucky and spot the car at one of them. If Sara's abductors are Americans then they might have driven back across the border with her."

"We will need something to go on we can't just drive down to the States and search for blue cars." Brand replied. "Hopefully Darcy will have some luck with the camera feeds."

The two of them sat on the deck talking as Brand finished his smoke.

"I better head in. I'm going to contact my office and get them involved with the search," Brent explained and stood up, Brand close on his heels.

Darcy spoke to the two as they joined him in the dining room; his eyes remained locked on his computer screen.

"I was just about to come and get you guys. I have found six crossings in Alberta and one a short drive into B.C. which ones would you like to start checking first?"

"What I can do is download a camera feed onto each of our computers that way the three of us can search through the feeds a lot quicker," Darcy explained to them. "How close can you come to guessing the time she disappeared Brand?"

Chewing on his lip Brand was slow to answer as he pieced together the timeline. "She would have been abducted Wednesday morning. That was the day after she left Brent the message then she never called him back like she promised. Also, that was the day her neighbour said she saw her get into the blue car. So if we go on the theory that she was driven into the States, let's see…the Coutts border crossing would take them say two and a half hours to reach. The one below Cardston is probably at least three hours or more and if they went through B.C. that would have to be four or five hours. I would think that we are looking at early afternoon on Wednesday at least."

"Alright, I'll cue the cameras to noon on Wednesday and we can start there. Are those the three major crossings?" he asked Brand. "You don't think that they would try to use a less traveled route?"

Brand thought about that for a minute. "No. I think whoever took her would want a bigger and busier crossing, less chance of having their car thoroughly checked."

"Okay. Let's start with the bigger ones and if we don't come across the car there, I can always bring up the camera feeds from the smaller border crossings." Darcy was already configuring the computers to show video feeds from the three busiest Alberta/Montana border crossings.

The three men watched hour after hour of video showing the back end of vehicles pulling up to and then driving through the crossings. Early afternoon passed into late afternoon and than early evening. Finally Brent broke the silence.

"Let's take a break and find a restaurant for supper. I'm starving," he said. "Grab a quick bite to eat and give our eyes a chance to focus again. What do you guys think?"

Darcy was quick to agree. Brand was more reluctant, he wanted to find the car, find out where Sara had disappeared but after some urging from the others he gave in.

Chapter 12

The three men returned to Brand's house in the dark. The hour was getting late, but neither of them was willing to give up for the night. They agreed that they would only watch the video feed from each crossing until midnight of the day Sara went missing.

Brent finished his scan of the first crossing and had Darcy retrieve the feed from the next crossing on the list. Darcy set up Brent's computer to view the Roosville/ Grasmere station between B.C. and Montana and set up the final two feeds on the other computers.

Around three Brent called the other two over to look at his computer screen. The time stamp on the video read 1:57 06/07/15. Frozen in the picture was the back of a blue Chrysler Three Hundred bearing a Montana license plate with the same number Betty Anderson had supplied.

Darcy switched places with Brent in front of the computer, manipulating the image, zooming in on the back of the car. After several minutes, Darcy had provided a very clear picture of the plate. They now knew where the car crossed and had a general area where to start looking for it.

"Can you see if there are any other cameras around the booth? One that would give us a view inside the car?" Brand spoke, looking over Darcy's shoulder. "Something... anything that would allow us to know for sure if Sara was actually in that car."

"Give me a few minutes and I will see what other cameras are in the area," Darcy replied, his fingers dancing across the computers keyboard. Images appeared and then were replaced by new ones, one after the other. Brand watched, the excitement of a breakthrough giving him a renewed sense of optimism, finally a tangible lead to point the group in the right direction.

"Here we go gentlemen, this camera is stationed above the guards head and shows the car's driver. It looks like there are two men in the car with her. I can slow the video down so we can view the feed frame by frame. We will be able to get a look through the car windows."

Brand and Brent crowded closer to the computer screen. Their attention focused on the still pictures they were viewing. The three men collectively held their breath as the still frames marched across the screen. Darcy paused the video slide show once the back window of the car crept into view. Sara's face appeared through the glass. Bingo. Her features were not easy to read, but now they knew that she was in the car.

"Rewind the video feed and try to get a picture of the driver," Brent asked. He had straightened up and let a sigh out. Looking at Brand, he said, "I guess a road trip is in order."

"Here is a fairly clear picture of the driver's face as he turns his head toward the booth. I can send the picture to your phones," Darcy told the men as they started to move into action.

"I'm going to grab a few clothes. Brent, leave Darcy the keys to your rental, we'll take my truck," instructed Brand.

"Sure thing," Brent replied. "Give me a few minutes to take a quick shower and grab my suitcase and I'll be ready to go."

Before the two left the house, Brent plied Darcy with instructions. "Keep trying to find more information about those men and see if you can find any more security footage of the car and where it may have gone. Find out where the vehicle is registered that will save us some time."

Four o'clock in the morning, the two of them climbed in Brand's truck and headed for the border between B.C. and the United States.

Chapter 13

For the better part of five days, Sara was kept locked in the room of the cabin in the mountains. The only time she had any contact with anyone was when the men guarding her delivered her meals. The men bringing her food would never answer any of her questions. She had made no progress toward finding out why she had been abducted and brought to this place.

The upside of being left alone was that no one had questioned of assaulted her. The men responsible for her detention were even what one would describe as hospitable. The accommodations and civil treatment only proved to be frustrating. Why did they take her and how long would she be held? At times, the only reason Sara was aware she wasn't alone was the noise made by the people guarding her door. Not a lot of comfort in that, she thought to herself.

From her view of the driveway and the front of the house, she had not spotted very much activity the last few days. Most of the people who were at the cabin when she arrived now seemed to be gone. From the minimal noise throughout the house, she imagined that there were not too many people left on the property.

She had no idea what type of gathering had taken place when she arrived or what was in store for her, in fact, she would have thought that she had been forgotten about if it weren't for meals arriving at her room regularly. She tried desperately to talk to the person on the other side of the door when the meals arrived but so far her pleas went unanswered.

She had not seen the two men who had abducted her since she first arrived. The man who delivered her food appeared to be the same person and always ignored her. Now and then she could make out faint sounds of conversation. The voices seemed to come from the same two people over the last couple of days leading her to believe that they were the only ones left in the house besides her.

Her mood swung between bouts of fear for her life to anger towards her captors. In her frustration, she would throw various items she found in the room at the door in an attempt to gain someone's attention. No one ever came in response. Her meals were the only contact she had.

Silent Crusade

The TV mounted on one wall provided her with a constant companion, at least, something to break the monotony of the day and offer some small bit of distraction. She had turned the television on shortly after she had been locked up and hadn't turned it off since. For five days she listened to the drone of the voices from the TV that kept her up-to-date on the world outside the locked bedroom door.

Although she feared for her safety, she found herself wishing for something to happen. Anything would be better than being kept a prisoner in this room. One way or the other, she thought, for better or for worse, let it end. The solitude, the uncertainty of what was going to happen, the endless wild flights of her imagination were wearing on her nerves. She found herself talking to the daytime TV hosts, and she was sure they were starting to answer back. Even screaming would not shake the sense of desolation anymore.

Chapter 14

By Thursday morning, two days after the young lady arrived at his retreat, August's other guests had all left. The last member left at the cabin, he gave the order to have the extra security assigned to other details. Four men stayed behind. Later in the day two of the men would escort him, the other two would staying behind to watch the property and to continue to watch over the girl.

Here she would remain out of sight, locked away until Christianity delivered the final blow against the hated Islamic religion. For the last three months, the cabal of devout Christian crusaders had very carefully manipulated the leaders of the Western World forcing their hand to remove the spread of terror in the world. The containment of the information and the young lady's silence was imperative. August deemed this necessary for achieving the Cabal's goal, for this, he was truly sorry.

He reflected on the road the Cabal had traveled down for the protection of their religion. How for decades this secret Christian alliance had steadily built up a network of dedicated followers sworn to protect the Christian faith. Leagues of men and women around the world willing to do whatever the Cabal asked of them in the name of the Lord.

The army of loyal soldiers the Cabal had amassed would be the envy of any country in the world. A shadow army of men and women buried deep inside all walks of life, many deeply planted inside the governments throughout the world, all doing their part to bring about the balance of power in Christianity's favour.

Since Nine-Eleven and the rise of Islamic terrorists to the forefront of the world's collective view, August's Alliance had fought hard to stem the tide of terror and bring the lost masses back to the folds of Christianity.

The ongoing battle currently being fought against the Muslim's had been carefully planned, and every step meticulously thought out well in advance to prevent detection. The other two bombings the cabal had initiated had been flawless in their execution and the group felt as confident about the one in the Toronto subway as well until this Canadian woman discovered the video of the bomber.

63

August thought how fortunate the group was in apprehending the Canadian women once she had discovered the accidental video of the Toronto bomber. Years of careful planning could have been washed down the drain if she had time to expose the bombing as a charade. His group had been careless.

The world could not know; the uninformed masses would never understand the sacrifices that this secret army was willing to go through to save the millions of lost souls. So for this, the girl would have to remain his guest in the cabin until the mission was complete. Then and only then she would know the reasoning for her imprisonment and he was sure at that time she would be thankful.

The burden of this crusade weighed heavily on August mind. The loss of innocent lives caught in this battle was something that he, and he alone would have to answer to God. He was prepared to spend eternity in hell for his actions so that the souls of humanity remained with the Lord.

Sitting at the desk in his study, August picked up the phone receiver off his desk. The landline in his house was a secure phone line, and it needed to be. He placed a call to his asset in Afghanistan. The need to check on the progress of the bombing in Chicago, the timetable moved up. The risk of discovery had exponentially increased; the plan carried out quickly and furtively.

August wanted an update and wanted to stress the need for urgency. The sooner the American President saw the light and pushed the button, the sooner the world would be released from the grasp of the devil, its faith once again returning to the welcoming hands of the Lord then the need for secrecy would no longer be warranted.

In his opinion, the Muslim religion of Islam was spreading across the world like a fourteen-century plague; it was time to administer a twenty-first-century cure!

Chapter 15

Brand pulled his truck alongside a gas pump at a twenty-four-hour gas station topping the gas tank as Brent went to purchase coffees for the trip from the store. Once they left the city limits behind finding gas stations that were open at this time of morning would be doubtful.

Turning onto Highway Two, they headed south toward the southwest corner of the province that led into the province of B.C. and down to the Montana border. The traffic was almost non-existent because of the early hour. Brand set the cruise control to a speed that he hoped wouldn't encourage any cops on the highway to stop them. Enough time had already elapsed since Sara's abduction; he fought an overwhelming need to rush that included wasted time getting written up for speeding tickets.

Brent told him that he was going to grab a few hours sleep and then he would take over driving when Brand got tired.

"Wake me up when you're ready to switch," Brent said as he rolled up his jacket and placed it against the truck window to use as a pillow.

Poor radio reception left nothing to listen to besides Brent's snoring, so Brand was alone with his thoughts, thoughts consumed by worry over Sarah's abduction. He figured if he kept a steady speed they would reach the border around eight AM. Early enough that traffic at the crossing would be light.

The two of them weren't on official business, so Brand decided against asking the border guards about the suspect's car and its occupants. The guards would probably wonder about Brand's intent if he probed and delay his entry into the States. He decided to wait until the crossing was behind them before inquiring about the car and showing the driver's picture in Montana. There were not a lot of towns close to the Canadian border so the pool of witnesses in Montana who had noticed the car should be small, hopefully speeding up the search.

Brand fought to keep his eyes open about two hours into the trip; just miles shy of the Crowsnest Pass. He pulled the truck off to the side of the road and woke Brent up. Exchanging positions, Brent climbed behind the wheel, and

Brand got comfortable in the passenger's seat, within minutes the truck was speeding toward the border again.

The next time Brand opened his eyes; the truck was crawling forward behind several other vehicles waiting in line for their turn at the crossing booths. The sky was bright and sunny, and the cab of the truck warmed up even at this early hour. Brand looked around at the buildings and other vehicles, his brain still foggy from the small amount of sleep he'd had since Sara's disappearance.

Brent tossed a good morning at Brand as he fiddled with the radio. Stopping at a classic rock station, he turned his attention back to the line of cars, a smile on his face.

"What is so amusing?" Brand asked.

"Nothing really," Brent responded, the smile still lingering on his lips. "I was just thinking back to the old days at the Agency when we were sent out on assignments like this."

Brand and Brent met when they were both working for the Canadian Security Intelligence Service, better known as CSIS. Brent's comment awoke memories of their team and the recent deaths of the other three members. The pain was still fresh in their minds, and a wave of doubt followed the reference intruding on Brand's thoughts. If his team of highly trained operatives could be taken out, what chance did Sarah have?

"I suppose, but those missions were never as personal as this one," Brand replied grumpily.

"You're right. That was a long time ago. Now you fish for a living, and I've got more headaches than I can count from running my security firm. Those were the good old days..." Brent finished, the smile still stuck to his face.

"Quit grinning. The guards are going to think we're up to something besides; you look like a flipping idiot.

"Here, let's switch places. I'll drive us through," Brand said and opened the passenger door, stepping out of the truck. Before he climbed back into the driver's seat, he opened the back door on his truck and rummaged under the seat pulling out two cases containing fly rods and some wading gear. He set the gear on the back seat and took his place behind the steering wheel.

Rolling up to the crossing booth, Brand lowered the driver's window as the truck pulled even with the guardhouse. "Reach into the glove box and grab out the truck's registration?" he said to Brent.

The border guard looked up as Brand stopped the truck.

"Where are you guys from?" The guard asked.

"Calgary," Brand replied passing the trucks papers along with their passports.

"Your friend's from Ottawa?"

"Yes. He came out west for a visit."

"Reason for entering the United States? Business or pleasure?"

"Pleasure," Brand explained. "We are going to try our luck fly fishing on a few of the rivers." Brand passed one of his business cards from his guiding service to the guard.

"How long do you plan on being in the country?" The guard quizzed.

"Two or three days probably, all depends on the fishing."

"What all do you have in the truck," The guard inquired further.

"Just a couple of small suitcases and our fly gear," Brand he pointed to the back seat of the truck. The guard rose up from his chair and looked past Brand into the interior of the cab.

"Okay. Drive through," the guard handed back their paperwork. "Enjoy your visit!" he added.

Brand put the truck in gear and rolled through the lane into the state of Montana. A short distance from the crossing gates at a cluster of buildings the men climbed out of the truck and walked inside for coffees before starting the next leg of the trip.

When they were back in the truck, Brent turned to him, "What's our plan now?"

"There isn't much between here and Eureka. That's the next town down the highway. I was thinking that we should stop there, grab a bite to eat and spend some time showing the locals the picture of the driver. Somebody might have noticed them as the car passed through," he answered in a matter of fact tone; his eyes glued to the road. Montana was a big state; they would need a good bit of luck to locate anyone who had noticed the car or the man driving it.

Eureka, Montana lay only miles from the border. A little under an hour after entering the state, Brand passed from table to table showing the picture of the driver he had saved on his phone to the early morning breakfast crowd.

From the restaurant, the two split up and concentrated on the main thoroughfares in the small town. No one recalled seeing the man or the car. After spending a couple of fruitless hours in Eureka approaching businesses and talking to strangers on the street they climbed back in the truck and left the town following the highway further into Montana.

Brand felt somewhat disheartened as he passed the town limits of Eureka. He knew going in that finding the car, and driver were a long shot to begin with, but that didn't make it any less disappointing. He grabbed his package of cigarettes off the dash of the truck and lit one. Drawing the smoke deep into his lungs, Brand held it there briefly then slowly exhaled, his thoughts racing ahead. Whitefish, Montana was the next stop on the list.

Chapter 16

The secure satellite phone that Michael Johnson had carried along for this mission started to ring. He excused himself from the group of tribal elders he was in conversation with and walked past the scattered array of tents towards some large boulders. The calls that this phone was meant for his ears only, thus he took the utmost care to keep these conversations private.

After several minutes on the phone, Johnson disconnected the call and went back to his meeting with the village elders. A grim comfort settled over him. His plan had received the green light. His job now was to find volunteers willing to martyr themselves as suicide bombers and escort them to the United States. Once in America, another group would handle the details of hiding the Afghanis and preparing the Jihadists for the fatal attack.

With the resources, which funded this mission, transporting the Afghani men into the States would be relatively easy in comparison to finding volunteers brave enough to die for their cause. Lots of the boys living in the village talked a good game, bragging about how willing they were to sacrifice themselves in the name of Islam. It turned out that talk was cheap, and many of the people just liked to boast among their friends when they knew they would not have to follow through with their rhetoric.

He wanted, no he needed devout Muslims, who wouldn't turn tail and run once faced with the inevitability of certain death.

Johnson asked around for Nabi Hussoini's location. He needed Hussoini's help in selecting reliable young Jihadists for the mission. After choosing the candidates, Johnson and his crew would arrange to smuggle these men across the Pakistani border and on flights to the States.

He would be sending his men to escort the three recruits on the long journey. The plan would require him to arrange three different routes to the states with no apparent connection to each to avoid detection. With the added security now employed at the western airports, too many suspicions would be aroused by a group of Middle Eastern men flying into the States together.

After that last phone call, time was now also a factor with a visible deadline. He was prompted to execute his part of the plan within the next week.

By the time, he found the volunteers and arranged safe passage to the United States it would not leave much time for the group stateside to carry out their part of the arrangements.

What the hell, he thought to himself. He only had to smuggle some men from out of Afghanistan into Pakistan and then make certain they were on planes headed to the United States without being detected. The success of the rest of the mission would then be out of his hands and placed into God's.

Chapter 17

The two ex-CSIS agents arrived in Whitefish, Montana by midday and much like Eureka, the pair set out checking popular establishments where travelers were most likely to stop in the town. After a couple of hours flashing the picture and of talking to the locals without luck, they pulled into a drive-thru burger joint for a bite to eat. Waiting at the window for their food, Brand showed the driver's picture to the attendant at the window.

The young man passed a bag of food to Brand before stopping to take a look at the picture on Brand's phone.

"Yeah. I've seen him around here a lot lately."

"Anything you can tell me about him?" Brand prodded.

The drive thru attendant eyed Brand for a minute, "You a cop." "This guy do something wrong?" The kid questioned.

"No," Brand replied. "Just trying to locate him."

The kid thought about Brand's request.

"I'm not positive, but I believe he works at a cabin up the mountain from here. Some old man from the east coast owns a big ass house and uses it as a retreat in the summer. I'm sure this guy said he is involved in security for the property."

Brand remained at the drive-thru window talking with the kid and collected a few vague details about the property. The kid didn't know a lot about the owner or the cabin and most of what he knew he had heard was from people gossiping. Before leaving, Brand asked the kid for directions, thanked the kid and pulled away from the window.

Setting the food on the seat beside him, Brand navigated his truck through the town. On the eastern limits, he turned the truck onto the tree-lined road leading up the mountain in the direction of the cabin.

"How do you want to approach this?" Brent asked.

Silent Crusade

"I'll pull off the road short of the property, and we go by foot and check the place out. When we have an idea what we're up against and who's all there, we can come up with a suitable plan. The only other option is to drive right up to the house and knock on the door, but that's just foolish."

"Maybe, maybe not," Brent looked at him, a grin lighting up his face.

"What are you thinking?" Brand looked back at Brent.

"Eat your burger, let me give this some thought." The two ate in silence while Brand steered the truck around the sharp curves, the road winding back and forth along the side of the mountain. Rounding a final curve to where they were told the cabin lay; Brent shoved aside his food and explained his plan.

"What the hell kind of sauce did they put in your burger? You can't be serious?" Brand exclaimed.

"If you have a better idea now would be the time to speak up, don't keep it a secret," Brent replied the grin still fixed on his face. "Stop the truck before the driveway and I'll switch places with you."

Grudgingly Brand steered the truck to the side of the road. Brent hopped out the passenger's door, reached into the back seat of the truck to retrieve his suit jacket and walked around the hood to the open driver's door.

Putting the truck into gear, he looked at Brand.

"You ready?" He asked.

"Sure, why not," Brand replied. The smile clung to Brent's face as he turned the truck into the shaded driveway. He had started to whistle, a smile appearing on his face as He brought the truck to a halt in front of the steps to the large cabin stepped free of the cab with his suit coat in his hand. Brent started to whistle as he reached into the backseat and grabbed a hand full of papers. He swung the truck door shut and walked briskly toward the cabin door. Brand shook his head in bewilderment at his friend, climbed out of the cab and followed.

The wooden door of the cabin had opened before Brent finished climbing the steps. A man clad in a plaid work shirt stood in the entrance, one hand on the doorknob ready to close the door once he dismissed the unwelcome intrusion.

Silent Crusade

Chapter 18

Over the last few days, the house and surrounding grounds had fallen deathly quiet. Sara was going out of her mind, her overactive imagination conjuring up all sorts of different scenarios that had her suffering at the hands of her abductors. Slowly she started wishing, almost begging for them to come finally get her and do their worst. She just wanted this nightmare to end.

Even the few routine activities that she now associated with the place had stopped since the old men in the suits, and their drivers had departed. Three times a day her meals would show up at her door and then the place would return to a tomb like a state.

Standing by the barred window, she stared hopelessly outside at the blue sky over the mountains. Under any other circumstances, she would be thrilled, almost mesmerized with the views the area had to offer. The bright sun on the majestic mountains framed by the thick forests of evergreen trees was breathtaking. For a brief second her mind drifted, she could almost smell the fragrance of the trees and hear the birds playing and singing in the tree branches.

Sadly she found that being locked in a room diminished the pleasure of the beauty right outside of her window. She sighed and was about to turn away from the window when the sound of an approaching drifted up to her ears. Pressing her face tight to the glass, she craned her neck to get a view of the driveway at the front of the house.

She continued to wait with her face against the bars. She had given up all hope of being rescued, but the approaching vehicle, at least, broke up the monotony of her day. Her breath fogged the pane of glass as she watched the trail of dust that rose up from the graveled entrance. Like a mirage, a truck emerged from the haze and pulled into the driveway

At first, she didn't register any of the details about the vehicle; it was just a distraction to break up the boredom. The longer she stared at it, the more the familiarity of knowing the truck seeped into the back of her mind. She realized that she had seen it before. In fact, she had seen it a lot of times before.

Why would Brand's truck be here? Then it donned on her. Brand's truck was pulling up in front of the house…the same house she was being held a prisoner.

She could feel the elation pushing away the depression that she had been feeling the past few days and then just as quickly she started to panic. What if he didn't know she was here and left? She was locked in this room with no way to signal to him, and she was pretty certain her guards weren't about to brag about her presence to some stranger at the door or anyone for that matter. Isn't that how kidnapping worked?

Her mind fought to seek a solution to the problem. She could not let him leave without her. Looking around the room, she did a quick inventory of the now all too familiar contents; her excitement mixed with panic caused her to struggle to figure out a way to signal him.

Then she paused to clear her mind. Panic was not going to help her figure a way out. If she could not get out the room, maybe something else might be able to. She grabbed a floor lamp and turned toward the window. The base of the floor lamp was too big to fit between the bars. Swinging the light by its trunk, she smashed it against the solid frame of the bed. Once, twice, on the third try the base broke off.

With the broken lamp held firmly in both hands, Sara rammed it repeatedly against the window shattering the glass. Once a hole in the glass appeared, she took a deep breath and started screaming Brand's name.

The man at the door was about to speak when Brent's foot hit the top step and stood in front of the door, his hand extended in greeting.

"Good to see you brother," Brent beamed at the man standing in the doorway, the words flowed out of his mouth with a smoothness that would make any religious door knocker proud.

"Brother Maxwell and I are from the Church of Better Judgement. We are traveling around the countryside looking to recall lost members of Jesus's flock…" Brent intoned with a vigour that would put a lot of backwoods pastors to shame. The man at the door stared at Brent before interrupting.

"Buddy, I ain't lost. Your standing on private property so the two of you had better make tracks out of here before even Jesus won't be able to help you."

The conversation at the door was interrupted by the sound of breaking glass followed closely by a woman shouting. A puzzled look crossed the face of the man at the door. It took a split second for Brand to realize that it was his name that he was hearing. He drove a hard right fist into the doorman's jaw at the same time grabbing the guy's collar with his left hand to stop the man from tumbling back into the house.

A movement farther in the house caught Brand's attention. A second man had stepped out of an inside doorway. Brand noticed the man's hand rising, the barrel of a pistol pointed toward the tussle at the front door.

Before he heard the bark of the gun, Brand's years of training and experience allowed him to react instinctively. He continued pulling the dazed doorman across this own body using the man as a shield.

The doorman's body jerked twice as bullets thudded into his back. The man's last breath gushed out of his open mouth as the impact from the bullets pushed his body into Brand sending the two stumbling backward out the door and onto the concrete step.

Brent was standing to the side of the door when he watched Brand and the doorman tumble past him. Spotting a gun tucked into the waistband of the doorman's pants, Brent reached out. His outstretched fingers curled around the gun handle as he dove inside the house. Brent tucked his shoulder under his body in a forward roll. Quickly coming out of the roll with his body low to the ground he traded bullets with the gunman.

Brent's shots found their mark. The gunman was spun around and sent crashing into a wall, the gun falling from his hand. Jumping to his feet, Brent took a couple of long strides and kicked the gun out of the fallen man's reach; his gun pointed down at the wounded man.

Brand recovered from his fall, rolled from under the dead man and bolted into the house close on Brent's heels. He bent down and picked the up the gun lying on the floor.

Without speaking, the two men crept through the main floor of the house clearing each room as they searched. In the kitchen, they found a pair of women busy preparing a meal.

Leaving Brent to secure the women Brand climbed the stairs two at a time as he raced to the second floor. He hesitated at the top of the stairs and quickly assessed the long hallway. Starting closest to the stairs he cautiously opened the door after door eliminating several rooms before he found a door at the far end of the hall locked.

Brand loudly called out Sara's name and waited. Hearing her voice behind the locked door, he warned her to stand clear. Lifting his foot he repeatedly smashed it against the panel beside the lock. After several attempts the door splintered and violently swung open crashing into the wall behind it.

Sara stood in the middle of the room staring wide-eyed at Brand. She rushed to him, threw her arms around him and buried her face tight against his chest releasing muffled sobs of relief.

Brand stood still, his arms automatically wrapping tightly around Sara for comfort. Holding her shaking body, he quietly soothed her refusing to let her go until she got control of herself. Stepping back from his embrace she looked into his eyes, her own red-rimmed eyes still wet.

"I didn't think you would be able to find me," she said in between staggered breaths.

"You had me worried, but I've got you now," he hoarsely whispered, unable to trust his voice as he fought between the elation of finding her and rage at the ones who abducted her. He felt a shudder run through his body. As the concern, he had felt earlier subsided a burning anger deep within Brand started to return.

He ached to question the man downstairs, find out why Sara was whisked away from her home, why she was being held captive? What possible reason did someone have for taking her? A flood of heated questions ran through this mind, but the answers could wait a few more minutes. He wouldn't move until he was sure she was all right.

Chapter 19

Sara began to relax and regained her composure. Brand led her back downstairs where they found Brent in the front room of the house attending to the bullet wounds of the second gunman. With the man restrained the women from the kitchen assisted Brent while he cleaned and bandaged the wounds.

Brand and Sara wandered through the house. In a large conference room, Sara spotted her computer sitting closed on a side table. She rushed over to it, opened the computer and turned it on. After a quick scan she could tell that somebody had been searching through her stored files, but, fortunately, no one had bothered to delete any of them, so she closed the computer and carried it with her as she followed Brand back into the living room. There the two stood aside watching Brent finish up treating the wounds of her captor.

"I called the local police in Whitefish...I told them to bring along an ambulance," Brent explained. "They said they'd be here a.s.a.p. We should be able to leave once they've taken our statements."

"I haven't found anything in the house so far that sheds any light into Sara's kidnapping. We did find her computer in a room in the back. After a quick look, the files seem intact." He pointed to the wounded gunman. "How about this guy, did he tell you anything?"

"Nada. I looked at both guys' ids. The body on the front step worked for the state police, which is interesting and I think this guy is either too scared of the people he works for or just plain stupid."

Brand looked at Sara. He did not like the idea of questioning her, but he had little choice.

"Did anyone explain to you why they abducted you or why they brought you here, any idea at all why they thought they should need to detain you?" he asked, patiently waiting for an answer.

She shook her head no. "These two aren't the men who showed up at my door and kidnapped me," She quietly stated then motioned to the wounded man. "When I first arrived here there was a large gathering, a lot of..." she searched for the right words, "... Old, prominent men, judging by the way they acted…the type of men who are used to luxury cars with drivers and have the need for armed personnel patrolling the grounds.

"Shortly after I was locked in the room, I watched some of them as they were leaving," she hesitated, still reeling from the ordeal. "I was taken directly to that room, so I never saw any of the old men up close. Nobody would tell me why they were all here and what they had to do with my kidnapping."

She told Brand about the men who had abducted her, the drive from Calgary and her worries about being killed somewhere along the way, how they crossed into the states one of the men pulled out a wallet containing a badge that he showed to the border guard allowing them to leave the country. "An official badge of some sort," she tried to describe its appearance, "but I couldn't see it very well from where I was sitting."

She recounted the events at the house, taking her time, long pauses of silence mixed with bouts of agitation as she relived the mental ordeal of her captivity.

Ever since he found out Sara had gone missing, Brent couldn't shake the feeling of the coincidence where Sara had no sooner thought she had made a breakthrough on the Union Station bombing only to get abducted along with her computer hours later. He had to see if Sara had connected the same pieces he had. He waited for her to finish reciting the events of the past few days and had calmed back down before he quietly raised the question about the video.

For a minute, she forgot about the trauma of her ordeal. Her face lit up while she explained about the discovery of the video, a video she was certain contained footage of the Toronto bomber. The video showed part of an alley and captured a person changing into a burka and hijab before leaving the alley. The same description several witnesses had stated to the police. Well, she was almost sure that she had seen the bomber, she gushed. Thus, the reason she had left the message but the next morning before she had a chance to search further and confirm her suspicions the two men took her.

"Do you think that the video would still be on your computer?" Brent nudged her along relieved to see her forget if even for a short time the anguish she had just been through.

"I had a quick look when I spotted my computer in the other room, and it doesn't appear tampered with," she replied hopefully.

"Since we have to wait for the police can you see if you can find the video?" Brand asked her.

Sara approached one of the household staff and requested the Internet password then proceeded to log onto her computer. Her fingers danced across the computers keypad forcing the screen to change rapidly. Several minutes of her searching through her downloaded files resulted in the video. She hit play and spun the computer to face the other two.

Without any questions, they watched the out of focus video portraying the details as Sara had described them.

Brent asked her to email the video to Brand's home computer. He would call Darcy, who he explained to Sara, was still in Brand's house and have him start combing through government databases. Starting the process of putting a name to the face in the video. Thinking ahead, Brent thought it would also be a good idea to have another copy of the video someplace safe in case the three of them ran into any other problems on their way back to Calgary.

Silent Crusade

Chapter 20

The state police arrived at the cabin by mid-afternoon their sirens screaming and gravel flying as they raced into the yard. Brand leaned against the front door of the cabin smoking a cigarette as he watched the police cars raise dust coming to a sudden stop in the yard, an EMS rig following close on their bumpers.

Officers from the Lincoln County police department jumped out of their cars using the car doors as shelter, their revolvers held at the ready as they surveyed the house and grounds around them.

Brand pushed away from the door, flicked his cigarette onto the gravel driveway and with his hands held in the air while he waited for the approaching officers. He greeted the team, and when they made no move to restrain him, he turned to go inside stepping over the dead body lying in front of the door. One of the officers bent over to check the body. Behind his back, Brand heard the trooper swear as he checked the identity of the man on the step. Still other guardedly followed a few feet behind Brand.

Brand was explaining to the local police Sergeant about the shooting when they were interrupted. The trooper from the front step pulled the Sergeant aside. Brand watched the two men. The conversation was too quiet for him to hear the words spoken but he was certain what it involved. The officers repeatedly glanced at the body lying on the front step.

The Sergeant returned to where Brand stood. He skipped to the part where he and Brent had found the cabin and wrapped up his story with an explanation of Sara's calling to them from the upstairs room leading to the gunplay on the main floor. While he told and retold his story to a couple of officers, other police members moved through the house and surrounding grounds. One cop motioned the ambulance attendants inside.

The sergeant regarded Brand suspiciously. His attention split between the two gunmen; his gaze kept returning to the dead man on the front step, the man's body partially blocking the doorway. From the officer's facial expression Brand knew the local cop recognized a fellow officer. Whatever the Sergeant was thinking he never raised the subject with Brand leaving him to wonder if the dead cop was dirty or there was more to this than met the eye.

One Lincoln County police officer took everyone's statements, pulling each aside and talking privately with him or her. The day drug on while the police decided what to do about the three Canadians involved in the shooting and abduction.

Brent grew tired of the local police and their bullshit, so he took an opportunity to step aside. Out of earshot, he dialed the number of a friend currently working for the FBI, a contact he had made while operating his security business. The cases his company often dealt with had him crossing paths with several federal agencies in both Canada and the United States. Through these dealings, he had made some very influential friends in high places. Friends that he maintained close relations with, including the heads of some three-letter law enforcement agencies. He felt that now was a good time to flex a little muscle.

The private number he called was to a top-level colleague of his stationed with the FBI in Washington. When the call was connected, Brent had a brief conversation and then passed his phone to the sergeant in charge of the scene at the house. The sergeant looked at Brent with a quizzical look on his face as he reached for the phone. The sergeant left the noisy room to speak on the phone.

On his return, the sergeant thrust the phone back at Brent and with a scowl on his face he told the three Canadians to get the hell out of his county and fast before he changed his mind and hauled them off to jail to wait while this mess was sorted out. Brand was about to say something to the police officer when Brent grabbed his coat and dragged him toward the door.

*****

At the truck, Brand helped Sara into the back seat and then along with Brent climbed into the front seats. Turning around in the driveway, Brand stepped on the gas and left a trail of rocks and dust flying.

The mood in the cab of the truck remained somber. Sara pushed Brand's fishing gear off the seat, stacked the suitcases and leaned against them. The adrenaline in her body was wearing off leaving her exhausted, so she closed her eyes and was soon fast asleep.

Brand drove straight from Montana back to Calgary; the only delays were a short stop at the border and stops for gas and coffee.

It was close to midnight by the time the trio saw the lights of Calgary on the horizon. Brand drove the truck down his back alley and parked in the garage. He stepped out of the vehicle and helped Sara to the house.

The bright interior of the house met them when they opened the back door and entered. At the first sight of Sara, Darcy jumped up from behind his computer and ran over to her grinning like a fool wrapping her up in a huge hug.

After Darcy had satisfied himself that Sara was unharmed and finished gushing with joy at her return, the four of them discussed the trip, and the many questions about Sara's abduction left unanswered.

Brent eventually directed the group's focus back to the bigger problem at hand starting with the alleged bomber video. He was eager to hear about what Darcy had discovered in his efforts at uncovering the identity of the man in the video.

"It took some doing, but I did get a hit on CODIS," Darcy told them. "The face in the video belongs to a drug addict and small-time crook. His name is Dougie Phearson. The Toronto police apparently have quite an extensive file on Mr. Phearson. I haven't contacted them yet; I thought you might want to handle that?" he said to Brent. "I printed out his file and some other background info on him."

"Perfect," Brent said. "It's late, but I can still get in touch with the RCMP in Ontario and give them the heads up on the bomber's identity. I think we can be of more use if we catch an early flight to Ottawa and continue this search with the resources from my offices." He looked around at the others, the three of them nodded in agreement.

"Darcy, see if you can book us some seats on an early morning flight out of here?"

"You all right with the trip East?" Brand asked as he studied Sara's face.

She returned the look with a weak smile and nodded her approval.

Chapter 21

Sara and Brand spent several hours rehashing the last few days, from the moment Brand left on his fishing trip until they were reunited at the cabin, before they fell asleep. The next morning, after a good nights sleep, Sara's demeanor was much lighter. She was more talkative and looked refreshed. Brand kept a close eye on her as if some one might snatch her away right before his eyes.

Before they boarded the plane, Brent called his office and arranged to have a car meet them at the airport when they arrived. The flight from Calgary left early in the morning. By mid afternoon, Ottawa time, they were being driven to Brent's offices.

On the ride to his office, Brent kept busy on the phone, getting updates, checking with sources in the RCMP and talking with other law agencies concerning the identity of the Toronto bomber.

Now that they had a face for the bomber, they needed to understand why a junkie in Canada would dress up in Muslim women's garb and blow himself up. It was an unusual move for Islamic extremists, one a lot of intelligence people did not see coming. This was just another angle for western countries to add to their watch lists in the war on terror.

Back in his office, Brent forked out assignments of his computer techs. They now had a face and a name for the bomber, what they needed next was a thorough background file on him. Where was he before the bombing? Who was he associated with, were the two other guys in the video involved in the bombing? The thought of a junkie and small time crook planning and carrying out the bombing on the Toronto subway on his own was theoretically improbable.

The techs were divided up into groups: some would dissect the bombers background, others were to search the net for any pictures of him and his friends captured in the pictures, and still others had the task of hacking into any phones or computers the bomber owned.

Brand wandered around the office, this type of investigating was beyond him. He was accustomed to face-to-face interrogations, tracking felons in the real world not by their cyber footprints. At least Sara had started to come out of her shell; she settled in front of her computer and reveled in the digital world she felt most at home in.

Brent called Brand into his office.

"I just got off the phone with Jack Presswal with the Criminal Intelligence Directorate of the RCMP in Toronto. The perp's mother has been located. Constable Presswal said that since we were the ones to give them the heads up on the bomber, he would gladly take one of us along while they speak with her."

"It's going to take me a while to get there," Brand stated.

"I already told them that. Presswal said that they would keep an eye on Mrs. Phearson until you arrived. He will have an officer at the airport to pick you up."

"Sure, sounds good. Better out there doing something than stuck in here," Brand said gesturing to the office full of computer geeks staring at monitors.

"Good. I'll get you a ride to the airport and have a ticket at the airport waiting for you. Do you need some time to grab anything for the trip?" Brent asked.

"No. I'm good. Don't let Sara out of your sight while I'm gone, I will hold you personally responsible," Brand threatened Brent as he headed out of the office on his way to tell Sara.

Brand sat down next to Sara's workstation once again checking to see how she was doing and if she wanted him to stay for a while. She assured him she was good and to go do what he was good at. He left the office in search of Brent's driver.

Chapter 22

A plainclothes officer of the Criminal Intelligence branch met Brand in the terminal of the Lester B. Pearson airport. He was several years younger than Brand but he had a self-confident look about him.

Brand watched the man's approach and thought the man was clad more for the streets of Calgary than Canada's largest city. The officer wore scuffed cowboy boots covered by faded jeans, a blazer worn over a button-up shirt and hair that hung below the collar. Without knowing better, Brand would have had a hard time pegging this man as a cop he determined as he watched the policeman approach. As the two met a hand was thrust in Brand's direction while the RCMP liaison introduced him.

"Constable Bronson. Glad to meet you Mister Coldstream," Brand's contemporary said as he raised his other arm to point to his left. "My car is parked in front of the main doors. I thought that we could head over and have a chat with Dougie Phearson's mother. Do you have any baggage to collect?"

Brand shook the hand offered to him. "No, this carry-on bag is all I brought. Lead the way officer," he said as he followed the man outside of the terminal and over to a shiny new sports car. A silver Dodge Challenger sat waiting, the polished paint sparkled in the sunlight.

Brand let out a soft whistle. "What year's your car?" he asked.

"Twenty fifteen. I've only had it for a couple of weeks now." Constable Bronson beamed as he told Brand all about the car, the horsepower, torque and miles per gallon admitting that he may have secretly taken it out on a deserted road to see what the car could do. Then with a wink added that the car handled very well indeed.

Like the officer, Brand appreciated a nice ride, and this one was not a terrible way to travel, but it simply wouldn't do for him. Where would he put his fishing gear? That didn't mean he couldn't enjoy it now.

Constable Bronson filled Brand in on the way to the suspect's mother's house. The bomber was basically a small time crook involved in petty thefts to feed his drug habit. Never really in any serious trouble aside from a few small misdemeanors, he was just a guy who could not shake the drug habit and move on with his life. He informed Brand that he had talked to some officers with the Toronto Police Service who had dealings with Phearson over the years and they were quite surprised that he would strap himself to a bomb.

"The officers I talked all agreed that he was harmless, just a mixed up kid with a weakness for shitty drugs. He was arrested a few times for break-ins and once for a botched armed robbery where he stuck his finger in the pocket of his coat and pretended it was a gun. Penny-ante shit at the best but no violence. They tell me that the guy was scared of his own shadow so they certainly wouldn't pick him for a violent offender, never mind a terrorist."

"We have a lot of manpower checking into the backgrounds Phearson's friends," the officer continued. "There is a small group of addicts that he hung around with regularly, but again, these people aren't the type to go blow up subway trains. The whole picture is off if you know what I mean."

"It certainly does seem odd. How does a small-time drug user end up in cahoots with radical terrorists? Do you think he was searching for salvation and converted to the Muslim faith?" Brand asked the question; rhetorical since even he could not imagine the scenario he described.

"Hard to say. I doubt it," Constable Bronson replied. "He lived with his mother in a low-rent part of town. She's single from what I've read. I guess raising him alone, a rough part of the city, anything is possible."

The two men continued exchanging notes as Bronson wove his car through the midday traffic to the Yorkdale-Glen Park district of Toronto. As they got closer to Dougie's mother's house, Brand saw what the other man was saying. The houses in this area were older, postwar or slightly newer, but not much. Most of the houses Brand saw were well maintained although a few houses really stuck out. In Brand's experience these were the rental properties and they housed the hard luck tenants.

Driving down several blocks they came to a street of neglected townhouses. Bronson parked the car and led the way up a cracked, weed-filled sidewalk in front of a dirty brick townhouse. The front lawns were unkempt and littered with trash. Small clumps of grass struggled to survive through and around the trash. Some of the windows were cracked, a few covered with greying plywood. Bronson knocked on an old wooden door, the paint faded and peeling.

The sound of heavy coughing came from the other side of the closed door. As it opened a sliver, a disheveled older lady, wearing a tattered robe cinched tight around her shoulders, peered at the two men on the step. Before she could speak, she was gripped by another bout of hacking.

"Mrs. Phearson?" the officer asked launching right into an introduction. "I am Constable Bronson; this is Brand Coldstream. We would like to talk to you about your son Dougie if you don't mind?"

Without saying a word, she opened the door and beckoned them in as she once again went into a coughing fit.

Brand and Bronson stood just inside the door waiting for her to finish coughing.

"Please excuse me," she told them. "Come in and have a seat. What has Dougie done now?" she asked in a tone that said this wasn't her first time with this song and dance number.

"Do you know where your son is?" the officer asked, a troubled tone to his voice.

"No, not really. He only calls me when he needs money or a place to stay when he gets booted from wherever he hangs out. I haven't talked to him for a while now." She stopped and thought. "

The last time he called me, he told me that some men had offered him a good paying job and he would have lots of money. He sounded very excited." The coughing wracked her body again. "The doctors say that I got terminal lung cancer. There is nothing they can do for me but they say there is a new trial drug that might help." She motioned around her run down house. " But I certainly can't afford them." "Dougie is trying to help me."

"Dougie, he is worried about me. He's such a good boy. I know he may be a little mixed up with the drugs and has had some trouble with the law, but he is a good son." Another coughing fit shook her frail body.

"Did your son happen to mention who the men were that offered him the job?" Brand asked her when a break in her coughing occurred.

"No... no, he didn't, only that he would have lots of money shortly and that he would take care of me," she said, her face lighting up with the thought.

"You may want to have a seat ma'am," the officer told her. "I need you to look at this picture I brought." Bronson then showed her the picture. "Is this your son, Dougie?"

"Yes. That is my Dougie?" A puzzled look showed on her face. "He...he's not..."

"I am truly sorry ma'am. This picture is on a video taken near the Toronto subway just before the explosion almost a month ago." Constable Bronson broke the news to her.

A look of horror settled over the elderly mother as the officer's words sunk in. Brand gazed around the house waiting for the grieving mother to compose herself. The woman's body was wracked with convulsions as she wept for her son. Brand was starting to get concerned about the woman, between the hacking coughs and the dreadful sobs.

The RCMP officer tried to console her until she was able to regain some control over her grief. Brand was doubtful that they would get any useful information from her but he had to try. He asked her about her son's habits. Where he was likely to hang out and with whom. Where he had last lived, did he have a girlfriend?

The distraught mother tried to be helpful but she didn't know much about her son.

"What about the money that your son said he would be getting paid?" Brand asked. His gambit of questions was running out.

The mother avoided his eyes when she answered him. "He...uh...he never sent any money like he promised to." Then to change the subject she blurted out, "Sneazy or Squeaky... whatever his name is... he would sometimes come by the house with Dougie. The man's name was something like that. Dougie said that he met his friend at one of the drug clinics he frequented."

Brand coaxed a description of Dougie's friend from the mother The description could fit hundreds of different men but the unusual nickname gave them something to go on. Brand thanked the lady and the two men walked back to the car.

"How many drug clinics are in this area?" Brand asked the constable.

"I'm not sure, but I can call the district police station, they would know, and they might even have heard of this Sneazy fellow." With that, the officer dialed information and had his call directed to the local precinct.

"Do you think she has her son's money?" he asked Brand.

"What I think is if we don't find any other clues you may want to go back and have another talk with her." Brand replied.

Silent Crusade

94

Chapter 23

After a brief talk with the captain at the local precinct, Brand and the constable set out in search of a place to get a bite to eat and kill a little time. The Captain had asked Bronson to give him a few hours and he'd call him back about the clinics and druggies with the name Sneazy or whatever the hell else sounded like that. He wanted to talk to some of the beat officers in the vicinity; they are the ones who knew the street people in the area better than anyone.

The two men found an Italian restaurant not far from Dougie's mothers. Through lunch and coffees, they chatted about the unusual case. Neither believed for a minute that some down and out drug addict suddenly became a suicide bomber, well, not of his own free will.

Two hours later Bronson received a call back with the information he was seeking. One of the Captain's beat officers was familiar with the name. Allan "Sneazy" Swiderski, the officer, had informed the Captain. He was a cocaine addict who made a habit of frequenting the drug clinics in the area. Arrested for larceny, break and enters along with drug trafficking and a hand full of other minor crimes. The Captain provided Constable Bronson with a location where the perp usually hung out.

Finishing lunch the two men left the restaurant and went in search of Sneazy Swiderski.

Constable Bronson drove to a collection of run down businesses not far from the restaurant. Here he parked the car, and the two set out on foot looking for Dougie's friend.

The neighbourhood was not one advertised in any tourist pamphlets. The pothole-filled streets were cracked, garbage strewn along the curbs and the few businesses that were still in the area had bars on the doors and windows. Graffiti covered most of the building walls and the rows of smashed light standards lined the street.

The men walked down a sidewalk in front of a string of boarded up businesses that had seen better days. On the far end of the block, Brand pointed to a group of people huddled in front of a store in one of the small, decrepit buildings. The neon sign above was askew; the faded writing covered by a myriad number of spray paint colours.

Brand walked up to the crowd and waited until they acknowledged him.

"Whada ya want man?" someone from the group challenged him.

Brand took his time looking at each separately.

"I'm looking for Sneazy?" he broadcast to the gathering. He realized that no one in the group was about to answer him, but his eyes followed their faces. Several people unconsciously glanced in the direction one of the men. The guy they inadvertently looked at when he asked the question told him all he needed to know.

Brand concentrated his attention on the man. The guy had a bad habit of sneezing. Probably caused by repeated sniffing of cocaine Brand guessed by the guy constantly dabbing at his dripping nose.

The man Brand studied was barely over five feet. His hair was sticking up in all directions, and his face was a canvas of acne scars. The small man withered under Brand's scrutiny slowly daring to return the look showing a weak smile of sorts, exposing sparse, yellowed teeth.

'Whatca staring at me for, I dun know ya. You a cop or something?" he asked trying to put on a show of bravado for his group of friends.

"Not really. The cops have to be nice to assholes like you. I don't have that problem," Brand replied crowding the smaller man and forcing him to back away from his crowd of buddies. Brand continued driving the man farther away from his friends until a brick wall stopped the small man's retreat.

Over his shoulder, Brand heard the guy's buddies start to object with shouts of police brutality. Before the group worked up the courage to interfere, Brand heard one of them yell, Cop. He glanced back in time to see the constable returning his police badge to his belt.

"We need to talk about your buddy Dougie, Sneazy," Brand said. "What's with the funny names?" he asked. "You guys have Dopey and Wheezy around here too?"

Richard Cozicar

"Why ya hassling me man, I ain't dun nuttin' wrong?" Sneazy whined. "I don't know no Dougie; ya must have the wrong fellow."

"I got to ask you Sneazy, how is your health benefits these days?" Brand moved a step closer. Sneazy looked as though he hoped the wall would swallow him in order to avoid the bigger man.

"The...the clinics are alright, the people there treat us fair... why... why da ya ask? Sneazy stammered.

"I'm glad you like them, I think you might be in need of one very soon." Brand said.

"No. I feels fine, honest." Sneazy looked at Brand, confusion on in his eyes. Then he went into a sneezing fit. Brand took a step back. Lord knew what this guy carried.

"So about Dougie?" Brand asked again, this time, he delivered a smack to the side of Sneazy's head.

"Ouch! Hey man, ya can't do that!" the addict spat the words at Brand as he raised his arms to protect his face.

"Sure I can. Make you a deal. You tell me about your friend Dougie, and I promise to keep my friend from roughing you up. I have to warn you. I certainly am the nicer of the two." Brand said motioning toward the intimidating looking detective who stood a few feet away with his arms crossed and a scowl on his face

Dougie's friend looked back and forth between Brand and Bronson. A look of terror crossed his face.

"Okay...uh, Dougie. Ya...what cha wanna know about Dougie?"

"For starters, who were the guys that Dougie was going to work for, the ones that promised him the money to help his mother?" Brand asked. He crossed his arms and tapped his foot: his impatience starting to show.

"Those guys...they some mean dudes man. Real buzz heads, ya know. I... I never knew their names, I don't think Dougie did either," the small man stammered.

"What do you mean buzz heads?" Brand prodded.

"Buzz heads…ya know…army types, all short hair, and muscle, buzz heads." Sneazy looked at Brand like he was from a different planet.

"How did Dougie meet them?"

"Dougie didn' meet them, they come around lookin' and found Dougie."

"Could you describe them, there are thousands of guys in the army that fit that description."

"Na didn't see them that well. They was dealing with Dougie. He asked me to go with him one time when he was to meet them. I stayed out of site... hey, wait!" Sneazy exclaimed as he fumbled in his pocket and removed his phone. "Dougie asked me to take a picture of him with da two guys. Said he wanted to prove to his mom that he really got a job this time, just like he told her."

Sneazy thumbed through his phone. When he found the pictures he shoved the phone in Brand's face. "There, these two. I got a couple of pictures for Dougie." The addict swelled to his full height of five feet, proud that he remembered the pictures.

"We will need to borrow your phone," Brand told him while flipping through the pictures on Sneazy's phone.

"Na, I can't let you take my phone. What im I gonna do without it," Sneazy said shaking his head. He stood firm; his mind made up.

"How much?" Brand asked.

"How much what?" Sneazy shot back.

"How much for the damn phone?" Brand repeated.

"I dunno man, what do I look like, friggin Wal-Mart?"

Brand was starting to lose his patience. He looked the small addict in the eyes. "Is there a phone store around here?" Brand said sarcastically. "Gas station, convenience store, anywhere that sells phones?

"Sure…" Sneazy stammered. "A few blocks away is all."

"Well let's go then. The detective's car is just down the block." Brand said and herded Sneazy down the sidewalk.

Silent Crusade

Chapter 24

Johnson was lounging with his crew when Wasim Zawar sought him out. Nabi Hussoini had returned from his voyage into Pakistan, Wasim told him and would meet with them now. The Foreign mercenaries reluctantly left the coolness of the shade where they were hiding from the scorching sun and followed Wasim. The trip to Hussoini's tent taking the group past a scattering of tents and tribesmen, most of the people in the village were clustered under awnings avoiding the midday heat.

The American was not worried about going to hell for his part of this mission, even if it did involve harming his fellow man. He couldn't imagine that hell could be any hotter than this god-forsaken region of the world he was in right now. How these people could live here, he had no idea. He was probably doing them a favour by facilitating the destruction of this hellhole.

Wasim stopped in front of a large tent, announced the group's arrival then motioned the westerners inside. Johnson ducked his head and entered the tent followed closely by the rest of his group. Wasim waited for the foreigners step inside before entering. On the inside of the tent, the men were motioned to spread out and find space among the circle of seated tribesmen that had already gathered. Johnson and his men sought out open spots on the rug-covered ground before lowering themselves down.

Hussoini waited quietly for the foreigners to sit before he introduced everyone. The other tribal elders had abruptly stopped their conversation when the Americans had entered.

"Michael Johnson," Hussoini said, "Wasim tells me that you are planning an attack against your country this time. Is this correct?"

"Yes," answered Johnson. "As I discussed with him earlier I will need three Jihadists to travel to my country, men who are great in Allah's eyes and who are not afraid to sacrifice themselves for a greater purpose. Three of your bravest men who will be revered as martyrs," Johnson claimed in an exaggerated tone, trying to sell his conviction to their cause.

"I see," Hussoini said as he peered at Johnson. "Once again, I find myself wondering why you would come here and join in our fight bringing destruction and harm to your people? I must say I am skeptical of your motives, but thus far you have remained true to your word."

"As I've explained, Nabi. The group I represent sees the injustice brought against the Muslim faith and your people. They are only trying to aid you in your Holy War, a war of which you are at a great disadvantage," Johnson continued.

We just need you to keep being gullible and help one last time, and you will never have to worry about us again, the American thought. He had grown weary of appearing sympathetic to these people and their ill-founded beliefs. Johnson longed for the completion of this mission. He wanted to get back to civilization, things like lattes and bacon. The sand and heat of this Afghanistan village were starting to fray his nerves.

"Okay, Mr. Johnson. The money and weapons you've provided so far speak of your commitment to our cause, so I have taken the liberty of picking out three young mujahedeen. Men who will be proud to serve when you are ready to strike this blow against our enemy."

The American explained to the group of tribesmen how he planned to smuggle the men into the U.S. He would make the arrangements for his men to travel with the three Jihadists across the Afghan border into Pakistan and then continue with them on flights heading west. Johnson outlined the basics of his plan, enough to suit the tribesmen without putting all his cards on the table.

He told Hussoini that he planned to start for the airport in Peshawar, Pakistan before first light the following morning. It was imperative to get the Jihadists to the States as quick as possible, and with Hussoini's help, he figured they could follow the same route that Hussoini himself used to transport his drugs across the border.

After hours of discussions, Johnson had laid out his plan and was given approval by the tribal elders. The caravan of westerners, Taliban members, and the volunteer Mujahidin would be on the move the next day.

The trip would be routed through different European countries to avoid detection. He also had to notify the team in the U.S. so they could prepare arrangements for the arrival and hiding of Hussoini's men once they entered the States.

Chapter 25

John C. Monroe, the American President, sat in the situation room at the White House surrounded by his most trusted advisors. A memo circulated to the heads of all the American Intelligence departments, the Armed Service divisions, and Homeland Security. The meeting started with a videoconference involving similar heads of state and security leaders from the other western allied countries.

They met to discuss and work toward a more resounding solution to the escalated terrorist bombings that had recently taken place against the Western world. The allied countries combined efforts to stop the spread of terror was failing miserably despite the increase in ground troops and airstrikes they had been sending to the regions harbouring the extremists. Their joint effort seemed to have had little effect on stopping the siege.

President Monroe had remained the voice of reason in these ongoing talks. Using nuclear warfare was the last resort he warned the others. Various county leaders felt pushed to the brink by the random bombings and it weighed heavily on all their minds. With every new attack, more and more leaders rebuked the President's call for patience and demanded a stronger show of force. The President had held fast against such methods but despite his protests, his resolve was wavering with each new attack. The time was quickly approaching when debating and brainstorming alternate solutions would no longer suffice.

He had already begun to have his military advisors start the planning process for the seemingly inevitable conclusion to this war. The civilian advisors were dead set against such an unthinkable solution. Nuking another country was preposterous and evil; the killing of thousands of innocent people to stop a few tyrants was to turn your back on God himself they told him.

The military viewed the situation differently the crisis was already out of control and they were determined and fully prepared to carry out this mission and end the spread of terrorism without any delay.

The President spent hours on the phone talking individually with the allied leaders trying to gauge their support of the pending bombings. The States closest neighbour, Canada, was still reeling from the subway attack in Toronto, a city thrown into turmoil from the mass destruction and extreme loss of life.

The Canadian PM was enraged. The British PM and the French President harboured the same sentiments; they were both ready to bomb the bastards back to the middle ages. No more of their countrymen should have to die at the hands of extremists if there was a way to prevent similar terrorist acts. Stronger and more extreme measures should be used to answer the terrorist volleys.

After he had tallied the votes, the United States President was the only voice of reason against the use of nuclear bombs. He knew if another country were to suffer a bombing he would have no choice but to give in to the mounting pressure.

Chapter 26

After Brand had bought Sneazy a new phone to replace the one Brand confiscated the two dropped the addict off where they found him. Brand asked Constable Bronson to drive them somewhere private where he would be able to make some calls.

"What hotel are you staying at?" Bronson inquired.

"Honestly, I didn't think I'd be in Toronto that long so I don't have a room booked," confessed Brand.

"No worries, There is a hotel not far from our offices. Makes sense for you to stay close in case something comes up or you need any of our resources," Bronson said as he pointed his car in the direction of the RCMP building.

Bronson relaxed in a lobby chair while Brand acquired a room. When he finished at the check-in desk, the two men walked across the lobby to the bank of elevators. Brand led the way into the room and threw his luggage on the bed, followed by Bronson, who quietly shut the door and took a seat in a chair by the window. Before getting down to business, Brand picked up the hotel phone and called room service; he wanted a pot of coffee.

The men discussed the information they had gotten from Allan "Sneazy" Swiderski, information that they both found interesting. A small-time criminal and drug addict coerced into becoming a suicide bomber by two white men who could be military or even ex-military. The new information put a different twist on what law enforcement usually considered terrorist strategy. They agreed that some white guys would feel sympathetic or even be allured by the terrorist's ideals, but this was a very different approach. Suicide bombers usually martyred themselves because of their beliefs in Islam, not as a way to earn money.

Bronson had already emailed the photos from Sneazy's phone to the NSIS, the National Security Intelligence Section of the RCMP's Criminal Intelligence division. Finding the identity of the two men in the photo moved to the top of the list for the NSIS once Constable Bronson explained whom the men were associated.

Brand called Brent at his office. Before talking about the bombing case, he asked Brent if he had heard anything further from the Montana State Police involving Sara's kidnapping.

"I phoned the Police Chief at Whitefish. He said the man from the house wasn't cooperating, all he admits to is that he and his partner kidnapped Sara and wouldn't give the police any reasons why."

"That's bullshit!" Brand exclaimed. "Sara said in her statement that those were not the same guys who drove to her house and abducted her. What about the house, did they tell you who owned it, it certainly was not the guys we had the run in with?"

"The house belongs to a billionaire industrialist from the east coast. The Chief says that he talked with the house owner. The guy had no idea what was taking place at the mountain retreat. The men at the cabin were in charge of security the owner told the police chief. The house staff backed up their story."

"Did the Chief give you this industrialist's name at least?" Brand asked.

"No. I am afraid not. He told me that the owner was a very private person and insisted his name left out of this fiasco. And hey, get this, the Chief very curtly reminded me that they knew perfectly well how to do their investigations and that we should stay the hell out of the way," Brent finished with a laugh. "Some piece of work that guy is. Don't worry, though; I made some calls to friends of mine at the FBI, and they are going to look into it. If this dip shit Police Chief wants to get into a pissing match I would certainly hate to disappoint him."

"Okay, thanks," Brand said. "I'll be forwarding pictures of a couple of men that I need you to check out. I'll email them to you shortly. The two were associating with our suicide bomber days before the subway, and it seems that they might have promised the man money in exchange for his...how should I say this...his services."

"I'll get Sara to run a search as soon as the photos arrive," Brent said. "Speaking of Sara, while she was reading the paper this morning... hang on... I'll let her tell you. Give me a sec to transfer you over to her."

Brand waited as the call switched to Sara's desk.

"How are you holding up?" he asked her before she could say anything.

"I'm good," she replied. "Keeping busy helps."

"I am probably going to be another day at least," Brand explained to her. "There is an Imam here in town that I've dealt with before. I want to get his opinion on these attacks. I'm hoping that he might be able to shed some light on this latest surge of bombings. I know that he used to stay in contact with different factions in the Middle East, so I want to find out if he still does. Maybe he's heard rumours about the group responsible, or knows someone who does… by the way… Brent hinted that you might have something to tell me?"

"Oh…yes, this morning when I was reading the paper I came across an article about a Canadian businessman. I was going to skip the story except a photo of the man accompanied the article…" Sara grew quiet her voice barely a whisper. "Brand, This is one of the men I saw at the cabin in Montana. Remember I told you that I stood at the window and watched the old men leave the house the day I arrived. This guy was one of that group… I am certain of it," Sara blurted out then her voice grew quieter again as the memories of her recent kidnapping resurfaced.

"No shit!" Brand exclaimed. " Send me his name and a photo. I'll find time to have a little chat with him? Also, do some digging. Let me know everything you can about the guy and see if you can find his current location," he paused thinking. " Brent was going to ask you to run a check on some photos I'm sending him. The photos are of the two men with the subway bomber. Maybe ask Brent if he can assign someone else to identify those men while you're busy with this business man."

"Sure," Sara agreed. "But isn't identifying the men in the photo a lot more important than wasting time on some guy I think I saw in a cabin in Montana."

"I'm not so sure," Brand, said, "You got kidnapped right after you discovered the video of the bomber, a bomber who turns out to be a drug-addicted petty criminal. I am starting to think that maybe these aren't separate incidents," Brand continued. "I very highly doubt that the addict suddenly became a devout Muslim or, at least, he certainly doesn't appear to fit the profile."

"What do you mean… you think my kidnapping and the bombing are somehow related?"

"I'm not exactly sure what I mean," he tried to explain. "Too many unanswered questions remain."

"But now we have discovered a photo of two other white men, very non-Muslim looking white men who are meeting with this addict and potentially paying him to do a job for them. Then suddenly our guy dons a burka, straps some explosives to his chest and boards a subway train blowing himself and countless others up. Too many coincidences all at once," he paused, thinking, fitting the pieces together in his mind.

"Now combine that with a Canadian businessman who just happens to be at the same cabin where you were held hostage right after you discovered the video of the bomber.

I am starting to wonder that maybe everyone is looking at the attack on the subway from the wrong angle. What if this attack was not carried out by some radical Islamic group but instead by someone trying to make it look that way?"

"But the Taliban have been all over the news taking the credit for it?" Sara argued.

"I don't know," Brand replied. "I don't have all the answers yet. After I talk with the Imam, I will hopefully have a clearer picture," then he added. "Might as well keep an open mind."

"I'll give you a call as soon as I have a chance to check into this businessman's background," Sara said.

"Nelson Bakker," she added after a quick pause, "That is the name of the old guy. The man I recognized from the cabin."

Chapter 27

In the encroaching dusk, Michael Johnson gathered his men. In silence the foreigners walked in the cool evening air away from the scrum of activity in the tent village. As a group, they climbed a small rise that overlooked the bleak, dust filled valley surrounding the village.

Johnson wanted complete privacy from the villagers before discussing with his men the plans he had made for the next day's journey to Peshawar. His men huddled in a tight circle, some smoking, others sombre with the anticipation of what was to come.

Johnson meticulously walked his men through his preparations often stopping to make certain that the men understood his instructions. When he was satisfied that each and everyone was on the same page, he told them to get some sleep, the trip to Peshawar would begin long before the sun rose.

He expected to make the Afghan crossing into Pakistan as early as possible. He reasoned that the night guards at the border would be tired as their night shift drew to an end. Hopefully, this would make them less enthusiastic and thorough with their job.

Michael Johnson and his men had been in the company of this Pashtun tribe for over six months. During that time they had adopted the traditional garb of the tribal men wearing turbans on their heads, loose-fitting, long-sleeved shirts that they wore outside their wide trousers and gathered tight around their waists with a drawstring.

The clothes combined with the all the months of exposure to the hot Afghan sun and the facial hair each member had grown, his men could now easily pass as Afghan countrymen. The last piece was the mannerisms, while they were able to replicate the movements and actions of the Afghani men, the majority of his men could speak little of the native tongue fluently. To deal with this Johnson planned to let Hussoini and their other escorts do the talking. He was banking on their physical appearances to camouflage the group and the early morning hour to prevent the weary guards from discovering the disguised foreigners. The overall appearance of a caravan traveling between Afghanistan and Pakistan happened all the time.

*****

At three a.m. the following morning the men leaving with the caravan to Peshawar were attending to the final preparation for the trip, Johnson and his men separated and were to ride interspersed with the locals in different vehicles. Along with Johnson's crew, Wasim Zawar and Nabi Hussoini were making the trip. Six other tribe members joined the group and climbed into the waiting vehicles. The main reason for the drive to Peshawar was the human cargo, the three young Muslim men who were willing to sacrifice themselves for a greater glory.

Nabi and Johnson rode in the back of the lead car. Nabi Hussoini would be calling the shots as the group made the crossing into Pakistan. Hussoini was well known in these parts and being a Pashtun he would have a better chance of ensuring the caravans safe passage through the Federally Administered Tribal Areas that rested on the Pakistan side of the crossing.

Not long into the trip, the group rolled up to the border. A sleepy guard sauntered out of the guardhouse under the glowing lights that lit up the caravan of vehicles. Nabi lowered his window as the guard approached. The guard stopped short of the car and looked over the trail of vehicles. Nabi called to the man, but the guard veered away from the lead car and started walking down the length of the caravan.

Nervous that the guard would screw things up, Michael Johnson reached for his gun. Nabi noticed the American's reaction and put a hand on Johnson's arm telling him to relax. Opening the car door, Nabi climbed outside and hurriedly walked after the guard. Halfway down the length of the caravan, he stopped the guard. The American turned in his seat and carefully watched the two men.

A spirited conversation took place alongside the waiting vehicles. Johnson pulled his gun out and set it on the seat, his hand resting on the reassuring metal, the pistol ready in case the conversation went in the wrong direction.

A few tense moments passed before Nabi pulled a wad of money out of his pocket, counted off a generous amount and placed the bills in the guard's hand. A smile lit up the guard's face. The two spoke a while longer before Nabi patted the guard on the back in a friendly fashion then returned to the car.

The crossing guard stuffed the money into his trouser pocket then turned to motion the guardhouse for the crossing barrier to be raised. Nabi glanced at the gun that Johnson held as he got into the car. With a look of disgust on his face, he told the driver to get the car moving.

Another hour passed. The sun started to rise chasing away the darkness while the heat of the morning streamed through the cars windows starting to tax the air conditioners. On the Pakistan side of the border, the highway had taken the company of vehicles on a circuitous route north across the Kurram River and topped out at Alizal before turning south for Thal At Alizal.

There the cars and trucks would be refueled before the journey continued on the Thal-Parachinar Highway to their next stop on the route at Thal. The scenery outside the car windows showed a broken, desolate land with several outcroppings of large boulders set among patches of flat brown meadows and lonely trees scattered sparsely throughout.

From Alizal to Thal the road travelled through a vast valley. On the other side of Thal, the caravan continued toward Thal-Parachinar Rd.; the line of vehicles pointed northeast in the direction of Kohat.

Johnson and Nabi reviewed the details of the mission as the hours of driving passed.

Johnson worried that the number of vehicles showing up at the airport could draw the attention of the Pakistan Airport Security Force. The two men agreed that only a couple of men must escort each of the three volunteers into the airport and book the flights, the smaller the number of men, the less attention drawn to them.

From Kohat, the group merged onto the Indus Highway and drove almost straight north to Peshawar. The midmorning traffic on the highway out of Kohat increased closer to the city. The job of keeping all the vehicles in the caravan clustered together became a chore. Nabi kept busy talking with the other drivers trying to maintain their positions. Despite this, a few of the vehicles had fallen behind the rest of the group by the time they passed through Dara Adamkhel.

The convoy worked their way through the rugged hills north of Dara Adamkhel as the highway descended into the flatter terrain of the valley on the last leg of the journey. Ahead, Johnson could see the open fields of the valley on the horizon. He talked to Nabi and suggested that they pull off the road into an area of large boulders to regroup and take one last break before driving on into Peshawar, but the Pashtun disagreed. They were only a short distance from Peshawar the Taliban leader argued but finally gave in to Johnson's insistence.

Nabi contacted the other drivers and explained the unscheduled stop and then he instructed his driver to pull the car off the highway toward a group of outcropping boulders where they parked and waited for the rest of the vehicles to arrive. Once the others stopped, Michael Johnson got out of his car and walked to the shade of protruding boulders and addressed the group. As the other members gathered in the shade, Johnson's men slowly separated themselves from the Afghanis.

Wasim Zawar, seeing an opportunity to relieve himself wandered from the group. In his search for privacy he climbed the rough terrain toward an outcropping of rocks a few hundred yards from the vehicles. Shouts and loud talking drifted up the hill after Wasim. Curiously he peered around the rocks at the sound of a heated argument from the group of men below.

The Westerners had separated from his fellow Afghanis. The men stood with their guns drawn surrounding Wasim's countrymen. Wasim crouched behind the rocks uncertain what to do, and watched the surreal scene unfold. He was too far away to hear clearly what transpired between the two groups but what he saw frightened him.

Chapter 28

The American mercenary waited until the Afghan men from the caravan wandered over to the spot that he and Nabi stood. None of the Afghanis took noticed of Johnson's men as they stepped back from the group and took up positions surrounding the tribesmen. The mercenaries remained on the outside of the gathering and waited for Johnson's signal at which time they withdrew their firearms and covered the Afghanis.

Nabi and the other tribesmen looked at the Westerners in disbelief. Johnson told Dean Adams, the former Special Forces member, to take the three Jihadists and walk them back to the vehicles. Johnson and his three remaining men kept their guns trained on the other men. Johnson's men had removed the three volunteers before he ordered the remaining Afghanis to kneel on the ground and place their hands on top their heads.

Nabi Hussoini stood alongside his men and stared defiantly at the American mercenaries. He had never fully trusted these men, and now it appeared he would die for not following his instincts.

"You have been a big help, Nabi Hussoini, but I am afraid your use has come to an end." Johnson addressed the Taliban leader. "No hard feelings, but I can not leave any witnesses privy to what we have been doing these past months. The American people must have no doubt that the bombings were the work of Islamic terrorists.

"What do you suppose the world would think if they found out that you cooperated with us and were used as puppets in the terror attacks?" Johnson said with a smirk. "You have my permission to meet your God knowing that you were paramount in bringing a rain of fire down against your beloved Arab countries. Will Allah reward you for the destruction that will follow your traitorous acts and be used to annihilate every Muslim within these borders laying to waste your pagan countries that harbour your religion?" Johnson laughed. "Enjoy paradise, my friend."

Nabi glared at the American. He had ignored his instincts about the foreigners and now he and his men would die for his lack of judgement. He faced the American with his held high, his faith intact, not begging for his life die but defiant to the end in front of his men. The Americans would not see him cower.

With a nod of his head, Johnson signaled his men. Gunfire echoed off the rocks, the acrid smell of gunpowder mixing with the dust in the air until all the Afghanis had fallen and were stretched out on the ground, blood pooling around their dead bodies.

Johnson looked at them counting the dead bodies. Someone was missing. He squatted in front of the dead men and checked their faces. "Where is Wasim?" he bellowed at his men.

The mercenaries looked at each other and then around at the hills surrounding them. George Williams, the former American Marine, pointed behind the group to a hill of rocks that climbed away from the dead bodies.

"There!" he shouted. The men watched as Wasim scrambled higher using the boulders as cover. A few of the men raised their guns and fired at the running Wasim but the distance was too great, the shelter of the rocks protecting the fleeing Afghani. The former SAS member, Dexter Tranter dashed to the bottom of the hill ready to climb after Wasim.

"Stop!" Johnson ordered. "We don't have time. We'll take a couple of cars and get to the airport. Make damn sure the other vehicles are disabled... I don't want him to be able to come back and drive off in one of them."

Before the group of mercenaries left the scene, Johnson talked with the volunteer Jihadists. He warned them that changing their minds after what they had just witnessed would be a dangerous idea. They might be willing to die but if they caused any trouble, they would be guaranteed not only of their deaths but also the torture and deaths of the families they left behind in Afghanistan. The mothers, fathers, brothers and sisters would die very slowly and painfully, he assured them.

114

Richard Cozicar

"The members of their families would beg to die by the time his men finished torturing them," Johnson stressed as he stared into the eyes of the young Jihadists. The young Afghanis exchanged looks then in unison they nodded their acknowledgement.

Wasim stopped to give his legs and lungs a rest, blood seeping from wounds he suffered from the sharp rocks he scraped against as he fled in panic. He had climbed high among the strewn boulders of the mountain as the gunfire chased after him. Bent over behind the shelter of a large rock, Wasim panted as he drew air into his burning lungs.

The last echoes of gunfire reverberated off the boulders. From behind a large outcropping, he warily looked back in the direction of massacre. Wasim watched dumbfounded as the traitorous Westerners climbed into several vehicles and drove away. Between panic and uncertainty, sadness for the loss of his countrymen settled upon his mind. Wasim knew he had to hurry back to his village and tell the elders of the deception and slaughter he had witnessed.

At the Bacha Khan International Airport the men left their vehicles and parted, walking off in separate directions, blending in with the crowds streaming into the terminal. The plan was for them to enter the airport at different locations. Johnson had previously paired each of his men with one of the Jihadists. A large group would be noticed and draw suspicions something Michael Johnson planned to avoid; they were too far into this mission to risk discovery now.

The members of his group were instructed to book tickets out of Pakistan to layover destinations. One coupling would head for Germany, another pair to buy tickets that would take them to Italy before rerouting to the States. The third pair headed for Canada by way of Turkey.

The men would all land in different cities in North America, making their detection by American authorities much harder. From there they were to be met by contacts working in the United States who would assist them to their final destination.

Silent Crusade

Chapter 29

Midday arrived with Brand and Constable Bronson leaving the hotel and driving east out of the downtown core. Bronson expertly navigated through the cumbersome traffic that clogged the arteries leading away from the skyscrapers of Toronto's crowded center. The two men were driving to Markham for a meeting with an Imam that Brand had dealt with years earlier while an agent for the Canadian Intelligence service.

The trip took longer than Brand expected. The Don Valley Parkway was busy at the best of times; today it seemed overly slow to Brand considering it was just the start of the rush hour. He had planned to arrive at prayer time. During his time with CSIS, he had studied the practices involved with the Muslim prayer schedule. One of the best lessons he had learned while in the Intelligence field through dealings with other countries and their diverse cultures was that knowledge was something you went to great lengths to acquire to maintain the advantage over your adversary.

He knew that the Dhuhr or the midday prayer would be coming to an end by the time they reached the Mosque. His intention was to speak with the Imam before the afternoon, the Asr, prayer began. He no longer had the Imam's number so he could not call ahead. He would have to risk that he could get an audience with the Imam when he arrived. Brand impatiently tapped his fingers on the window trim before glancing down at the time displayed on the car's dash then back up at the crawly lanes of traffic willing the volume of cars to move faster.

The traffic started to thin as the two neared Markham. Years had passed since Brand last visited the Mosque, but with the help of the GPS in Bronson's car, the men arrived minutes before the afternoon prayer was preparing to start. Bronson spotted the overflowing lot at the mosque when he turned onto the street forcing him to park the car on the road.

The two men walked across the parking lot toward the entrance. Several men eyed them suspiciously as they drew closer to the ornate front doors of the Mosque. Imam Khak Pasoon stood on the steps in front of the door greeting the afternoon worshippers. He watched the men approach.

Climbing the stairs to where the Imam stood, Brand called out the Imam's name. Khak Pasoon stared at the ghost from his past, then with a warm smile, the Imam held out his hand.

"Brand, my friend. It has been a long time." Imam Pasoon embraced the hand of his long time friend. "What brings you to my humble house."

"Nothing good I'm afraid," Brand offered. "Imam. Constable Bronson with the RCMP." Brand pointed to the officer. The Imam shot a puzzled glance at the two newcomers.

"I had heard that you retired from the service long ago. What brings you around?"

"It's a long story," Brand paused carefully choosing his next words. "I'm helping with the investigation of the bombing in Toronto," another pause. "Khak…do you still have your contacts in the old country."

"I may. Why?"

Brand pulled the Imam aside, apologized for interrupting his day and asked if they could continue this talk in private.

The Imam led the way back down the steps to an alcove on the side of the building. Brand quickly explained how he got involved in the investigation of the Toronto subway bombing and his reason for seeking out the Imam.

"A sorrowful day indeed," the cleric frowned then explained that he was well aware the tragedy, as was every other Torontonian.

"Have you heard any rumours, anything about what terrorist groups may be involved?" Brand searched the Imam eyes for an answer. "At one time I know that you were very well connected back in your country."

"Amazingly enough, there has been little talk about the bombings or who is responsible. That's very unusual," the Imam admitted. "These terrorist's like to boast loudly about the fear and destruction they cause in the world. But this time, things are different. Whoever is responsible for these attacks remains quiet about them. Not the usual bravado."

The three men had continued talking for several more minutes before the Imam excused himself. Brand was aware that the Imam had to return to prayer, he pulled a card out of his pocket and passed it across to the cleric before bidding his old friend farewell.

"If you hear anything," Brand added pointing to the number on the card.

"If I hear anything I will not hesitate to call," the Imam smiled and assured Brand. "Give me time to contact some family members who remain in the old country."

"People talk," he went on. "Maybe someone will have heard things about the attacks or who is behind them."

Brand apologized again for the interruption and left with Bronson. The RCMP Constable echoed the Imam's observation about the recent attacks not having the fanfare that had followed similar events. He agreed that most terrorist groups responsible for scenes of carnage and death seemed to relish the attention from the destruction they caused almost more than the acts themselves. They liked to brag and remind non-believers around the world that they were not safe no matter in which country they lived.

Brand thought about this. He hadn't stopped to consider it, but Bronson and the Imam were right, another strange twist in the way the strikes differentiated from the ones of the past. The two men contemplated the importance of this change to the terrorists' M.O. on the way back to the center of the city. As they closed in on Brand's hotel, he asked the constable to drop him off explaining that he had several calls to make and that he would see him again in the morning.

In his room, he went straight to the phone and called Brent's office asking to speak to Sara. The two of them engaged in small talk until Brand nudged the conversation back to business. Sara updated him on the info she had so far managed to find on the Canadian businessmen.

"He lives a couple of hours north of Toronto on the south shores of Georgian Bay on an estate close to the Victory Harbour," Sara read the directions to the property. "I found several news references about Nelson Bakker; he is the acting CEO of an energy giant despite being eighty-five years old," she continued. "Apparently he is still deeply involved running the energy empire he built... Also, let's see..." More clicks of computer keys followed.

"He is a widower with two daughters, both married and also involved in his business. His wife died several years ago from cancer."

"Can you find me any specs on his house? I need to know if it has a security system and if it does try to find out what make it is. Knowing what type of system could prove to be very helpful later," Brand asked and as an afterthought he added, "Do his daughters live with the old guy or do they live elsewhere?"

"One second, I have that information somewhere…" Brand could hear the sound of paper as Sara searched before replying, "Bakker lives alone from what I see. The info doesn't list any house staff, but I would assume he employs someone to attend to his house. At his age and that size of the mansion, a person would certainly need some help," she speculated.

"Good. Concentrate on finding out about the security system and figure out how to hack into it? I'm going to go and have supper and then after I've rented a car we can talk. Give me a call in a couple of hours if you have anything more." He hung the phone up and walked out of his room. He took the elevator down to the lobby and made his way to the hotel restaurant. The day had already been long enough and with hours to go, he did not feel like wasting time wandering the streets in search supper. His mind was preoccupied with the information Sara had provided so he decided that anywhere with food would be good.

Upon ordering a rye to accompany his meal, he sipped from the glass pulling together a plan for the evening along with mulling over the possibilities of a meeting of a soon to be new, old friend. While he ate, he was engrossed with the idea of a surprise visit. The idea intrigued him and by the time he finished eating and rented a car the hour had grown late, but, maybe still too early for what he intended.

Chapter 30

The American President sat forward in his chair with his elbows propped on his desk, his chin resting on his tented fingers. Hal Jorgenson, the Director of the CIA, had called him earlier in the day and requested an impromptu meeting.

The Secretary of Defense, the Director of the FBI, the President's Chief Advisor and the head of Homeland Security were all present, all requested by the CIA Director to attend the meeting. The Director of the CIA stood and waited while the other men sat. His eyes looked each man in the face before beginning his update of the news out of the Middle East.

Hal Jorgenson informed his colleagues of the reports that had crossed his desk filled with news of an attack currently being plotted against America. Overseas assets of the CIA had been picking up lots of chatter about a mounting threat, and the lines of communication were rife with rumours of the upcoming attack.

The Director informed the gathering that his department had yet to confirm the rumours but the sources that had forwarded this information were positive this was not just idle talk. He explained in detail to the president and his peers of the requests sent to every resource in the Middle East imploring them to work their contacts and nail down a confirmation of the Intel. With a reminder that threats against the U.S.A. were not uncommon, and that to verify the rumours he had all the resources available shaking every source for solid leads and workable information. What dates were suspected? What factions were supposedly involved and most importantly, where was the attack supposed to take place.

Jorgenson apologized to the President for not being able to answer these questions, but considering the tone and urgency of the messages detected by his office; he felt that the warning of an imminent attack should be brought to the President's attention immediately.

President Monroe, his jaw still resting on his hands addressed the room as a whole.

"Gentlemen, what do we make of this?" he asked. The President remained motionless as he let the conversations in the room die down. Leaning back in his chair, he looked at the head of Homeland Security.

"Mike," he said, "I know this is hypothetical but what kind of resources and response time would you need?"

The head of Homeland looked back at the President.

"I don't know if I can answer that, Sir, without details of the time or place, I would have no idea where to stage the responders. I can have everyone on alert, but where and for how long?" the Homeland Director answered, shaking his head and shrugging his shoulders.

"Yes. I know," the President conceded. "What else can we do? If such an attack is in the works then we need to be prepared," he slammed his fist on his desk in frustration. "We need more than suppositions," he stopped and searched for the answers in his advisor's faces. "How do we stop the unknown?"

"Gentlemen, I know we don't have any solid facts yet, but given the bombings against our allies, we have to be proactive, not reactive, not when American lives are at stake!" the President added forcefully. He knew that the men gathered in this room shared his concern. The difference was that they weren't under constant pressure to respond with the force of nuclear bombs. The President bolted upright. He had grown tired of trying to persuade the leaders of the free western world that the use of nuclear warheads was not the answer. He now realized he might be wrong. The powerful weapons might be the only way left to stop the increasingly violent acts of terrorism. Yes. He realized. Maybe the time had come for him to consider this situation from the other side and adjust his thoughts.

Chapter 31

Standing back from the line lines of passengers waiting to purchase airline tickets, Michael Johnson surreptitiously surveyed the airport concourse then rode the escalator up. From a second-floor vantage point, his eyes persistently roamed the crowds for signs of trouble while his men prepared for their flights. The other mercenaries had disappeared into various restrooms throughout the concourse with their cargo in tow.

His men would swap out the Pashtun garb that they had worn to the airport for more conservative western clothing before purchasing airline tickets and checking passports. The men's beards shaved, and their hair trimmed to reduce the chances of being identified as Muslims. Changes to aid passage through customs smoothly and unnoticed.

Johnson remained wary. This part of the trip was crucial and not until his men and the Afghanis were safely on flights out of Peshawar would he relax. Once this stage of the plan was complete, Johnson would then change his appearance and book his passage out of Pakistan.

He wandered back down to the main concourse and walked among the waiting passengers, frequently moving to avoid drawing suspicion. At a predetermined time, his men left the washrooms and one pair at a time approached him. To each pair, he passed an envelope of money for the flights and instructions followed by a handshake and a curt, "Good luck".

Leading the first pair to buy tickets was Dean Adams. Adams and his guest booked flights on Air Blue airlines. The next stop for the duo was Abu Dhabi and then onto Germany. From there they would take a plane to the United States, landing in Cincinnati.

The other members of Johnson's group followed the same procedure. Same idea, different routes back to North America. When the other men were booked and ready to depart, Johnson sought out a restroom. Hidden inside a stall, he stripped off the clothing he was wearing and dug through his duffle bag until he retrieved a t-shirt and a pair of jeans. After six months of walking around clad in Afghani robes, the western clothing felt strikingly odd.

He stuffed his old clothing into a garbage can and parked himself in front of the bathroom mirror. Taking his time he shaved off both his beard and moustache while scanning the mirror watching the room around him. He washed the remainder of shaving cream off his face then exchanged the razor for a pair of scissors from his pack cutting off months of sun-bleached hair. Laying the scissors down he stood back from the mirror and gazed at his reflection.

Pulling off his t-shirt he shook the loose hair away, dug to the bottom of his pack and retrieved a new set of identity papers that he brought with him from the states and tucked it in his back pocket. The identification he entered the country with including the passport under the name Michael Johnson he buried in a different trashcan.

The identity switch complete he walked out of the bathroom moved in line at the ticket counter. His route out of Pakistan was supposed to mirror his men's flights to Europe. Michael Johnson had been in the game too long to follow instructions blindly and to advertise his moves.

When he stood in front of the ticket window, he booked a ticket on Air Blue Airlines, but instead of a stopover in Dubai; he paid for a ticket to the U.K., Birmingham England. The direct flight would put him ahead of his men, and he would be back in the States before anyone suspected the deviation of his route.

Johnson felt relatively confident that his team's actions in Afghanistan went undetected, but Wasim's escape troubled him. If the man returned to his village and were to tell his story, would word of the massacre reach the States, he wondered. Johnson didn't think so, but one could never be too careful.

Chasing the thought away, he concentrated on the present. At the moment, there was a deadline to meet. Once his feet were safely planted back in the U.S., he would come up with a plan to deal with Wasim if the problem arose. There was nothing he could do about it from 30,000 feet.

He reclined his seat on the airplane and for the first time in months he relaxed. The desert and the people had gotten to him. Not letting your guard down for six long months was hard on the body and strained the mind. The day the Americans bombed the shit out of that hellhole could not come soon enough for him, then he would have his reward for the months he spent there, detesting every minute of it.

Chapter 32

Brand drove the rental car away from downtown Toronto a little after eleven in the evening. The trip to Georgian Bay was at least two and a half hours so he timed the drive to arrive at his destination in the wee hours of the morning. It took Brand several glances at the cars GPS until he found the Four-Hundred Highway. He double-checked with his map. The Four-Hundred would take him straight north toward Georgian Bay.

Greater Toronto was a massive city and home to millions of people, so even at this late hour the traffic leaving the north end of the city was heavy. It wasn't until well into his trip the traffic thinned and eased to a reasonable volume. Winding his way north, Brand talked with Sara on his cell phone. She had called with the info he requested for his business in Victory Harbour at the south end of Georgian Bay.

Brand explained his plans when he arrived at the oilman's house. Once he had a chance to check out the place, her task would be to hack into the alarm system clearing the way to enter the house unannounced. His intentions weren't legal he confided to her but he wasn't concerned, he had given up being a cop long ago. Besides, he reasoned, at the moment his only intentions were to have a short talk with the man, find out what he knew about Sara's abduction.

Brand stopped at a gas station in Barrie for a coffee and to stretch his legs. The traffic had all but disappeared as he continued heading north. A little over an hour later he saw the sign for Waubaushene. There he turned onto Highway Twelve for the final leg of his journey. He seemed to be the only one on the road when he drove into the deserted streets of the resort town of Victory Harbour.

Pulling off to the side of the road, Brand typed the address for Nelson Bakker's house into the cars GPS. The town was small, the house taking minutes to locate. Parking his car a few blocks away, he locked it and sauntered back down the block. The spacing of the streetlights left enough light for him to see but still left enough shadows to provide him with cover. The neighborhood remained quiet and still at this early hour.

He sauntered down the block reading the numbers posted on the fronts of the houses. When he found Bakker's home, he stopped on the sidewalk and stared at the house for several minutes before walking on. No lights shone from inside, and the yard lay quietly in the darkness.

Brand ambled down the block a few houses before he removed his phone from his pocket and dialed. Whispering into the phone, aware that his voice would carry in the silence of the night he spoke to Sara.

"How long will it take you to shut the alarm system down?" he asked her.

"Not long," she replied. "I have everything ready to go. I need a few minutes."

"Okay. I'll set my phone on vibrate. Call me back once you're finished. I'll check to make sure that it's you who called, then I'm going in," he explained. "It sure would be funny if someone else were to call and I go in before you've finished," he joked.

"Do you usually get calls in the middle of the night?" She asked, a hint of mocking laughter in her voice.

Brand ended the call and after a quick look around he crossed the lawn and made his way down the side of the house. Placing his phone in his mouth, Brand pulled a thin pair of gloves out of his back pocket and worked his hands into them. Grabbing the phone again, he rounded the corner of the house into the back yard. Keeping his body bent over and tight to the house he checked for a rear door. The days of climbing through windows was behind him he acknowledged grudgingly?

A painted wooden fence surrounded the property but lay open on the side of the house. Brand thanked his luck. No gates meant no dogs were waiting for him to enter the yard. He followed along the edge of the house to the back yard and had to skirt around a deck. From there he followed a stone walkway to the deck stairs that led him up to the back door. Crouched by the door, he studied the lock while he waited for a call from Sara.

His phone vibrated in his hand. Checking the number, he put his phone away and removed a slim leather sheath from his pocket. Slipping two thin pieces of metal out of the sheath he inserted them into the door's lock. Brand found that he was a little out of practice. His current employment as a fishing guide meant he hadn't had to break into a house for the past several years. He released a sigh of relief when the last tumbler lined up, clicking into place. The lock released. With a learned patience, he twisted the knob and slowly pushed the door inward prepared for the sound of barking and a guard dog rushing to greet him.

Seconds passed as he waited to let his eyes acclimate to the shadowy light. He breathed a few deep slow breaths, let his eyes adjust to the darkness, and listened carefully for noises in the house. As he stood in the doorway, Brand realized he should have asked Sara if she could have found a layout for the interior. Oh well, he thought. The house was two stories; chances were good that the bedrooms were on the second level.

Careful not to disturb anything and cause a racket, he stealthily moved through the house looking for the stairs. Cautiously placing his feet on the sides of the stair stringers to prevent the stairs from creaking under his weight, he climbed to the second floor. At the top of the stairs, he paused again. In the dim light, he could make out four doors lining the hallway. Three of the doors yawned open, the one at the far end stood closed.

Brand crept down the hall stopping to peer into each open door as he passed. In the dim light pouring in from the street, he noticed the empty rooms with their beds all neatly made. He stepped gingerly on the carpeted floor as he approached the end of the hall. Pausing outside the last door, he hesitated for a second letting his ears sort out the night sounds of the quiet house. Then lowering his hand he reached for the doorknob. Gently Brand tested the knob with his hand and found no resistance, the door unlocked. Silently he pushed the door into the room as he eased through the opening.

The bedroom was at the front of the house, and the light from the street seeped through the curtains. Standing in the doorway, Brand looked over the room. Straight ahead of him on the opposite wall stood a massive bed with end tables on either side. To Brand's right was a table set up as a desk with two chairs next to it. On one wall, a TV was mounted; pictures hung from the other walls. The open door blocked his view of the corner, but he was confident it was safe. Still years of fieldwork made him advance cautiously.

Stepping lightly into the room Brand grabbed a chair from beside the table and carried it over to the bed. Setting it down, he reached behind the nearest end table and pulled the plug for a lamp out of the wall. Placing the chair about a leg's length from the bed, he sat down and carefully considered his next move, an occasional snore emanating from under the bed covers. Brand took a breath debating whether this was the right address, if not this situation could get very embarrassing.

What the hell, he thought, and then he raised one foot and shot it forward giving the bed a sudden kick. The bed's occupant groaned and rolled over. Brand raised his foot and kicked the side of the bed again. The bed shook jarring the sleeping man awake.

Brand watched the closed eyes slowly flicker open while Bakker struggled awake. The startled old man tried to sit up, his eyes flashing wide open when he realized there was an intruder in his room. Turning his head, he strained to see through the gloom in Brand's direction.

A look of anger crossed the man's face as he glanced at the phone sitting on his bedside table.

"Don't bother," Brand barked at him.

"What are you doing here?" Bakker demanded. "Get the hell out of my house!"

"Shortly," Brand calmly replied. "I need answers to few questions first. A young lady was abducted from her home in Calgary a few days ago. Two men abducted her and drove across the border taking her to a cabin in Montana." Brand felt his emotions begin to surface. The anger building in the pit of his stomach crept into his voice. Fighting down the feeling, he continued, "she was held against her will, locked in a god damned room." He drove his foot into the bed once more releasing some of the bottled up anger. "This lady is a very close friend of mine. She saw your picture in the today's paper, told me she recognized you from the cabin. I want to know why she was abducted and held hostage and what part you played in her kidnapping?"

The Canadian businessman lay defiant, through the faint light he glared up at Brand. Brand returned the stare, the seconds ticking down in his head while he waited for the old man to answer. The room remained silent. When Brand had counted off a minute, he drove his fist into the pillow narrowly missing the white hair on the man's head.

"Mr. Bakker, believe me when I tell you, it'll only take me seconds to end your miserable life so I'll give you one more chance to convince me that you should go on breathing," Brand uttered through clenched teeth.

"I don't have a clue what you're talking about," the frightened man replied.

Before the old man could say anything else, Brand stood up and placed a hand on the prone man's chest pinning him to the bed. With his other hand, he yanked out a pillow from under the white head and squashed it down on the senior's face. The old man thrashed wildly, clawing at Brand's hands struggling to remove the pillow that was now suffocating him. Brand swatted away the feeble attempts as Bakker fought to free his face.

Continuing to hold the pillow clamped tight over the old man's head, Brand stood looking down at Nelson Bakker letting the panic build up inside the old man as he squirmed and twisted fighting to breath. Brand lifted the pillow and dropped it on the bed before he sat back down.

"Mr. Bakker. You are old, probably ready to meet your maker?" Brand stated in an even tone. "If you are, that's fine. I'll happily oblige you…but what about your daughters… you do have two daughters, do you not? I can't imagine that you would want the same fate to fall upon them or their families?" Brand looked at the old man. "I'm sure you're not naive enough to think you will be able to protect them?"

"Look, you leave them alone, or I'll…" the man replied, the quaver in his voice betraying him.

"You'll what?" Brand questioned. "I'll tell you what I'm thinking. I came here with the sole intention of meeting you, have you answer a few question, and see what kind of bastard would participate in the abduction of an innocent woman, a woman from Calgary who happens to be very dear to me.

I wish there were more time for me to finish this chat, but right now I have far more troubling problems to sort out, so you think about tonight and get back to me." Brand stared menacingly into the old man's pale face.

"I am going to leave a number with you and very soon I expect you to call me and enlighten me. I want to know how you are involved with the kidnapping and the reasons behind my friend's detainment. And I stress, very soon Mr. Bakker, or I'll be the worst fucking nightmare you and your family ever had… Capiche,"

Brand clenched his fists struggling to refrain from driving them into the quivering body cowering on the bed. "Now you get some sleep and tomorrow you think seriously about your families safety," Brand stood up and put his hand on the bedside phone yanking the cord loose from the wall and sent it crashing across the room.

Regaining his courage, Bakker glared at Brand.

"I will find out who you are you know and then the shit will hit the fan!"

"Mr. Bakker, Nelson, you don't mind if I call you Nelson do you? Nelson, I might not be a plumber but I sure and the hell know which direction shit flows and I can assure you, I have no problem stepping into it when I have to. But make no mistake, you, my friend are on the bottom of the pile I'll be stepping on." Brand pulled a pen out of his pocket and scratched the number of a burner phone he possessed into the surface of the end table. "Don't make me wait too long." Brand turned rapidly and drove a fist into the old man's stomach.

By the time Nelson Bakker regained his breath and was able to move, Brand had strolled onto the street.

Chapter 33

The American President paced circles in his office. All the countries defense departments and the whole American Intelligence network were scrambling to either verify or prove the rumoured attack false. The threat level remained high until proven otherwise.

The President knew that if an attack happened within American borders while he railed against bombing of the terrorists, the American people would take to the streets in a massive uprising. Honestly, he could not blame them. All the manpower he had beating the bushes looking for Intel of the threat had better come through. Not just for him, not just for the American people, but also for the millions of Muslims who would die should he be swayed to annihilate any Middle Eastern country.

Someone was talking. The President Monroe snapped out of his musing looking around the table in search of the voice. The Secretary of State, William Kendal, was staring back at him.

"As I was saying," Kendal repeated. "In my opinion, we are wasting our time playing out this charade. Instead, Sir, I vote to have the military begin preparations for the bombing strike. Hit the bastards before they can take any more innocent lives," he said.

President Monroe looked woefully at the Secretary. William Kendal had been a long time running mate of the President and a trusted friend. Secretary Kendall was also one of the most vocal in taking the fight to the terrorists. How many more lives, he kept asking are to be lost. The President nodded his head indicating he didn't know.

"We are running out of options and time," President Monroe admitted. He looked across the room at the White House press secretary. "Jim," he said. "I suppose it is time to at least inform the American people about the rumours circulating of this attack before it gets leaked to the media.

While we do that, I'll want statements added to convey our message to the governments in the Middle East. Strong statements to outline what we suspect and what we are prepared to do if any such attack is carried out against our country. Get your staffs busy writing the drafts immediately? I plan to be live across the country during the supper hour tonight." The President then turned his attention to the defense and intelligence directors in the room. "Gentlemen, we need some proof, we need to get ahead of this situation. Preferably before I go to air," he said bringing the meeting to an end. "I would most certainly appreciate it."

Richard Cozicar

Chapter 34

Brand woke up to the sound of his phone ringing. He had not returned to his hotel until almost six in the morning, and it felt like he had just fallen asleep. He glanced at the clock beside his bed. Nine twenty-seven.

Brand sat up in bed, the lack of sleep made him irritated by the phones interruption. With the back of his hands, he rubbed the sleep from his eyes, and then swung his feet to the floor. Brand shook his head to drive off the lingering effects of sleep that still clung to his brain before he reached for the phone.

Raising the receiver to his ear, he answered. Khak Pasoon's voice greeted him from the other end of the line.

"Did I wake you, my friend?" the Imam apologized.

"Not a problem," Brand replied, "I had a late night. Go ahead Khak, what's on your mind?"

"After our talk yesterday, I made some phone calls back home," The Imam explained. "A few minutes ago I received a call from an old friend of mine, another Imam from Khost, Afghanistan. My friend heard about my inquiries and called me back. He had heard news of a Pashtun tribesman near the Pakistani border who had barely escaped a massacre by a group of mercenaries from the West."

"What type of mercenaries?" Brand asked.

Imam Pasoon related the story from the other Imam. The news out of Afghanistan included a small band of American and British soldiers who had been living among the Pashtun's for the past several months.

"The part of the story I think you will find interesting," the Imam paused, "the mercenaries drove away from the massacre with three young Afghanis. Young men from the village who volunteered for a suicide mission in the United States."

"When did this happen?" Brand asked, the lack of sleep now forgotten.

133

"Yesterday, before noon," then the Imam clarified, "Afghanistan time."

The investigative part of Brand's brain took over. He had the Imam repeat the story as he asked several questions to collect even the minute details. Hanging up the phone, Brand remained seated on the edge of the bed, the new information swirling in his head. Suddenly like small collisions, the seemingly scattered fragments started coming together. The clarity of the puzzle unfolded to reveal itself. Brand had been suspicious about the bombings and how they had a different feel to them. Now he was positive.

The phone on Sara's desk rang. "Can you find me a number for Nelson Bakker, the old guy I talked to last night?" Brand asked and waited as Sara searched for and found the phone number and read it back to him. Brand punched the number into his phone, and while the dial tones rang in the background he thought about this new information and how it mixed with the other scraps he had collected to this point

"Hello. Nelson Bakker, who do, I owe this pleasure?" the Canadian businessman asked.

"You could say the Boogieman," Brand replied.

The oil executive released a short laugh.

"The Boogieman, indeed Mr. Coldstream. Brand Coldstream, isn't that your name? I have resources too, Mr. Coldstream and from what I hear, the Boogieman is certainly accurate."

"If your resources are competent then you know that I am most capable of keeping my promise," Brand stated.

"Yes, from what I've learned about you, I have no doubt...so why the call?

"I just finished a call from a friend of mine." Brand continued, not only retelling the Imam's story but also including what he had pieced together about the bombings, Sara's abduction and how all the little scraps of information were now forming a bigger picture.

"That is a very compelling story indeed, but I am not sure why you would be bothering me with this?"

"I have a feeling you know exactly why I am calling you." Brand replied coldly. "I also believe that any light you can shine on this situation, the better off you will be. Understand."

"I hear what you are saying," Bakker replied, "I will have to get back to you,"

"The sooner, the better." Brand said sternly and ended the call.

*****

Nelson Bakker hung up the phone and sat at his desk. Despite his voluntary involvement, he had begun having doubts about his part in the crusade as the weight of the journey that he had been a willing and eager participant in settled over him.

The stark reality of what the Cabal had undertaken. The loss of innocent lives and the horror they had caused stared him in the face when he had briefly locked eyes with the young girl standing at the window of August's cabin. In that short interlude, the morality of right and wrong brought on by the Cabal's actions broke through barriers in his mind forcing him to rethink their war on the Muslims and his role in aiding them.

The thousands of lives lost in the Cabal's battle against Islam and the eternity of being condemned to Hell, he had long since prepared his soul for, but from that moment he felt his principles change. Maybe he still had time in this life do something on the side of Angels.

Maybe there was still a chance to help prevent the further loss of innocent lives. The message he was receiving from God lately wasn't to hold to the path for the re-emergence of Christianity by annihilating the Muslims; instead, maybe he could be of better service to the Lord by helping prevent the Armageddon he saw the two religions racing toward.

Silent Crusade

Chapter 35

Disconnecting the call to Nelson Bakker, Brand dialed Brent Gallow's office and eagerly waited again while his call connected. His mind focused on the sequences of the plot, as it grew continually clearer. The destruction brought on by the bombings, all the dead and wounded, the families that were torn apart and left to mourn and all for what. The why he still didn't know, but he was getting closer to an answer.

Brand took his time briefing his friend on the new information and expanding on his theory. Brent listened attentively to his friend, every now and again asking a question, trying to make sure that he understood what he was hearing. When Brand finished, Brent added a few pieces that he now knew would fit.

"I have some calls to make. There is going to be a lot of people that will need convincing; everyone has been going on the assumption that these attacks were solely the doing of the Islamists. Some people are going to cling hard to that theory," he told Brand. "When are you heading back here?" he asked.

"I need time for a shower and some food after that I'll head straight to the airport. Can you have a car waiting when I arrive?

"Sure. Give me a call once you have your ticket booked and tell me what time to expect you."

"Will do," Brand said. Leaving his phone on the bed, he padded over toward the shower. Things were about to get very interesting he thought as he turned the water on.

*****

Brent Gallows spent the rest of the morning on the phone in conversations with different heads of the Canadian Intelligence agencies. Some of the men he talked to balked at Brand's theory, others took less time to see that the possibility of the scenario they had been working hard to prove could be wrong. Late in the morning, Brent had set up a conference call between all the Canadian agencies, shared Brand's report and led the groups in a discussion to decide on whether to take the investigation in a different direction.

By early afternoon, Brent had one call left to make. He knew the bureaucratic layers he would have to swim through to get this information to the Americans and the time that he would waste. This next phone call he decided provided the quickest way to contact the White House and update the American Intelligence community plus inform them of the change of direction the bombing investigation was now leaning.

Brent waited on the line for Canadian Senator Audrey Meadows. The Senator had walked the halls of Parliament for as long as anyone cared to remember and over the years she had earned the respect of her colleagues and many high-ranking officials outside of Canada's borders.

The Senator was in charge of a special black ops division assembled a year earlier by the Canadian Prime Minister. A task force that had been formed to investigate and bring to an end a devious plot involving Russian sleeper agents inside the Canadian government and fanatic environmentalists.

The shadow operation mirrored the Canadian Intelligence Agency while remaining unknown to other countries and their intelligence services. Prime Minister Reynolds had formed the unit when he not known how deep his government had been infiltrated and wanted the knowledge of the operation limited.

Since the successful closure of last year's investigation, the Prime Minister decided that having a secret arm of the intelligence community waiting in the shadows would allow his country to handle certain affairs without all the bluster of committee hearings and red tape that normally restricted their movement and speed.

Senator Meadows was a close, trusted friend of the Canadian Prime Minister. With the PM's consent, Senator Meadows, in turn, convinced Brent Gallows to allow the use of his security firm as a front for this covert Department of Canadian intelligence. A department that his friend Brand had assisted last fall while exposing the plot aimed at usurping the Canadian government.

In his head, Brent reviewed and rehearsed the argument he would need to make in convincing the Senator about Brand's theory. Subconsciously his fingers tapped on the surface of his desk in rhythm to the music being piped across the phone line while his call sat in limbo waiting for the Senator.

"Senator Meadows." The Senator's tired voice answered.

In a subdued tone, Brent meticulously described the theory he and Brand had pieced together about the bombings. Taking his time to answer the Senator's queries Brent made a solid case for the mostly circumstantial evidence that constructed their theory.

The bombings were a high priority and the Senator held on to reserved doubts of her own. She grilled Brent repeatedly always returning to the most obvious question, his degree of certainty regarding the conclusion he was drawing from the evidence.

Playing devils advocate with Brent; Senator Meadows stressed that this new information would change the course of the investigation and could have dire consequences if Brand was wrong with his timelines and assumptions. She attacked the line of reasoning from all angles as she looked for holes in Brand's theory but found few. The whole thing smelled of deception Brent argued, and the evidence pointed to some other group using the Islamic terrorists as scapegoats.

After a long and sometimes heated conversation with the Senator, Brent prevailed then expressed the urgency to inform the American intelligence agencies. He ended the call by adding that he had not been in touch with the Americans fearing their outright refusal of the theory if the message came from him.

"This information is crucial," he implored, "they need to act."

"Yes. A soon as I hang up the phone my priority will be to get in touch with the Director of the CIA, Hal Jorgenson; he can brief the others," She agreed. The Senator let out a troubled sigh. "What the hell is going on, Brent? It is almost like there's some secret fraternity waging a war of their own against Muslims." She speculated, not knowing exactly how close to the truth she was.

Chapter 36

By five o'clock in the afternoon, President Munroe's meeting with the countries security agencies had wrapped up. Not one of the intelligence agencies tasked with defending the country had so far corroborated the attack or proved the rumours wrong. The President reread the press release one last time then took a few minutes to gather his thoughts.

The perceived threat against this country and the steps that he as the President would officially order in retaliation for such an attack, that he was about to explain the American people, and thus the world, was something he would have never foreseen doing. The use of nuclear bombs was the last possible resort left to any President and certainly not one to be taken lightly.

The bombs were not discriminatory in who they killed. Therefore, a lot of innocent people would suffer because of the misguided beliefs and devastatingly violent actions of a group of radicals. The President had steered away from this course of action as long as he could, but the violence was escalating. Despite his best efforts on the ground, there was no way to identify all of the terrorist operatives and no other solution to stop the killing except to eradicate the source.

President Monroe stared off into space. His eyes blurred, a sheen of tears forming as he forgot to blink. He had only moments before he would be standing in front of the cameras, warning of the suspected attack and at the same time, trying to comfort the American people. His glanced back down at the words of his speech that soon would be broadcasted across the nation and around the world.

His press aide caught his attention and gave him the five-minute warning.

God help us, the President thought.

*****

The white haired matriarch of the Canadian Senate sat at her desk. The phone call from Brent Gallows was disturbing. If an anonymous group was manipulating the investigation down a false trail straight to the Islamic terrorists, then the real perpetrators gained the advantage to organize and perpetrate more heinous attacks unchallenged.

Finally settling on a decision, she had picked up her desk phone and dialed the office of the CIA Director. While the Senator waited for the phone call to connect, she turned the previous conversation over in her head. The more she'd thought, the more she'd realized that the theory made sense. All the little pieces of the puzzle that didn't seem to work before now seemed to fit together perfectly.

While President Monroe prepared to step in front of the cameras, the phone in the CIA Director's office rang. Hal Jorgenson tore his eyes away from the breaking news banner on the television and picked up the phone.

"Director Jorgenson, this Senator Audrey Meadows."

*****

The Canadian Senator had wasted little time as she explained Brand's theory detailing the misconception the allied countries' intelligence communities believed. Point by point Senator Meadows championed the working, yet unproven theory that the Canadian intelligence agencies were now exploring.

Jorgenson listened intently; occasionally interrupting the Senator seeking clarification of a specific fact and, like the Senator had done to Brent, repeatedly questioning her certainty.

Senator Meadows stubbornly reasoned with the CIA Director that the information she had in her possession pointed overwhelmingly to an unknown group being the driving force behind the recent explosions. A group unknown to either countries intelligence communities but one that disguised their work as terrorist attacks, laying the blame at the feet of the Muslim community while remaining out of sight.

She argued with the CIA Director that the information she was sharing should provide more than ample reason to halt or at least postpone the planned counter-attacks and possibly save hundreds of thousands of innocent lives.

"We need to slow things down and gather further Intel," she stressed to the Director. "The most pressing objective," she said, "Was to prevent the President of the United States from making an irreversible mistake, one that history would show far outweighed the current loss of life attributed to the current radical terrorists."

Jorgenson commended the Senator for her countries help and assured her that he would inform the President at the earliest opportunity. He bid the Canadian Senator goodbye and contemplated the phone in his hand while he digested the Senator's words.

"DAMN!" he shouted to the empty room. Director Jorgenson stood up, stepped around his desk and stormed to his office door, insured that it was locked then returned to his chair. His position as the head of the CIA came with the benefit of having one of the most secure phone connections in the world. Right now he was glad.

As Director of the CIA, he had been able to divert the investigations progress into the bombings with subtly placed misinformation leading away from the Cabal and narrowing everyone's focus on the Muslims. Now with the Canadian's so close to the truth he would have to change strategies and limit the flow of information to avoid any suspicion. He sat at his desk wondering how else he could impede the investigation and the sharing of resources and if he could buy enough time for the final act to be played out?

If he was too obvious and simply withheld information or tried to curtail the new investigation he risked exposure both for him and the Cabal. Damn...so close, he fumed. No, he decided, continue the charade and subtly sabotage and delay what he could. After all, what other choice did he have left?

Jorgenson dialed a number, his anger building while he waited

The CIA boss spoke when the call was connected.

"August, it's Hal. We have got a problem." Quickly briefing the billionaire on the Canadians investigation he slammed the phone down and remained at his desk staring blindly at the television. The President stood in the

Whitehouse media room, the news cameras broadcasting his dire message before the world.

*****

President John Monroe stood before the television cameras; staring forward steely eyed trying not to portray his concern that the inevitable fear his words would ignite throughout the country. He forced himself to shove those thoughts aside and proceed with the prepared speech he held in his hands.

He talked briefly about the bombings of the past months and about the concerns that rippled through the international public, emphasizing how he shared the same worries and how his responsibility to keep his country and her people safe was his number one priority.

"…Recent information uncovered by our nation's Intelligence community, the world's best intelligence agencies," he added to boost the confidence of the American public. "The men and women assigned with protecting this great country have reason to believe an attack is being planned against us and is to be carried out inside our nation's borders." The bright lights from the cameras highlighted the dark bags under the President's eyes, and the worry etched into his face. The Commander and Chief read the speech with confidence even he was having trouble believing himself.

"I ask each and everyone of you to be vigilant and watchful," Monroe continued, "my office along with every government and security department across the country will remain on high alert. I assure you that we will not rest as we work night and day to prevent such an attack. The terror alert in our country has been raised to its highest level and will remain so until we uncover this plot. No one," he stressed, "will rest until the perpetrators of these heinous crimes are caught and dealt with to the fullest extent of American justice."

President Monroe looked down as he lifted a glass of water and took a drink. The moment had come; it was too late for him to stop now he decided. He cleared his throat and returned his gaze to the cameras,

"…And to the leaders of the countries that continue to produce and harbour these terrorists, heed my warning, the United States of America will not be sitting idle and waiting for another attack to happen. If one small shred of evidence is discovered confirming an attack, we will be proactive, not reactive. The consequences of an attack on the American people will be unlike any ever witnessed by the world in the last seventy years…" the President stopped for a long pause to let his words reverberate around the world. "…This new era of terrorist activity will be removed from the face of the earth once and for all!" He sternly stated and turned his back to the cameras leaving the podium.

Silent Crusade

Chapter 37

Brand took his phone out of his pocket as he walked across the Ottawa Airport and turned the power back on. He had shut the phone off before boarding the plane. When the phone powered up, he noticed a message icon flashing but decided against retrieving the message at the moment and stashed the phone back in his pocket. The idea of walking through the bustling airport while being distracted by his phone did not appeal to him. With a mental reminder to review the message once he left the terminal and its crowds behind or seated in the car sent for him.

*****

Brent spent the morning on the phone with British Intelligence. With the new information, the British forces reviewed their investigation into the bombing and like the Canadians uncovered a similar situation.

The intelligence community revisited the evidence and after countless man-hours and thousands of CCTV videos, they too now had a positive lead on the London bombers identity. There too videos were uncovered showing a British national disguised as a Muslim woman minutes before the explosion.

The activity in London mirrored the Toronto subway incident and yes, like the Canadian bomber, the man responsible had a rap sheet of petty crimes.

"Our perp was born in England and a Caucasian male," the British agent read off the bio sheet to Brent. "Our investigation is far from complete, but one thing is sure, our man's background closely resembles that of the Toronto subway bomber. We've still got a lot of legwork to do, friends and family to hunt down and interview," the Brit confessed. "Without your tip, we would have likely missed this. The initial M.O. for the attack matched other attempts in our country, so that was where we were focusing our search. Thanks again old chap, we'll talk soon once we've had more time to sort this out."

Brent returned the phone to its cradle and looked up as Brand walked through his office door.

"That was British Intelligence. The bomber in England shared a lot in common with our subway bomber. Caucasian, small time crook, not Muslim, nothing in his background so far to indicate he had terrorist connections. No doubt his story will unfold in the same way," and as an afterthought, he added. "I talked to a guy at the General Directorate of Internal Security in France; so far they haven't found any footage or evidence that helps them identify the bombers there yet. They'll get in touch if they find some."

Brand shook his head and seated himself. The cell phone in his pocket jabbed him when he sat down reminding him that a voicemail message was waiting. He stood up.

"Give me a minute," He apologized as he turned to leave. "I forgot I had a message on my phone." Walking out of the office into the hallway, Brand leaned against the wall and retrieved the message.

"Holy shit!" Brand exclaimed and rushed back into Brent's office.

Brand set his phone on the desk and set the phone on speaker, "Hey Boogie man, I gave some serious thought to our conversation from the other night...." Began a voice that sounded old and tired.

"Boogie man, are you kidding me..." Brent said through his laughter. "...So you're the reason I check my closet and under my bed every night before I go to sleep?"

The ends of Brand's mouth curled up a bit at the sides as he chastised his friend for the remarks.

"Shut up and listen!" Brand scolded while he restarted the recorded message. The tired old voice started over again; the recording played out of the phone's speaker. The caller blamed a change of heart for his decision to call and then provided Brand with information about a group of mercenaries from Afghanistan. Men, who at the time of this message, had already left Pakistan and are now on indirect routes to the United States.

The same group of men had boarded at the airport at Peshawar Pakistan a day ago escorting three potential suicide bombers from Afghanistan.

The plan called for the mercenaries, along with their Afghani guests, to cross into Pakistan and board planes to different European destinations. In pairs, the individuals were to book flights heading west toward North America with the leader of the group arriving on a separate plane. The four flights heading west were destined to arrive either tonight or early tomorrow morning." That is as much of the plan that I was privy to." The weary man's voice apologized.

The voice droned on reading off a list of names for the mercenaries and the North American airports the planes were to land. Three of the airports were in the States and the Pearson International Airport in Toronto was named as the fourth.

"…Hope this helps…now you can go and haunt someone else's damn dreams for a while," the message ended. Brent looked at Brand.

"Who was that?" Brent asked.

"That's not important right now, what about the message, though," Brand said changing the subject.

"How credible is this guy? He's not some crazy kook out to waste our time and then sit back and laugh at us as we chase around looking for ghouls where there are none, is he?" Brent grilled Brand as he sat up at his desk, his attention focused, his disposition growing sombre throughout the call.

"I think we should seriously consider what he had to say, Brand assured him and proceeded to explain what he knew of the Canadian industrialist.

"Wow…I guess we had better get busy and make some calls. There's going to be a lot of scrambling to verify the information from this call and have these men apprehended when their planes land," Brent replayed the message and with pen in hand he furiously wrote down the names and arrival times of the incoming flights. Brent set down his pen and passed the paper to Brand.

"Take this to Sara and Darcy. We're going to need everyone with access to a computer to research these names plus we are going to need photos of the men for distribution."

Brand left the office as Brent picked up his phone and started dialing. He had to notify Law enforcement in both countries, a lot of manpower was going to be needed, and the clock was ticking.

Brent realized that keeping the operation contained and out of the media before the suspects were in custody would be near impossible but he would have to do his best. With so many agencies and the number of law enforcement required, a possible leak was inevitable. He would stress this with every department head he contacted, if the suspects were alerted before they were apprehended, the Intel would be useless, the conspirators could make a new plan and thwart any attempts to arrest them.

At Sara's desk, Brand handed over the paper and explained the phone message. When Sara had copied the names off the list, Brand sought out Darcy and repeated the process, and then he moved back to Sara's desk and borrowed a chair to sit in. While Sara typed away at her terminal, Brand told her a short version of his adventures earlier that morning. He also asked her about the photos of the two men in the video with the subway bomber.

Her fingers flew over the keyboard, the computer search started.

"The two men are both former Canadian military officers. We've circulated an APB already, alerted all the crossing stations into the States and a notification has gone out to the local airports," she paused, her hands resting on the computer keyboard." The OPP have found an abandoned car believed to belong to one of the men hid in a field south of here, but so far it looks like the pair has disappeared."

"Any luck tracking their cell phones?" Brand asked her.

Shaking her head, she glanced away from the computer screen, "No. So far there are no signals from the phones. I suspect they must be turned off, or maybe the men destroyed them. Right now we are at a dead-end in the search for those two."

Chapter 38

Sergeant Dan Quails, the on-duty officer at the RCMP Airport Detachment snagged the ringing phone off his desk. He listened as the Deputy Commissioner of the O division alerted him about a plane that was due to land at the Pearson Airport later that evening. An ex U.S. military ranger and a young Afghanistan man were on that plane and were to be taken into custody once they left the plane.

The commissioner was very exact in his instructions on how he wanted the arrests handled and told the Sergeant that he would be sending extra men to assist. There were five other officers currently on duty at the airport, which should be more than enough, the Sergeant told the Commissioner. The Commissioner ignored the Sergeant's statement; the ex-army ranger could be very dangerous and if these men had anything to do with the bombings the more manpower, the better.

Sergeant Quails hung up the phone and spoke into his body mike; all other police officers were to meet him near the gate scheduled for the flight from Milan. Once assembled, the squadron of police was instructed to clear the arrival area before the plane landed. The Sergeant supervised his men as they cordoned off the area. His men rapidly swept the area ensuring all non-essential personnel had left before he circulated a photo of the mercenary, a picture provided by the British Military. The picture was old, but it was all they were able to supply on such short notice.

Detective Bronson led another a group of uniformed officers as he rushed into the airport. He was aware that the Airport police were at the international gates in the process of clearing the concourse as the planes arrived.

The plane from Italy had just entered Toronto airspace, the tower's instructions to the pilot were to circle the airport; he would receive permission to land very soon.

When the plane ahead of the Italian flight was offloading its passengers, Sergeant Quail contacted the tower, "Tell the pilot its time to land." The squads of police finished clearing the concourse around the arrival gate and took their positions.

The plane taxied down the runway and came to rest at the terminal. An airline attendant bid everyone welcome to Toronto and opened the plane door. Most of the passengers had removed their carry-on baggage from the overhead compartments and in a single file left the aircraft. A long line of people walked down the passageway toward the customs desk and then down the long hallway to the concourse arrival area. There, the first departing passengers walking through the doors were stopped by two RCMP officers. The officers asked them to divide into two groups, women on the left, men on the right.

The confused passengers reluctantly separated into groups. The line of women escorted away from the arrival door while a set of officers scrutinized the male passengers. Barret Hammond, the ex-British SAS member along with the young Afghani, walked down the long hallway past customs with the rest of the crowd. In front of the two, the line of passengers slowed as they entered into the terminal. Barret became suspicious of the delay into the building. Grabbing the arm of the Afghani, he stepped to the side of the hallway and let the other passenger's stream by.

He stood against the wall and watched the travelers from the Italian flight bunch up as they rounded the corner into the airport. His entry into Canada should have gone unimpeded. At the airport in Italy, he bought tickets with a passport under a different identity, an identity selected to bypass scrutiny by Canadian airport security.

He wondered at the possibility that the authorities were looking for another passenger, but the coincidence was too great for him to accept. Motioning for the Afghani to stay behind him, Barret stepped back in line behind the last of the departing passengers. Preparing for the unknown, Hammond nodded to the young Afghani and the pair moved toward the exit. Resorting back to his military training he studied the desolate surroundings for any means of an advantage he could use in his favour. As the two moved slowly forward in the long tunnel, Hammond accepted the fact that very few options presented themselves; surprise was the only tool available at the moment.

The months he had spent in Afghanistan had changed his appearance. His hair was much longer, and his facial skin burned to an almost black hue from the hot Middle Eastern sun. Even if the Canadian authorities had an old photo of him, the picture couldn't possibly resemble the way he currently appeared.

Barret stepped around the bend in the hallway. The passengers from the plane were being directed to separate lines as they passed through the doors. The British soldier moved casually toward the waiting officers; the Afghani youth followed close on his heels. Barret smiled at the officers as he closed the distance. If the police weren't looking for him he was about to make a huge mistake, if they were, it was better he use the element of surprise while he still had it in his favour.

The officer in front of Hammond extended his arm and gestured to the line on the right. Barret took a step forward as if to comply then in a fluid motion he spun and grabbed the officer's outstretched arm, twisted the outstretched arm behind the cops back the man while he relieved the officer of his weapon and pressed it tight to the man's spine.

Before anyone realized what had taken place, Barret Hammond dragged the officer backward, the body of the cop shielding Barret in the front. Using his gun hand, he shoved the Afghani behind. The remaining police reacted, scrambling the remaining passengers away and seeking cover, their pistols were drawn and pointed at the mercenary's retreat.

Hammond had been in a lot of tight spots before, but he had always managed to escape. He understood that under no circumstances were the police going to let him walk out of the terminal. If he tried to cross the concourse using the police officer as cover, his back would be fully exposed. Barret quickly came to the conclusion that there was only going to be one ending to this standoff. He said a silent prayer, raised the confiscated gun and shot the Afghani youth in the head. He then pushed his captive to the floor in front of him, raised the gun and fired a round into the ceiling above the approaching officers.

Suicide at the hands of the police, it was not the way he had pictured his life coming to an end. In a short span of time Hammond contemplated that if the police knew about his arrival on this flight, they probably knew about his involvement in the bombings. He was not prepared to spend the rest of his life in prison. As for the Afghani, Barret's loyalties to the Cabal allowed him to die knowing he was protecting the cause he had been fighting for; the police would not be able to get any information from the two of them.

Barret Hammond felt his body jerk as the bullets entered his body. He tried to make his peace with God as the guns continued firing. A smile came to his face as he slid down the wall; his days of crusading were over.

*****

Dean Adams' fate was not much different when the German Airlines flight landed in Cincinnati. The State police didn't have the same lead-time as the police in Toronto had. Adams and the man he was escorting were already in the terminal and wondering about the airport when the police stormed through the buildings doors. With the help of a squad of National Guardsmen, the airport exits were sealed off as the manhunt began.

Adams quickly realized that something had gone terribly wrong as he watched the police pour into the building. He grabbed the young terrorist by the arm and sought out a place to hide. Spotting a cluster of people gathered around a bulky work of art near the luggage carousel Adams hurried for cover, dragging the young man with him into the crowd. Hiding behind the art display he watched as the police spread throughout the main concourse. His eyes roamed the large crowded floor of the terminal. Opportunities to escape shrunk with every passing minute. From his position the routes out of the building filled with the bodies of law enforcement. More officers with flak jackets and assault rifles raised spread around the concourse floor. Adams chances of leaving the building were not good from what he stood but the term surrender wasn't in his vocabulary.

His eyes followed the armed members of the task force as they swarmed the arrival gate he had entered minutes before and as a group, the cops slowly worked their way to the carousel. The confusion of the other travelers in the area was hampering the cops as they searched. The task of finding anyone in the melee was damn near impossible. One officer stepped within feet of where Adams had taken refuge, the man's attention directed toward the baggage carousel as he walked closer to the art display. The mercenary stepped behind the officer and used his arm to drive the gun from the unsuspecting cop's hand.

Adam's then shoved the officer forward and snatched the gun off the floor. With the gun in hand, Adams grabbed the frightened Afghani and pulled him in the direction of a pair of huge sliding doors that led out of the terminal. Chaos erupted as the fleeing men struggled for the exit.

"DOWN, EVERYBODY GET DOWN!"

Crowds on the concourse looked around, noticed the police then started dropping to the floor. Adams took aim and fired at the security personnel

154

blocking his path to freedom. The bullet that connected with the first man spun him around; the impact of the next bullet toppled a second man backward.

Screams of hysteria filled the air adding to the chaos. Adams attempted to fire the gun again when his body started convulsing, bullets tearing into his body from several angles. Time stopped for him as he watched other officers firing their guns. He was barely aware as he felt his weapon slip from his finger and fall to the ground, his hand no longer able to grip it. The noise in the airport ceased to exist in Dean Adams' mind as a feeling of peace flooded his brain. Seconds later he lay crumpled on the floor in a growing pool of blood.

The State Police rushed cohesively towards the spot Adams had fallen. Lying beside Dean Adams was the young Afghani man, his body riddled with bullets as well, but he was still breathing. The chaos inside the airport settled then came the scream of sirens as they too joined melee from outside the building. Paramedics pushing gurneys rushed inside to attend to the wounded.

A sergeant with the State Police waved a paramedic over to the fallen body of the Afghani man. The man needed immediate medical attention if he was to live long enough to be questioned.

*****

Dexter Tranter and George Williams were also supposed to enter the United States the following morning. The Afghani man they were escorting was in tow. A mix up with their flight in Germany had caused them to rebook with a different airline. The change in plans changed their original time of arrival; the men entered the States earlier than their previous flight. The plane touched down at the Detroit Metro Airport late in the evening, over seven hours ahead of their scheduled flight.

When the three men had claimed their baggage, Williams walked up to the counter of a rental booth in the airport and signed out a car. Keys in hand the trio left the building and walked to the lot unobstructed. George Williams had been given explicit orders to avoid contact of any type until he had safely arrived back on American soil. All the returning mercenaries had been given an address and directions to a safe house a short distance west of Chicago where they were to rendezvous upon entering the States.

Williams climbed behind the wheel waited for the other two to settle into their seats before leaving the airport behind them. Their Afghani companion huddled securely in the back seat. George Williams was familiar with this part of the country; he had grown up west and south of Detroit near the Indiana-Michigan border. The drive ahead of them was at least five hours. The time was of no consequence because they were not supposed to land in the States until the following day.

As Williams drove, he kept his eyes open for an all-night convenience store. Johnson was the only one of the men who had been allowed a phone while they were on mission. Now that they were back in the country Williams wanted a phone so he could make contact with the rest of the group.

*****

Michael Johnson stepped off the plane at the International Airport in Milwaukee, Wisconsin. His face lit up in a smile as he followed the other passengers into the airport. Finally back on American soil! He had never been so glad to return to the good ol' U.S. of A. No more dust and tents, or goats roaming about underfoot or living with the tribal people of Afghanistan.

Johnson walked passed the line of people at the luggage carousel. A small travel bag was all he returned to the States with. The travel bag by his side he bypassed the crowds at the carousel and crossed the terminal toward the car rental kiosks. Ignoring the Cabals offers of help upon his return instead preferring to take care of his own arrangements.

He left the terminal in high spirits, the sun high in the Wisconsin sky. Intent on savouring his peaceful return he waited until he was inside the rental car before activating his phone. He glanced at the message icon as it flashed on the lit screen. . Taking his time he methodically combed the rental lot, the instinct a side effect of his line of work. Satisfied that he remained unwatched he returned his attention to the message light, tapped the phones buttons and proceeded to listen to the messages.

His mood soured. The first message warned him that his flight into the states has been compromised. The FBI was acting on information about his groups flights are were coordinating raids at the airports in question. The message continued.

"If you are listening to this message, you obviously made it back into the country undetected so be warned and take whatever precautions you see fit."

The other messages changed from warning of the leak to the F.B.I. to instructions for him to make contact A.S.A.P. All the phone messages originated from the same number. A number that few knew but he recognized August Jackson's secure number.

Michael Johnson thanked his lucky stars that he had the foresight to change flights. He hesitated in returning Jackson's anxious pleas. Once he had driven to a secure location he then would call the man back.

On his drive away from the airport Johnson pondered his luck at avoiding detection by the American officials. He then mulled over the carefully crafted plans his men had followed in returning to the States. How had they been identified? Was his group being set up? And if so then why he wondered and what had happened in the short time since he left Pakistan?

Anger overtook him as he thought back to the months spent in that hellhole working side by side with people he detested. All in the name of accomplishing the goal the Cabal had assigned him, the righteous goal of driving a stake into the heart of Islam. Was it all for nothing he wondered?

Once he was safely out of sight he swore to himself that he would find the traitor. He and his men had worked too damn hard and sacrificed way too much to be cast aside because someone was getting cold feet. He didn't see any other possible way that the F.B.I. would have information on the attack. He banged the steering wheel in frustration as he guided the car down the highway.

Silent Crusade

Chapter 39

Brent was joined in his office by Brand and Sara as the three sat at his desk watching the early morning news. Brent's desk sat littered with containers of cold Chinese take-out. The three had been in the office through the night waiting for the news while police staked out the airports in question. Since early in the morning news reports started pouring in from both sides of the border pre-empting the regularly scheduled programming at all the major stations. Reports of the shootout in Toronto led the broadcasts. Police spokesmen released public statements regarding the deaths of two terrorists trying to enter illegally into the country. Several of the suspected men had died in a battle of gunfire, and a couple of police officers had suffered non-life threatening gunshot wounds.

Then the coverage switched to Cincinnati. News cameras showed the interior of the airport. Police and paramedics were attending to several passengers injured in another armed takedown. The police had killed the gunman and wounded the accomplice; the news report later said the wounded terrorist died en route to the hospital.

Brent flipped from channel to channel. Every major Canadian and American station ran a loop filled with extensive coverage of the airport shootings tossing in updates as they came across the news wire.

The phone on Brent's desk rang. Choking down a mouthful of cold food, he lifted the receiver and put the phone to his ear. He stared at Brand as he listened to the caller. For a long time, he remained quiet. Slowly a troubled look crept across his face. At the end of the conversation, he mumbled "Goodnight Senator." and returned the phone to its cradle.

Brent looked at the other two, "I guess we are flying to Cincinnati. Senator Meadows wants us to leave ASAP. We're to hook up with FBI and Homeland Security agents there. Apparently one of the men shot at the Cincinnati airport never died of his wounds like the news stories reported.

Homeland issued a false statement about the death," Brent paused for a minute. "The police checked the other flights on the list. The remaining men weren't on them," he glanced between Brand and Sara.

"If the information we have is valid, that still leaves three mercenaries unaccounted for and one of the Jihadists. Right now no one knows if they arrived in the country or not," Brent went quiet mulling over the gravity of the phone call.

Breaking his silence, he looked in Brand's direction. "The Senator wants the two of us to assist Homeland Security. They declined her offer but being the pit bull that she is; she left them no choice. The fact that we were already involved in this case because of the two terrorists at the Pierson airport, the higher ups at Homeland are allowing us the courtesy of joining them. Agents are waiting for our arrival before questioning the suspect they have sequestered away," he stood from behind his desk. "The Senator took the liberty of having our tickets booked. I'll have a one of the men drop us at the airport," he added and rubbed the weariness from his tired eyes, "She suggested we hurry."

*****

The Cincinnati Airport was still in disarray from the shootings of the previous evening as the two Canadians walked from the plane onto the concourse. Men from Homeland Security met them at arrivals and escorted them to a pair of waiting SUVs parked outside the airport's main terminal. Brent introduced himself and Brand. The lead agent turned to Brand and spoke.

"I hear that you were the one who figured this whole pile of shit out, thank you," he said. "Very impressive, glad to have you join us," the man commented as the group approached the waiting vehicles. "The location where we are keeping the terrorist isn't far."

Brand look out the window at the streets of Cincinnati as they wound through busy midday traffic. The building they approached looked like a cross between a hospital and a federal building. Their driver went around to the side of the building and took a ramp leading to an underground parkade.

Brand followed behind the Homeland agents into the building and down a series of hallways until they stopped at a door with more agents standing guard. The American's exchanged greetings with the guards at the door. Once the pair from Canada and the men from Homeland crowded into the room, the door was closed.

More men were already standing inside, another agent and a translator stood beside the wounded terrorist as he lay in the bed, hooked up to a tangle of tubes and wires.

"Anything new?" the Canadians escort asked the waiting agent.

"No. So far he refuses to say anything," the other answered.

The lead agent leaned over the bed and prodded the injured man with a couple of questions. The terrorist blankly stared at him and remained quiet.

Brand watched as the Afghani repeatedly ignored all the questions directed his way. "Enough of this shit!" Brand thought as he pulled his gun out of his shoulder holster and pushed his way to the head of the bed. Pressing his hand against a wound on the terrorist's chest, Brand stuck the barrel of his gun into the terrorist's mouth. The man jerked from the pain, his eyes bulging in fear.

"We're not going to ask again!" Brand said and jammed the weapon further into startled man's mouth.

The young Afghani tried to swallow; muffled words rushed out of his mouth around the gun barrel. Brand raised the gun. In broken English, the young man spoke rapidly his lack of the English language forming incoherent sentences.

"...Chicago, baseball game..." the scared man replied. Brand grabbed the translator and pulled him closer to the bed.

"Talk to him in whatever damn language he speaks. It's imperative we get the details correct." Then he stepped back and stood beside the other agents and listened as the two men conversed loudly in the foreign language.

The conversation lasted several minutes, the two men's hands wildly gesturing as they talked. The translator turned his back to the prisoner and carefully repeated the man's confession. Slowly, the translator explained a condensed version of the wounded Afghani's voyage to the States...he started this journey with two others from his village; the translator told the room, the men volunteered to come to America and participate in an attack in Chicago, supposedly during an afternoon baseball game.

"Ask him when and how many men are involved in the attack?" Brand prodded the translator.

Several more minutes passed while the translator spoke rapidly then listened while the suspect answered. When the young Afghani fell silent, the translator turned to the rest of the room with the translation.

"He heard the planned attack was for the twenty-ninth. That and an afternoon game are the only part of the scheme he knows. The men who tried to smuggle him into the country never revealed much. They told him that he would go to paradise for his part and that was all he needed to know."

"The Twenty-ninth, Jesus, that's only two days away..." Brand thought out loud.

Chapter 40

"What the HELL is going on?" Johnson barked when August Jackson picked up his phone.

"Michael, where are you? We worried that the police arrested you along with the others." August exhaled a long sigh of relief. "When we hadn't heard from you, we had to assume the worst."

For a second, Johnson thought he almost detected a note of concern in the old man's voice. Strange, everyone involved with the Cabal understood that the only thing of importance to the old man was the successful conclusion of this mission and Johnson had no misgivings that he and his crew were expendable.

August briefed Johnson on the arrests at the airports, the killing of the returning soldiers and the young Jihadists.

"The shootings at the airports have been all over the news, but the police have yet to release any names. As far as the rest of the men are concerned, no one has heard. So where does this leave us?" August wondered out loud. "We certainly don't have the manpower to go through with the attack."

Johnson confessed to August that he had changed his flight plans arriving at a different airport and was currently on his way to the safe house.

"Look, I'll call you back once I'm at the house. I've got a long drive ahead of me. I need some time to think," Johnson said to ease the old man's mind. "We've come to far, made far too many sacrifices to give up now." Johnson thought as he spoke. "If you hear from the others let me know. I'll find a way to finish this; I'm not ready to give up yet."

"You be careful," the leader of the Cabal warned before cutting the connection. August then dialed the private number for a Cabal collaborator in the Presidents circle of advisors.

Hal Jorgenson snacked the ringing phone off his desk. Hearing August's voice, Jorgenson stopped his friend.

"I'll call you right back," he said, nervous to even utter August's name in his government office. The director of the CIA set the phone back down, stood up from his desk and with long, hurried strides he closed and locked his office door, paranoid of having his conversation overheard. Jorgenson returned to his chair and dialed August Jackson's secure number.

The two men discussed the unfortunate circumstances leading to the discovery and killing of their men at the two airports and the consequences this had for the operation. During a lull in the conversation, August Jackson asked the CIA Director a question that the Cabal leader feared he already knew the answer.

"What about the President. Will he still believe that the Islamist terrorists are behind the bombings? What has he been saying? Is he still prepared to back up his threat?"

"Like everyone else in this country he has been watching the news broadcasts closely. I think that he may be having doubts about the attacks," the Director conceded. "I have taken every opportunity to advise him that this doesn't change matters. It's not the first time men from non-Muslim countries have taken up the torch for Islam and perpetrated acts of terrorism," Jorgenson assured August. "Fortunately, for us, none of your men lived to be questioned."

"I did have to admit to the President," Director Jorgenson warned, "that the takedown at the airports has to disrupt the attack against our country," Jorgenson paused. "The President remains worried, all the men on the list haven't been accounted for yet, so the threat remains. The consensus in the war-room is to send planes to the countries that are the breeding grounds for these terror groups." Jorgenson went quiet and for a time the line remained silent, both men lost in their thoughts.

"What else can you do to keep the President focused on his threat to bomb the Muslims?" August reiterated.

"Well, I can't come out and tell him that a secret Christian movement is behind the attacks and would like him to bomb the Middle East to stop the spreading Muslim plague, now can I?" Hal Jorgenson replied sarcastically. "We need to keep the attack in play. The outrage of the American people should be enough to force his hand and leave him with no option but to follow through with his threat."

"What about the terror alert levels?" August asked. "Can you have them lowered?" August added.

"No. I definitely can't do that! The country will have to remain on high alert for the time being. I can steer the investigation in another direction by leaking false information. That will open a small window for your men to operate but that being said, we have to be cautious. You need to find the traitor in your organization August. Any more screw ups and the President will have reason enough to back away."

"Keep The President focused," August said. "Johnson is back in the country. I'll talk to him and see if there's another way of pulling this thing off."

Silent Crusade

Chapter 41

Michael Johnson skirted along the edge of Chicago driving west toward the safe house chosen for its proximity to the target. Johnson's destination was Berwyn, Illinois, a short distance west of the major city and was a suburb of the larger Chicago metropolis with a population sitting near sixty thousand people. A population more than adequate to hide the Cabal's men while they gathered and waited for their next move.

Johnson pulled the rental into a deserted parking lot of a small pub on the outskirts of town. He needed a place to think and the fact that he hadn't had a cold American beer for the past six months now also swayed his choice of establishments. Seated in the air-conditioned bar, a frosty pitcher of beer in front of him, he stared absently across the bar his mind sorting through the change of events.

The question he kept returning to was exactly how much did the feds know and how did they know? That there was a leak was evident but how high up was the leak? Was the safe house compromised and could he expect cops hiding in the bushes waiting to arrest him?

Spinning the beer mug in his hand he thought about his approach to the safe house, if it were under surveillance would he be driving into a trap. His concentration impeded as his thoughts dwelled on the fate of his men. Were all the men who left Afghanistan arrested on their entry into the country? The stark realization hit him, if the men were arrested or killed; the plan had an almost zero chance of success. Good questions, but unfortunately he could find no answers in the bottom of his glass.

He sat at the table savouring the cold beer in the air-conditioned bar as he racked his brain for a solution that might still enable him to complete this mission. Johnson lingered over the cold beverage, his mouth a wry smile. If the authorities were waiting at the house for him, they could wait a while longer.

Johnson left money on the table when he finished his drink. Stepping into the sunshine of the early Illinois day. He breathed deeply sucking in a welcoming lungful of air, crisp and fresh, a pleasant change from the hot, scorched air he left behind. Walking to his rental car, he skirted the small city, the safe house only a short distance from town on a secluded acreage. A few short miles into his journey he turned off the highway onto a secondary gravel road for the last leg of the trip.

Slowing his speed as he topped a small hill on the road, he guided the car onto the shoulder. The rise provided an unobstructed view of the house and surrounding yard. Johnson climbed out of the vehicle and stood beside it looking down at the acreage. The warmth of the late morning warmed his back as he checked for signs of law officers waiting in ambush. Several times he observed men walk out of the house and light a smoke or to grab something from the vehicles parked in the yard.

He kept watch until he was satisfied that the house was not under surveillance, climbed back into the car and drove the rest of the way into the yard. Parking alongside the other cars in he got out and walked across the grass, hesitated for an instant at the door then swung it open.

Standing in the doorway, Johnson scanned the front room of the house. He spotted Tranter first, then Williams along with an Afghani. The two men who had coordinated the Toronto bombing sat beside each other on a couch.

A smile came to Johnson's lips. Not everyone had been captured or killed, as he had feared. There was still hope, a small a chance of the mission proceeding! The men in the room stood up to greet him, handshakes and questions mixed with greetings surrounded them while they all tried to talk at once and compare notes on the events of the few days. Johnson listened to the chatter, interrupted occasionally and asked questions of his own. He allowed himself a smile as he studied the group in the house. Yes, there was still hope for the crusade after all.

Once Johnson had spoken with the men, he walked outside and paced the yard. His elation of finding the men at the house forced an urgent need to develop a new plan, one taking into consideration the loss of men. A vague outline started to form.

The group only had one of the Jihadists; the need for replacements topped the list, but they didn't have the time to find new volunteers. He was back in States; people weren't lining up to sacrifice themselves for Islam.

Johnson put his planning on hold as he called August Jackson. When Jackson answered, Johnson told him about the men who had returned safely to the States. He asked August what had been happening on Capital Hill and about any insights he may have heard from the group's well-placed informants throughout the government.

August told Johnson about the President, still poised to follow through on his threat to bomb the terrorist nations. He informed Johnson that the FBI and Homeland Security were now aware of an attempt at Wrigley Field. The agencies weren't dumb enough to show their hand in public, but August had learned that the police presence at the stadium would be beefed up, and the Illinois National Guard would be called in to assist.

The buzz around the Intelligence community was the minimization of the threat, but they didn't want to ignore it outright. There had to be a traitor inside their organization the two men agreed but finding that leak would have to wait until after the bombing.

Until then, the President had to be forced to administer the cure against the Muslim plague otherwise all their work was useless! Then and only then they would flush out the traitor among the crusaders deal with them. At this stage there was little else the traitor could do to impact the final act of their plan and therefore no longer of consequence.

Michael Johnson digested the information August Jackson had given him. Johnson had fought on the field of battle long enough to be able to adjust his tactics quickly. That training came in handy. The start of a thought wormed its way into Johnson mind while he talked to the old man; he now knew how his group could get close to the stadium without being detected. He gave August a list of essentials that he would need to get his men past security and into the stadium. He also knew that August had a league of devout Christian followers all around the country, in all walks of life, so the equipment Johnson requested would be easily obtained with no suspicions raised.

"How in the world do you expect to complete the attack with only one suicide jockey?" August begged the question. "We don't have time to fly in backups?"

Johnson had thought about the shortfall of volunteers but being the good tactician he already had an idea to fix that problem. An American-made solution to the problem wormed its way into his brain, and he knew where he could find the volunteers

"Don't worry," he reassured August. "I think I know a way to find help." He ended the call, pulled the two men from the Canadian bombing aside and sent the men into Chicago with specific instructions.

Chapter 42

The pair from Toronto left the safe house and made the forty-five-minute journey back to Chicago their instructions understood. Their distorted version of recruiting coupled with a location of where to find new suicide bombers.

It was mid afternoon when they entered the busy city and went in search of a Mosque they had found online. The men parked their car down the block from the Mosque and watched men entering the place for the midday prayer. The men drank coffee and remained nearby until the prayers finished, and the Muslim men reappeared. The pair was watching for a couple of very specific targets.

After the service finished up and the men from the Mosque started leaving, the men spotted their likely targets, a pair of young Muslims. Their quarry walked out of the parking lot and headed down the block engrossed in conversation. Johnson's men followed the young men, the car rolling quietly behind them until the youths turned onto a deserted section of sidewalk.

The driver stopped the car in front of the two Muslims and rolled down his window. He waved the pair closer. When the young men wandered over, he pointed a gun at them and told them to climb into the back seat. The terrified young men obeyed and once they had climbed into the car and closed the door the car raced away from the area.

The passenger spun in his seat, his gun covering the men in the back. He demanded the two men pass him their wallets from which he removed the driver licenses and threw the wallets back. He studied the men's ID's and then spoke to them.

"We are in need of a couple of volunteers, and it seems you two are going to have to do." He said. The young Muslims started to protest until the gunman explained what was riding on the line. "Volunteer without problems and your families will go on living happy and prosperous lives. Refuse or cause problems and your families will suffer torture beyond your imagination. Am I making myself clear?" he asked.

With frightened faces, the young men in the back seat looked at him. "What kind of volunteering are we expected to do?"

From the passenger seat of the car came their answer. "A chance to strike a blow against the heart of the enemy," the soldier said, an evil smile turning up the corner of his mouth. "Isn't that what all Muslim men want, to fight as Jihadists and die as martyrs?" Blood drained from the faces of the two Muslims in the back seat as they stared forward their eyes wide with fear.

One of the young men in the back seat broke down in tears. The driver told him to shut up, "You are going to do your religion proud...more importantly, the rest of your family will continue to live their miserable lives unharmed."

Chapter 43

Brand sat with his feet resting on a chair in the FBI regional office in Cincinnati. The fallout from the previous evening's airport shootouts still had the law enforcement offices on the Eastern Coast scrambling to deal with the aftermath. Brent sat across the table engrossed in a conversation. A combination of Homeland and FBI agents sat around the conference table discussing the investigation waiting for the Special Agent in Charge to complete his call with the FBI director in DC.

FBI regional SAC, Harold Sterns walked out of his office and took a seat by the two Canadians. "I spoke to the Director about the Afghani and the information he provided. In his opinion, the threat in Chicago is nullified with the disruption of the terrorist plans. With part of the terrorist unit killed or captured he can't see how they would be capable of carrying on," the SAC shrugged, signifying the case was out of his hands," but he will discuss the matter with Homeland, find out what they think. I did suggest someone contact the Illinois Governor with a recommendation to have the National Guard present at the stadium. At least as a show of force to put fans attending the game at ease."

"How about the President. Has anybody contacted him? These attacks aren't the product of Muslims or Islamist terrorists. It appears evident that a different group is behind them with an entirely different agenda?" Brand stated.

"The Director doesn't see it that way. He argues that Americans have voluntarily gone and joined the Islamist's numerous times in the past. He sees this no differently," the SAC replied.

"Bullshit!" Brand swung his feet to the floor and stood up. "The men at the airport weren't some smitten university kids looking for the romance and adventure the Islamic videos portray. These men are battle-hardened soldiers. Men who have probably fought against the same enemy that he now says they decided to join." He stopped and took a breath fighting his anger rising. "That doesn't make any god damn sense. There is not a terrorist faction that I know of that operates in North America."

Brand noticed the room of agents looking at him, calming himself he returned to his seat.

"Sorry," he apologized "This group is responsible for the abduction of someone very close to me. They held her captive in a cabin in Montana because she stumbled across evidence that disproves any theory of terrorists. This whole charade smells."

The SAC looked at Brand and then looked around the table, then back at Brand.

"The Director sure in the hell isn't going to go to the President and request that the President change his mind based on no facts. You don't think American of British soldiers will convert to other beliefs, fine until you can prove otherwise, keep it to yourself," the FBI Special Agent in Charge fired back.

Brand locked eyes with the SAC. This argument wasn't going to get him far, he realized.

"Can you make arrangements with the Chicago office for me to work with them. I've got nothing better to do, might as well take in a ballgame."

"Sure," the SAC agreed. "I'll be glad to have you out of my hair," and smiled at Brand breaking the tension. "I'll call ahead for you. They are planning to beef up the security there already. All the baseball stadiums in this general part of the country have been advised to increase police presence, not just for the next couple of days, but until the remaining men on the list have been apprehended."

"Good. Thanks," Brand replied. Looking at Brent, he motioned toward the door. "Is there someone who can give us a lift to the airport?"

*****

"You don't play well with others, do you?" Brent ribbed him as the two entered the Cincinnati Municipal Airport for their flight to Chicago.

"Their reasoning is all wrong," Brand retorted. To him, the answer to the attacks was apparent although it seemed to elude the American law enforcement agencies. They were ignoring the evidence and ploughed straight ahead with blinders on. Why?

In Chicago, an officer greeted the two of them as they got off the plane.

"Special Agent Ron MacLeish. Pleased to meet you." The agent said as he shook their hands walked them to his car. The three men chatted during the drive from the airport toward downtown Chicago.

"The office is fairly dead at this time of day, can I drop you guys off at a hotel." He suggested. "There is one close to our office, within walking distance, so you won't need a car to come by the agency in the morning."

"That sounds good," Brand quickly agreed before Brent had a chance to say anything. "What's the status of the bomb threat?"

"The National Guard will be sending troops that morning to help the local police monitor the grounds. Everyone feels that the threat has passed, but we don't want to take any chances. Contingents of agents, myself included, are going to be at the stadium, give the boys a hand screening the fans before they head inside. No backpacks or carrying cases of any type will be allowed past the screening line," SA MacLeish explained.

"Ask for me when you arrive at the office in the morning and I'll introduce you to the SAC. I don't think he'd mind you guys sitting in on our morning briefing."

When Brand and Brent were in the hotel, Brent turned to Brand.

"Didn't the agent appear friendly? That's unusual for the FBI," he joked.

"Times they are a changing, who knows what the world is coming to," Brand replied.

The two men checked into their rooms then caught the elevator down to the lobby, the hotel bar their next stop for the night. Relaxing over drinks and supper, they talked through the events that brought them to Chicago. Then prepared for the future.

"I don't know," Brand kept repeating. "Young, impressionable kids converting to Islam I can understand, even if they don't realize what they are doing. But soldiers who have trained and who have fought against terrorists suddenly switching sides, that doesn't make sense." Brand swirled the rye in his glass and sat back in the chair, his mind grasping at the unknown.

"What's not clear is why Sara would be kidnapped because she uncovered a video of the bomber, taken across the border and then locked away. That's out of context for today's terror groups. Why not they kill her like they've done with countless other captives that have gone before her? Instead, she's whisked off to a cabin in Montana and treated like a guest. I have a feeling this won't end all neat and tidy."

"Well, we'll perhaps get an answer in a day or so, and hopefully," Brent held up crossed fingers, "we are wrong. The terrorists on the list that eluded us are still a cause for worry. Who knows if they made it into the country or were they warned and told to hold back? What day is the twenty-ninth?" Brent asked.

Brand checked his phone. "Wednesday. Why?"

"Just wondering. Middle of the week, most people work through the week, with any luck there won't be a lot of people at the ball game that day." "But that doesn't make sense either, why not attack on a Saturday or Sunday when the ballparks packed?"

Brand continued punching keys on his phone. "I don't know. More security on the weekends I suppose." Then continuing the train of thought, he checked the weather report for the following Wednesday.

"America's favourite pastime and the forecast say sunny and hot. What would be more American than a beer and a hot dog while enjoying an afternoon ball game in the middle of the week? And, on a day not expected to be too busy so security at the stadium is lax."

"I wonder why they don't just cancel the damn game until they get a handle on this threat?" Brent said.

"I imagine that they don't want to run scared at every threat made against them," Brand countered. "If the whole country shut down with each threat, there wouldn't be a lot happening. Then the terrorists win, won't they"?

Richard Cozicar

"You're still convinced that Sara's abduction and the men in Montana are a part of this whole plot?" Brent returned to Brand's earlier statement. He felt the same way too, but maybe the two of them were looking for conspiracies.

"The way it has all come together. Well, a crew of former military merging with Muslim terrorists to kill Americans on their home soil is one question that remains out there as far as I am concerned. If we can find out what their motive is then the rest of the puzzle, I predict, will be easy to answer," Brand stood up. "I 'll see you tomorrow; I'm calling it a night," he said as he walked away.

The next morning after breakfast the two men made the short walk to the FBI building. At the receptionist's desk, Brand asked for Special Agent Ron MacLeish. The pair had waited several minutes before the agent stepped out of the elevator to greet them.

SA MacLeish led them to a conference room where a large number of other agents had gathered. Once introduced to the Special Agent in Charge, Glen Macalester, the SAC led a review of the latest Intel then the group gathered around a table laden with blueprints and schematics of the ballpark. A discussion followed outlining the FBI's plan of action before the agents received their assignments.

When the briefing ended Brand asked the SAC if an agent could be spared to give him a tour of the baseball stadium and grounds. The SAC obliged then reminded his men that there would be a final meeting on the stadium security early the next morning and that he expected the assigned teams to be at the field well ahead of the crowds.

Special Agent MacLeish drove the Canadians to the baseball stadium. He informed his guests that the team returned home tomorrow to start a six-game home stand. Arriving at the stadium, SA MacLeish parked, and the three men climbed out. Brand raised his head and whistled at the sight of the baseball stadium. The heat was rising off the black asphalt of the parking lot in the mid morning sun.

Brand stood by the car and surveyed the crowded street. A full parking lot of cars would make detection of any attempts of an attack against the stadium difficult. The saving grace was the buffer zone provided by the wide promenade

177

separating the street and the building. Brand was happy to note the vast landscape of flat concrete with only minimal blind spots, only a few scattered monuments and pieces of artwork on the promenade to obstruct the view of the entire space.

Brent and SA MacLeish trailed behind Brand as he strolled around the perimeter of the ball diamond walking past random pairs of police officers and soldiers from the National Guards inspecting the various entrances into the stadium. Brand was impressed with the security already standing guard the day before the game.

SA MacLeish showed his badge to the guards at checkpoints surrounding the park as the three stopped and talked with the men on duty. Taking their time, the three spent hours walking around and meeting the combined security details. When Brand had seen enough, the men climbed back into SA MacLeish's car and returned to the FBI office.

"Will tomorrow's security contingent be the same guys we encountered today?" Brent asked the FBI agent.

"Pretty much...enforced with an extra contingent from our office," MacLeish answered.

"How about the National Guard, they'll be the same too?" Brand added.

"Most likely, like the SAC said we'll see in the morning. Everyone, including the Guard, will assemble hours ahead of the gates opening before the crowds start showing up. We'll get a rundown of the final numbers then." MacLeish reminded them. On the sidewalk in front of the FBI building, the Canadians took their leave; there was nothing further for them to do until the next morning, the two walked down the sidewalk toward their hotel.

Chapter 44

Forty-five minutes southwest of Wrigley Field, on the secluded acreage outside of Berwyn, a different type of planning was taking place. Throughout the day, the reinforcements that Michael Johnson had asked August for slowly rolled onto the property. The acreage filled with vehicles as recruits continued arriving at the property. Throughout the day men showed up, a couple driving into the yard with large cargo vans. Vans that would be needed to transport the growing group of Christian warriors to Chicago the following day.

The amount of men crowded around the house and yard of the acreage was small compared to the army of security personnel that would be guarding the fans and building for the game tomorrow. The difference in size between the two groups didn't concern Johnson. His plan wasn't contingent upon outnumbering the enemy; his plans hinged on the art of deception.

Johnson assigned men to empty the contents of one of the vans into the house. The cargo consisting of military uniforms he had requested. Camouflage for tomorrow's big event. Other items like army-issued rifles were carried into the house and sorted.

Michael Johnson wandered the yard, checking on sentries he had stationed after his arrival at the house and taking advantage of the quiet to think. Later that evening, Johnson would call all the men together to do a final walkthrough for tomorrow's siege on the stadium.

The two young Muslims liberated from the Chicago Mosque were under constant guard inside the house. The jihadist from Afghanistan sat with them. He extolled the virtues of the Koran the rise to paradise the martyrs could expect for their glorious opportunity the next day. The young Chicago men pleaded for their freedom, their voices falling on the deaf ears of the Jihadist and the men holding them captive. They were peaceful Muslims they protested. They were not at war; their religion preached peace and forgiveness against non-believers. The Afghani laughed at them. The more heretics killed, the better the world would be.

The Afghani launched into a tirade of his radical interpretation of Islam. The young Muslims shuddered at the ideals the terrorist was professing to, it was entirely different from the one they learned at the Mosque, but whether they believed in the Afghani's version or not, they would be forced into his perverted world as unwilling volunteers. At prayer time, the young Jihadist led the prayers. His prayers and the two Muslim prisoners prayers could not be more different.

As night approached, Johnson gathered everyone together except the prisoners and the Afghani. With meticulous detail, he walked the men the series of events for tomorrow's raid on the stadium. Johnson emphasized to every single member that they had to pay attention to detail. He pointed out the disadvantage caused by the small number of men going against a much greater foe. For the plan to work, he needed them all to be focused. Surprise and the unexpected were their allies.

When the travesty was over, they would be hailed as heroes of the Christian faith. People the world over would rejoice when the Muslims were delivered a crippling blow from the American President.

The details were repeated one last time as Johnson looked at the brave men who would follow this crusade through putting their lives on the line to protect the faith they believed so fiercely in. Tomorrow's events would have world-changing effects as far as the war between the Christian faith and the faith of Islam was concerned.

Sending everyone off to rest, Michael Johnson crossed his chest and said a final prayer. These men were heroes in his eyes, may God help them achieve this mighty blow against the enemy.

Chapter 45

Wednesday, the twenty-ninth of June at Six o'clock in the morning Brand sat at a table in the hotel restaurant drinking coffee as he waited to meet Brent. A copy of the Chicago Tribune spread on the table in front of him. He leafed through the paper, his mind preoccupied with the upcoming events.

Brand quickly perused the paper, no big news stories from the night before. He worked his way through the paper; his eyes stopped briefly on an article about two young Muslim men who had gone missing the night before. The men disappeared the day before after leaving the midday prayers at their Mosque.

He continued leafing through the paper on his way to the sports section. He stopped at the MLB standings; the Blue Jays were currently holding onto second place in the American League East division. Brand read the stats and then an article on the RBC Canadian Open, the only PGA Tour event held in Canada. The tournament had ended the previous Sunday. He was in the act of folding the paper when Brent sat down at the table.

The two talked over breakfast. They would be riding back to Wrigley Field with SA MacLeish. They were to meet with the rest of the agents at the FBI building and suit up before the trip to the ballpark. The FBI contingent wouldn't be meeting until eight, so the two took their time with breakfast and coffees. As the time drew nearer, Brand let Brent pay for the food and he walked outside to wait on the sidewalk. When he was clear of the hotel doors, he dug into his pocket and removed his package of cigarettes. Seemed like forever since he had a smoke Brand thought as he shook one loose and lit up.

"That shit is going to kill you." Brent ribbed him as he walked outside to join him. Brand ignored him as he breathed the smoke deep into his lungs. The two left the hotel and made their way over to join the FBI agents at their offices. They stepped off the elevator onto the bustling, noisy floor; men crowded the room preparing themselves for the day ahead.

The assembled group donned Kevlar vests and checked firearms while the Special Agent in Charge ran through a checklist at the back of the room. A list detailing where he expected his men knew to be and what each was assigned. Brand was issued a Kevlar vest and a windbreaker with FBI stamped in yellow on the front and back.

When the morning meeting broke up, Agent MacLeish joined Brand and Brent, and the three climbed into his car for the drive to Wrigley Field. The FBI field agents would meet up with the police and National Guard in the stadium and divide up security tasks.

Brent whistled at the sight that greeted them as they turned onto the street leading to the stadium. Chicago Police cars and National Guard vehicles lined the streets fronting the stadium set up as barricades, sealing off the streets nearest to the main entrance and blocking all other entrances to the ballpark.

At various spots, the vehicles were parked two deep to stop any attempts by a suicide bomber to drive into the building. That was one of the favourite tricks employed by suicide bombers in Middle Eastern countries that they hoped to avoid here.

The three men left MacLeish's car and joined a cluster of men already gathered. Brand stood off to the side as a Sergeant from the National Guard, the man in charge of coordinating the defense of the ballpark, spoke to the group of individuals reviewing the potential threat and assigning duties. Being excluded from the assignments, he and Brent spent their time weaving through the throngs of law enforcement, paying close attention to everything and everyone.

Members of the Chicago police department along with several FBI agents stood guard at the gates leading into the ballpark. Spread loosely around the perimeter of the stadium the National Guard patrolled. The noise excited talk rose as the early crowds started to dribble into the area. Brand heard several ball fans comment on the police presence, but none let it hamper their spirits.

As the opening pitch drew closer, the crowds of fans grew. The queues to get through security and into the stadium started to backup as greater number of fans arrived. The increased screening process slowed down the typically quick lines as people were carefully searched before being allowed through the checkpoints.

Brand stood out of the way and watched, his eyes regularly scanning the crowds looking for anyone acting suspiciously. One by one the baseball fans walked up to the checkpoints, waited patiently and then passed through on their way to their seats.

The early morning sun shone high and bright in the sky. The heat of the day was chasing the mercury quickly up the thermometer as the warm morning gave way to a scorching afternoon. Despite the longer than usual times at the security points, Brand could hear the laughter coming from the late June crowd assembling in the baseball park.

Silent Crusade

Chapter 46

Morning at the acreage outside of Berwyn mirrored the activities at the stadium, the majority of the men with Johnson had at one time or another served their respected countries and were used to the rigors required to launch an attack. The mood among the men at the acreage was solemn. The killing of innocent people went against their nature and everything they had previously fought for, this understanding would haunt them the rest of their lives, but in the battle of good and evil, casualties were unavoidable. The men assembled at the acreage shared a single belief, to deliver a crippling blow against the spread of Islam. Without such an intervention the Christian faith would suffer irreparable damage.

With the same precision of armies throughout the passage of time, the small but dedicated group prepared for their tasks. Uniforms supplied by faithful supporters of the cause were donned, including pants, jackets, and caps. The shoes were the only things not provided, as the timeline was too tight to outfit each man with the appropriate footwear. Michael Johnson begrudgingly faced the fact. His attention to detail mollified with hopes that the chances of somebody noticing the shoes were a risk he had no choice but to accept.

Midmorning saw his troops dressed and milling near the trucks anxious to leave. Signalling out a couple of men, he gave orders to collect the guests of honour. The Jihadist smuggled into the country from Afghanistan was eager to go. By contrast, the new recruits fought their captures every step of the way as they reluctantly marched from the house.

Even with continued verbal threats to their family's safety, the young Muslims, now faced with the reality of their deaths, were not cooperating and Johnson could not blame them. He knew that he would not do what he was forcing them to do. He had no choice, though; he needed suicide bombers to add legitimacy to the attack.

It took several of his men to outfit the young men. The Muslim robes slipped over the men but when the vests containing the dynamite came in sight the young men fought vigorously to avoid being strapped to the bombs. The struggle was not ending until Johnson's men until finally fastened the vests in place and the two young men had their hands secured behind their backs. Michael Johnson had the foresight to wire the vests with remote triggers, devices he trusted to no one but himself. The two young Muslims, along with the Afghani Jihadist were loaded into the first of the waiting cargo vans; the second van would transport the remaining of soldiers.

Johnson looked at his watch. Allowing for minor traffic problems, he wanted the arrival at the ballpark precisely timed. If they arrived too early, they risked discovery, if they were too late, the effect would be minimized.

Johnson climbed into the backseat of the lead car. Dexter Tranter and George Williams rode up front, Williams in the driver's seat. Johnson looked back at the small caravan that would follow. He said a short prayer to himself and then caught Williams watching him in the rear-view mirror; he nodded his head.

"It's time," he said.

The caravan kicked up dust as it rolled down the gravel driveway and snaked it's way to the highway. The start of the next battle and hopefully the last one for the Christian crusade against the Islamists moved toward Chicago.

Chapter 47

Brand leaned against a car, Brent and Special Agent MacLeish beside him. The tension of the potential attack, the crush of baseball fans and the long security line-ups had drawn to an end. Brand lit a cigarette and let his eyes roam the deserted promenade fronting into the stadium. The only personnel he now observed were the groups of law enforcement officers that patrolling the area after the last of the crowds took to their seats before the start of the afternoon baseball game.

Some of the officers grouped sought out fellow members of their agencies. Troops of the National Guard remained at their posts, eyes alert, but he could tell that all the men were now confident the potential threat of attack was over, and they were letting their guards down. The men as a group had expected that if any attempt were to happen it would likely take place while the fans were gathered together waiting to clear security. There the crowds were at their most vulnerable.

Brand observed the groups of men start to relax as they talked animatedly with each other. The sounds of laughter could be heard rising into the air at broken intervals. The PA announcer's voice rang in the still summer air. He read bios of individual players and their hitting stats, his voice floating over the stadium walls as he occupied the crowds filling the gaps between plays. The home crowd cheered and stomped at every crack of their team's bats then clapped and applauded the defensive plays when their team took to the field.

Brand threw the remainder of his cigarette to the pavement and ground it down with his foot. He took his time studying the streets that led away from the entrance in both directions. Turning his head, he glanced up at the huge sign displayed at the top of the stadium, the sun reflecting back into his eyes.

Again the crack of a bat sounded from inside the park followed closely by the roar of the crowd then the excitement of the announcer's voice rose above the din. Chicago had just hit a home run. The game was now at the top of the fourth inning. The home team was up by a couple of runs over the visitors.

Brand found himself thankful that the rumours of an attack appeared unfounded. The worry of protecting the close to capacity crowd at this afternoon's game started to diminish. Alone at the far end of the parking lot, he swept his eyes over the streets in front of the ballpark, assured himself that the area was free of danger then sauntered over to where Brent and FBI agent MacLeish stood.

Standing beside the two, he turned his head, facing the street to the south side of the stadium. Without undue thought, he watched as a car, and a couple of cargo vans parked down the street. His mind had left the empty threat of the attack behind momentarily as he found his thoughts sorting through the information he had learned from the previous bombings.

His eyes followed the actions of the vehicles without focusing on anything in particular as the back doors of the vans opened and men in uniforms climbed out and assembled on the sidewalk. First, one van emptied and then the other. Three men stepped out of the lead car and stood on the sidewalk behind the men.

The sound of a well-struck baseball echoed through the stadium. The hometown crowd cheered again. The announcer described the play amid the cheers and foot stomping.

The double lines of uniforms formed ranks then turned on their heels and slowly started marching toward the front of the ballpark.

Brand continued looking in the direction of the vans; his eyes capturing the men's movements, his brain occupied with other thoughts.

*****

Michael Johnson watched his men climb out of the cargo vans and assemble on the sidewalk and lining up in double formation. The men's backs turned toward the entrance to the baseball stadium. Johnson gave the men the last bit of instruction.

Some of the officers assigned to guard the stadium were disciples of the crusade and on seeing the new arrivals would leave their posts as ordered. But, the majority men on duty were not. Those who remained behind could be expected to do their jobs and lay their lives down in the protection of the crowds in attendance at the ball game. Johnson reminded his soldiers that not all of them would live to see the outcome of the battle they were about to enter. Bowing his head he led them in a short prayer asking for forgiveness for what they were about to do, and for the strength to accomplish their goal.

Johnson finished the prayer and raised his head. He looked at Williams and Tranter. Both nodded their heads indicating they were ready. Johnson gave the order and like a well-trained unit the men spun on their heels and started a slow march toward the front entrance of Wrigley Field.

While the line of marching men blocked the line of view into the opened back of the van, both Williams and Tranter reached into the van and forcibly removed the two young Muslims. The Afghani Jihadist followed climbing down onto the sidewalk. The three suicide bombers draped in ill-fitted army coats, chosen to fit over the vests of explosives strapped to their upper bodies.

Johnson observed from the vehicles. In anticipation, he placed his hand into his uniform pocket, and he let his fingers curl around the detonators. His fail-safe and lack of trust for the two unwilling volunteers to follow through with their part of the plan. He would be notified on the radio when the two young Muslims were in the right position after that the remotes would handle the rest.

He stood tensely watching as his men marched slowly down the last block and a half to the stadium. He lifted his eyes to the area in front of the marching columns; a wry smile crept over his face. As planned, members of the local police left their posts at the front of the stadium walking away from the advancing force. Even with those men out of the picture, a lot of police and National Guardsmen surrounded the building. Johnson counted on the fact that the uniforms his men wore should buy a few crucial minutes to advance the bombers close to the stadium. He wanted the three young men well into the ball diamond before detonating the vests, that way the force of the bombs and the damage to the structure would maximize the impact.

Johnson's attention fell on a man in an FBI windbreaker staring back at him. The man watched but failed to react. Good, Johnson thought, the uniforms the camouflage effect he had hoped.

*****

Brand gazed mindlessly at the soldiers lined up and marching toward the ballpark. A niggling of warning alarms began ringing inside his brain.

"...Shit, I don't remember the briefing this morning including a change of guard, but it looks like the cavalry is here," Brent's words interrupted Brand's thoughts snapping him back to the present time. He looked again at the marching lines of men moving closer as if seeing them for the first time. He turned his head looked back over the other police and Guardsmen that had been on duty since morning. Several of them could be seen leaving their posts and walking away from the approaching soldiers. He turned his head to look ahead once again, his eyes scanning the new arrivals.

"They must be another unit of the National Guard," he commented. The approaching group wore the same uniforms, right down to the... Brand's comparison ended at the shoes of the oncoming soldiers, random footwear, certainly not army issue. Some wore runners; others had boots and since when did the U.S. Army allow that...the alarms in his head grew steadily louder.

"The shoes," he yelled at Brent and SA MacLeish. "Look at their shoes." Brand pulled his gun out of his shoulder holster. Something was wrong. The army did not waver; soldiers wore Army issued combat boots, end of story. Brent and SA MacLeish quickly followed Brand's lead and un-holstered their firearms. SA MacLeish turned to warn the rest of the security detail. A bullet struck him before the words left his mouth.

Brand took one final look at the man who stood behind the stream of marching soldiers. Burning an image of the man's face into his memory, he knelt down by the fallen FBI agent to check on his condition. The groups assigned to protect the ballpark were out of position. Under the warm sunny skies and the lull of the baseball game, the men had relaxed and now were caught in the open away from cover. With the advancing team using the element of surprise, the security detail took a few hits before realizing they were under attack.

Glancing back at the men assigned to protect the stadium he became aware that to a man they were reluctant to fire. Why and the hell aren't they shooting, Brand wondered and then he realized. The security forces at the park were tentative. The advancing lines of men dressed as National Guards caused confusion, the men from the stadium protection detail afraid of firing on the wrong soldiers. The advantage was to the new arrivals.

Brand grabbed Special Agent MacLeish's radio; an idea came to him. It would mean that his side would be briefly short of firepower, but it would separate the real National Guards from the imposters.

Brand keyed the radio.

"All National Guardsmen, who can hear my voice, drop to the ground. Drop to the ground NOW!" he repeated. He took the chance that the fake troops moving toward the ballpark weren't monitoring the protection details radio frequency. Brand clutched the radio in one hand as he fired at the advancing troops.

A few more seconds passed as the National Guards struggled with the order before they began dropping to the ground removing themselves from the confusion, then from their positions on the sidewalk raised their rifle and joined the gun battle.

The sound of gunfire increased from both sides. Brand lined his sights past the faux soldiers and focused on three smaller men near the back of the line. The three wore baggy army coats over their robes. Taking careful aim, Brand fired. The first bullet was high on the chest of one of the robed men. The man stopped as if he had run into a wall. Brand followed with two more quick shots; the man crumpled to the sidewalk.

Moving the sights of his gun, he took aim at a second man in the small group when a bullet found his Kevlar vest. The impact smashed into his chest and knocked his body back. A searing pain flared throughout his body. He gritted his teeth and fought to recover. A second bullet drilled into his vest. The impact of the bullet slammed his body back into a car door, the thin metal bending from the force of his body.

Brand knew couldn't remain in the open. Staggering to his feet, he dove across the hood of the car. His foot snagged a wiper blade as he slid sending him in an awkward tumble off the far side. Moving his head his shoulder took the force of the collision with the pavement; a groan escaped his mouth as he crumpled to the ground. Shaking his head to clear the cobwebs, he knelt tight to the car and peered through the windows at the onslaught.

The stadium guards were now returning fire at the advancing men. The advancing soldiers scrambled and searched for cover of their own. Brand frantically looked around for the radio he had retrieved from SA MacLeish's body. In his dive across the car, the radio had fallen from his hand. He found it sitting atop the hood of the car. Snaking his hand over the fender he snatched the wireless off the hood and pressed the talk button. Brand issued a warning to the men by the ballpark entrances. Keep an eye on the doors, nobody in and nobody out he shouted. The last thing the security team needed was a rush of panicked spectators streaming out of the stadium into the line of fire.

He had no idea how many of the men he had arrived with were still able to fight. The gun battle raged across the closed street and sidewalk in front of the ballpark. The FBI agents and contingent of police officers were drawing the majority of the gunfire, doing their best to return the fire from the cover at the base of the building. Brand swept his eyes over the National Guardsmen, lying on their stomachs in the middle of the promenade firing their rifles from the ground.

Slowly the men protecting the stadium halted the advance of the attacking group. The battle settled into a stalemate. Looking back toward the rear of the line of attackers, Brand watched as one of the smaller men with a baggy jacket rose to his feet and started to run the wall of the ballpark for the cover of a giant statue. Fearing the worst he continued watching as the man brought a hand up to the front of his coat. Brand stood up from behind the protection of the car to get a better view and fired a shot at the man.

The instant the man disappeared behind the statue a massive explosion erupted. Debris blasted through the air. Large chunks of concrete rained over the parking lot. A small piece grazed Brand's chest knocking him off his feet, his back shattering the window of a police car parked directly behind him. He slid to the ground in a daze.

For a second time, he had to clear his head. Brand rose up on wobbly legs. His ears rang from the explosion. He cautiously moved back behind the car he had earlier used as a shield. Glancing to the side, he spotted Brent lying on his back. His friend's body covered with broken glass, concrete, and dust from the explosion. Brand scrambled over to his friend. Brent's breath was shallow, his eyes shut, his face covered in cuts and blood plus a severe cut on one of Brent's arms. With strips of Brent's shirt, Brand wrapped the arm slowing the bleeding.

The ringing in Brand's head lessened, and then silence. The sounds of gunfire no longer filled the air. Carefully standing up, Brand looked around. The explosion had taken down a lot of the attackers. The ones that remained were slowly retreating toward the vans they had driven to the park. While the fake soldiers retreated, some members of the combined FBI, police, and National guards advanced on them. Between the fleeing group and the security team stood the last of the three young men in the baggy army jacket. The young man knelt on the sidewalk with his hands held high in the air. The young man's face a mask of fright as tears streamed from his eyes.

From a distance, Brand studied the youth then lifted his eyes to the attackers retreating to the cargo vans. His gaze stopped on the leader of the terrorists. The man stood beside his car shouting orders while his men clamoured into the back of the vans. The lone individual waited until the last of his men had climbed into the van.

Brand noticed the leader holding a small device his hand. A cell phone or a...

Too late, Brand realized that the device was a wireless remote. He switched his gaze back to the young man in the baggy jacket kneeling on the sidewalk. The advancing team of security personnel had closed the distance to the young terrorist on the sidewalk.

"STOP! Get back..." The words had barely crossed Brand's lips to warn the officers. Heads swiveled in his direction. Some members of the team stopped, others continued their slow advance.

The second explosion had no statue or wall to absorb the force of the blast. Brand and those immediately in the vicinity were tossed through the air like pieces of human confetti, flying in every direction. His head impacted the fender of a car. He crumpled to the ground. His consciousness momentarily registering the sounds of screaming before his world went dark.

Silent Crusade

Chapter 48

Brand struggled to open his eyes. His vision was blurry; his head felt like there was a jackhammer beating against the walls of his skull trying to get out. Through the haze, he watched a hand reach for his arm and saw a silhouette of a person blocking the light in front of his face. Fighting against the hammering in his head, he blinked his eyes rapidly to focus. The haze enveloping his brain slowly lightened. He saw the mouth of the person move as they spoke His concussed brain, the ringing in his ears and the hammering in his skull acted as a wall preventing sound to penetrate.

With assistance, Brand worked his way up into a sitting position. He leaned back against a car for support and opened and closed his eyes a few times, small explosions of light flashing behind his eyelids. He accepted a bottle of water that was forced into his hand and rinsed his mouth before taking a drink. Gradually his eyes cleared and the hammering dulled to a steady din.

The cacophony of sounds around him started to filter through to his brain. On unsteady legs, he stood up and looked around. His first rational thought was that the area looked like a bomb had gone off. Then the memory of the explosion flooded back. A bomb had gone off, and then another one. He swayed on his feet as he leaned against the car. Brent... he remembered Brent lying on the ground right before the explosion. He pushed himself away from the car and staggered off in search of his friend.

A police officer that Brand did not recognize walked up beside him and wrapped an arm around his shoulders to steady him. The scene was now overrun with police officers and paramedics. Firefighters were spraying down an area against the stadium wall. Ambulances and police cars had filled the cordoned off street, sirens wailing in the background.

As Brand walked he examined the carnage left from the gun battle and the destruction of the suicide bombs, behind him afternoon revelers from the ball game were herded out of the stadium from a far exit. Several paramedics were bent over fallen victims, checking vitals and attending to the wounded. Bodies lay scattered where the exploding bombs tossed them.

Brand's ears still rang from the explosion, his brain foggy and his body racked with pain. Determinedly he pushed aside his injuries to find out had happened to his friend. The sheer number of injured bodies made the task of finding Brent almost impossible. Turning to his guide Brand attempted to explain his dilemma. When the officer steered Brand toward the waiting ambulances he tried to shake him off.

"I am fine! I need to find my friend. He was right here!" But the officer's persistence finally made sense as they approached the waiting vehicles.

Lying on a gurney at the rear of an ambulance lay Brent. His face a muddy mixture of blood and dust from the explosion; his eyes closed. Brand put a hand on his friend's chest and felt the rise and fall of Brent's chest with each shallow breath his friend took. An EMT brushed him aside as the paramedics folded the gurney and lifted it into the waiting ambulance.

Brand shrugged from the officer's grip and staggered over to rest against the hood of a nearby police car, the car's flashing lights circling the area. Time passed as he sat against the car amidst the swarms of first responders attending to the wounded bodies splayed all around.

Bit by bit his hearing cleared. Gradually the sounds around him began to penetrate the wall of noise inside his head, and his vertigo lessened. Brand left the support of the car in search of agents that he had accompanied to the ballpark. He spotted a few FBI agents standing close to the building, so he picked his way through the debris and bodies toward them. The men were talking with a group of officials. He waited close enough to the gathering to hear their conversation but far enough away not to intrude. Brand stood silent until the impromptu meeting broke up before approaching one of the men he had met earlier.

"How bad is it?" Brand asked while he his eyes roamed the recovery.

The agent had a grim look on his face. "Pretty bad I suppose. We lost a large number of our men. The few attackers who couldn't flee also killed by flying debris because of their proximity to the explosions."

"So, no one to question?" Brand asked. Then he thought of the agent he had ridden with to the ballpark. "SA MacLeish. Where is he?"

The FBI agent lowered his chin to his chest and shook his head. Looking down at the sidewalk the man said, "He died when the attack started. Bullet through the neck, right above his vest."

Richard Cozicar

Brand drew in a deep breath and then slowly released it with a sigh.

"So what do we do now?" he asked the agent.

"We've been instructed to meet back at our office for a debriefing. From there it's up to the brass to decide how we continue...SOMEONE has got to pay for this!" the agent spat out the words as he turned away from Brand. He got that right, Brand agreed; someone WAS going to pay. He hadn't known Agent MacLeish long, but Brand pegged the man as an honest, hard working officer. He, along with the multitude of others deserved better than to be killed in their country protecting their fellow citizens.

"Can I catch a ride back to your office when you leave?" Brand asked.

"Ya, sure. I'll track you down when I'm ready to go," the agent promised.

Brand went looking for the man that had helped him earlier. Finding the policeman, Brand asked him where the ambulance would have taken his friend.

"Hang tight for a minute. I can find out for you," the officer said and pressed the button on his radio calling his dispatch. Together the two men waited while the dispatcher searched for the information. The minutes ticked away.

"St. Agnes Hospital on the corner of Wellington and Ashland Avenues." The officer wrote the address on a piece of paper as the dispatcher read it off and then handed it to Brand. Brand muttered his thanks and turned to leave when a small group of FBI and National Guardsmen approached him.

One of the men stepped forward and shook his hand.

"We would have suffered a lot more casualties today if it were not for you," the FBI agent stated grimly. "The guys here want you to know how thankful we are for your quick thinking." The man released his grip on Brand's hand. Brand solemnly acknowledged the praise, but a lot of people had still died he reflected.

Brand looked down the length of Addison Street at the police barricades holding back the throngs of onlookers and media personnel that had built out front the stadium. He felt useless standing among the responders as they combed through the destruction and dead bodies. If only they could have been better prepared.

Chapter 49

The President sat behind his desk; his eyes glued to the news reports running across the TV. The Director of the FBI, Homeland Security and the Chief of Defense along with several others sat nearby watching as the news reports showed the horrific scene that had unfolded earlier in the day. The reporter's voice droned from the television; the room otherwise silent as each separate individual dealt with the news. To the side of the President's desk sat a sombre looking CIA Director, his thoughts on the attack much different from the rest of the room's occupants.

The President broke the silence.

"Gentlemen, we tried to reason with them," he said stoically. His gaze shifted to the Secretary of Defense. "I want any and all battleships and carriers in the vicinity of the Indian Ocean moving toward the Gulf of Oman." He paused briefly, "Get our planes loaded with the nuclear warheads and have the men ready." Then he turned to the Secretary of State, "Inform Pakistan we will be flying over their airspace, and we seek clearance from them when we have everything in position," Monroe continued.

His attention focused back on the Defense Secretary, "Let me know an ETA for the carriers. When our troops draw close, I'll personally call President Baloch and let him know our plans. He can either be with us or against us; I do not care at this moment. One way or another our planes are going in!"

Next, the President gave the CIA director instructions. "Gather all the impertinent Intel you can; I want to know where the highest concentration of these terrorist cells is situated. But, gather the information discretely," he needlessly advised. "The last thing we want is for the bastards to hear of our plans and scatter." "General Farring," The President addressed a four-star general at the far end of the room, "I want these first strikes carried out with surgical precision. I know that some civilians are doing to die, the least we can do is try and limit the casualties."

Then President Monroe spoke to the entire group, "The orders I just gave today are to remain in this room. We will only inform any affected personnel of our actions immediately before we begin the airstrike. I don't want to start a panic, and I don't want those terrorist bastards escaping leaving innocent civilians behind to die! Do I make myself clear?" He paused to let his words sink in.

"I will be meeting with our Intelligence agencies and the Department of Defense and have them prepare our country for reprisals."

"How much time is needed to be mission ready?" he threw the question out to all the men in the room. The group of officials all tried to reply at the same time; each was offering different answers, hoping theirs was the response suitable for their Commander in Chief. The President's orders started a discussion that drug on for hours. Bombing a foreign country had consequences; both foe and friend would frown upon the use of the American nuclear arsenal.

The President found himself with his back against a very hard wall. Do nothing and worry where and when another terrorist attack would happen next, or follow through on his threat and pray he was making the right decision? He cast his eyes across the faces around the room; each face reflecting the troubled thoughts they confronted in this situation. The United States would avenge these cowardly attacks with a feeling of impunity. No longer, the President promised on the bodies of the dead Americans, never again would this happen in his country while he was at the helm.

Hal Jorgenson, the President's long trusted friend fought to keep his face impassive, inside he was relieved. The end was in sight; the crusade was almost over, and the good guys were going to win.

Chapter 50

The afternoon wore on. Brand had had more than enough of standing amongst the debris watching the bodies of the injured and dead being carried away. He wondered about the responders in quest of the FBI agent who had earlier promised a ride back to the field offices. Brand struggled to remove the jacket he had been wearing and threw it on a pile of rubble. The thing was full of holes from the burning shrapnel that had hit him when each of the bombs had exploded.

Finding the agent after a short search, Brand asked if he could get a ride to the hospital instead. The policeman was unable to leave but found Brand a ride to St. Agnes. The hospital was only a short drive from the ballpark but with the rerouted rush hour traffic, the best they managed to travel was at a slow crawl. When they finally arrived at the hospital entrance, a still dazed Brand thanked the officer and climbed out of the car.

He walked through the doors and inquired at the front desk for his friend's whereabouts. The receptionist typed commands into the hospital computer, smiled up at him providing the room number and directions. A private room down a couple of halls just past the emergency ward she told him.

The waiting area in the ER was chaotic. Brand dodged numerous hospital personnel as they rushed around attending to patients who had been steadily arriving for hours. He found his way to nurse's station on the next ward that housed Brent's room. The nurse at the station informed him that doctors were still treating his friend and that he would have to wait. Nodding, he let the nurse know where he'd be waiting as he left the desk.

The waiting room seats were full. He found a chair tucked into a corner and sat down to wait. Brand slumped in the chair and relaxed, the warm room and the steady drone of activity surrounding him preyed on the fatigue he felt. Fighting to keep his eyes open he sat biding his time, watching the other occupants of the room and the nurses and doctors rushing all around them.

He fought valiantly to overcome his fatigue while he waited for news. The next thing he knew, a nurse was gently shaking him.

"Your friend is out of emergency and is resting in recovery," she said and furnished the room number. As she straightened to leave, she commented, "Go whenever you're ready, but you might consider seeing a doctor yourself, you don't look too good."

He stood up and walked over to a dark window and stared at his reflection. The nurse was right. He looked like hell with the dust and blood that covered his wounds.

He gave the nurse a weak smile, "I'm fine…really!"

Brand stopped outside Brent's room. A thick curtain hid the room's interior from the traffic in the corridor. Pushing past the curtain he gazed down at his friend, as he lay covered on the bed, his eyes closed, his breathing even. One of Brent's arms was in a sling. His face was cleaned exposing the cut up, and black, and blue bruises already prominent against his skin. The noise of the curtain opening was brief, but Brent opened his eyes and his lips curled in a weak attempt at a smile as he looked at Brand.

"If I were you, I'd fire my plastic surgeon," Brand said trying to add a bit of levity to the situation, lightness that he was far from feeling.

Brent started to laugh, but it quickly turned into a painful sounding cough. When he finished coughing, he motioned toward a chair before asking Brand for an update from the stadium. He was eager to catch up on what he had missed after he lost consciousness. The two men talked quietly until a nurse poked her head into the room announcing the end of visiting hours.

"Rest up. We can finish this conversation tomorrow," Brand said as he stood to leave.

Brand stood on the sidewalk in front of the hospital. He fished a cigarette from the pack and held it to the flame of his lighter before dialling a number for a cab. He watched the cigarette smoke curl into the air as his mind replayed the attack at the stadium waiting for a ride back to the hotel.

*****

Brand walked across the lobby toward the elevators. Other hotel patrons in the hotel lobby moved aside as he crossed the floor, most stopped and stared. He couldn't blame them, not after seeing his reflection in the hospital window earlier.

He entered his room and went directly to the bathroom. The sight that stared back at him was almost unrecognizable. His hair plastered to his head, his face dusty and splattered with dried blood from several cuts caused by the flying debris. The sleeves of his shirt were torn and ragged, and his pocket hung torn.

Fortunately, the Kevlar vest had shielded his upper torso, its outline clearly visible with the lack of blood and dust from where it covered.

Brand peeled his shirt off and threw it to the floor. He examined the bruises from the bullets that had struck his chest. Two large black and purple bruises already appeared at the points of impact, both tender to the touch. Removing the rest of his clothes, he climbed into the shower and let the hot water cascade over his body. He had phone calls to make but not before his shower used all the hot water in the hotel to release some of the physical and mental pain he was experiencing. The steady rhythm of the water on his skin helped to relieve the chaos.

The hot water did as Brand had hoped and rejuvenated him. Reluctantly he stepped out of the shower and donned a robe. From the room's mini fridge, he poured a glass of rye and settled on the couch before picking up the receiver and dialling the phone.

His first call was to the Canadian Senator. She would most certainly be expecting a briefing of today's attack. It was early in the evening. He tried her work number. From what he knew of the Senator, she wasn't the type to abandon her office when national security was in question. The call rang twice before being answered.

"Hello," Senator Meadows said.

"Senator Meadows, this is Brand Coldstream," Brand quickly re-introduced himself. He assumed she would remember him from their dealings of the previous year. At that time, the Senator had excused Brand of wrongdoing but had informed him that should the country come calling in the future his answer would be yes. She knew he was with Brent in Chicago, and Brand apprised her of the situation and Brent's condition.

His report was short, strictly the main facts from earlier that afternoon. The Senator remained silent until he finished his briefing of the day's events. She reassured him that she already knew most of the details; the bombing had been all over the news. Furthermore, as soon as she learned of the attack she had ordered her contacts to flesh out any information that could assist Canada's neighbors to the south. Knowing Brand's value as a highly trained operative, the Senator asked his opinion of the attackers.

"Definitely not the Muslim terrorists that everyone has pinned for the other bombings," he told her. She asked him to explain. "Too military in the precision of the attack, the way it was carried out. Besides," he continued, "I can not wrap my head around the possibility of American soldiers aligning themselves with the enemy so wholeheartedly to attack their country in the name of Islam. The very groups they have been fighting against for the last, I don't know how many years. I just can't buy that."

"Have you found any proof or are you basing your assumption on a gut feeling?" she asked. "This wouldn't be the first time that home-grown sympathizers aided Islamic causes," she pointed out. "I can recall a few that have happened in both countries over the last several years. Oklahoma, Fort Hood, the attack on our own Parliament buildings."

"No. No proof yet," Brand admitted. "I don't even know if the men that were attacking the ballpark were actual soldiers. I imagine that it will be a while before forensics can identify the bodies," he conceded. "Regardless. You have to talk to the Prime Minister and tell him to make sure this does not get out of hand. It will be a travesty if the West retaliates like the American President had threatened to do in his speech."

The Senator considered Brand's advice, "without any solid, tangible proof; I am afraid that trouble may be heading for the Middle East, and I think that it may happen very soon."

"How soon?" Brand was eager to know.

"I can't say anything for sure, but if your suspicions are real, I would advise you to find me some proof quickly." silence gripped the line. "Call me back at this number as soon as you discover something. Until then I'm afraid there is not much I can do." Brand could hear the defeat in her voice as she ended the call.

He sat staring at the phone. Shit! He was positive that a shadow organization was running a False Flag operation. Some unknown puppeteer is pulling the strings and convincing the world the ploy was terrorist driven. Hell, he was all for destroying each and every terrorist on earth, but not if it meant killing thousands or hundreds of thousands of innocent people to do it.

Brand checked the time. He might have just enough time to make one more call before the meeting at the FBI office. He dialed Sara's number. She was probably beside herself with worry, and he wanted to reassure her that he was fine. He longed to be with her, but he had a feeling that he would be remaining in the Chicago area for a while longer.

Chapter 51

By the time Brand walked into the FBI Chicago headquarters and made his way to the conference room the meeting was already underway. The room was packed with agents reporting on the day's attack at the ball diamond and analysts reviewing the day's events. Every chair was full; the overflow of men stood around the perimeter of the office or leaned against the walls.

Brand stood in the entrance, his back against the doorframe. He kept silent and listened to the meeting. The underlying tone in the room mixed with tension and regret from an assignment gone terribly wrong.

The SAC paced back and forth at the front. All of the agents present felt responsible. Their job was to protect the American people, and yet this terrorist group had waltzed right up to them and a devastating blow while they practically watched. Their biggest contribution today was to the list of casualties instead of thwarting a violent attack against their country. Now they were on the defensive, checking sources, analyzing evidence and rushing to formulate a plan to right the wrong that had devastated their organization, the City of Chicago, and the American people. Brand watched and listened, his ears alert for any scrap of new information that may help reveal the group behind the attack.

The debate volleyed back and forth around the room between the agents and the SAC. The same conclusions surfaced at the end of each discussion. Everyone conceded that the disguised men could quite easily belong to one of the many terrorist organizations; help from the inside of the country was not withstanding.

Brand walked the room eavesdropping on the many discussions taking place. He was an outsider. It was not his place to interrupt. But he had let the American agents wrestle with it long enough. The foremost question he was concerned with was the man with the remote detonator. In his mind, the answer rested with the man, but they needed to come at the problem from a different angle. Finally, he spoke up.

"Has anyone identified the leader, the one who remained with the vehicles behind the attack? I'm sure he was the one who remotely set the bomb off, the one the second bomber was wearing under his coat." Every head in the room turned to look at him.

"No. No one mentioned him; I don't know if anyone out there got a good look at him. When the second bomb was detonated everyone dove for cover, or at least tried to, some weren't so lucky." The SAC replied. "Did any of you see this man?" the SAC called out the agents. The room full of men collectively shook their heads. No, nobody in the room had gotten a clear look at the man. Between evading bullets and getting out of the way of the bomb blast, they had been too preoccupied.

"I got a good look at the man," Brand told the SAC. "I can describe him or if you have a facial database I can look through them. Might be a good idea to start with any army databases you have first, though. The way the attack played out, someone knew their way around military strategies," he spoke as the scenes at the ballpark replayed in his mind.

The SAC ordered a couple of agents to get on their computers and pull up the entire local databases, the army database first. The men left the conference room and headed for their stations in the outer office. Brand took a chair at the table and worked to focus his mind. When he trained at CSIS, face recognition was the key tool. As an intelligence agent in the field, you often weren't afforded the luxury of carrying photos of the perps you were tracking. Every operative trained and perfected the skill to memorize and recall facial features.

The SAC walked over to Brand while the room cleared. He told Brand to wait while he sent for the sketch artist to get a rendering of the suspect while the man's features were still fresh in his mind. It would prove helpful and speed up the process in their hunt for this man.

The FBI offices were a flurry of activity around Brand as he sat in the conference room and provided a description to the FBI artist. After finishing with the artist, Brand was asked to join with other agents assist checking databases for a facial match.

For over an hour Brand worked with the FBI artist, the face slowly taking form. When Brand was satisfied the drawing closely resembled the suspect he was introduced to a couple of other agents waiting at their computer stations.

The clock had swung past midnight by now, but even at this late hour, the activity in the FBI office remained. Brand was supplied with coffee as he sat at a computer and scrolled through pictures in the FBI database looking for a face to match his description. As Brand's eyes studied face after face, in his mind he quickly did some math in his head. The number of military personnel, both enlisted and retired would have to be in the millions so even with all the FBI agents in the country searching at the same time, the amount of time and luck needed were tremendous. And that would never include the soldiers who were not on any databases, identities hidden from the public files because of involvement in covert operations.

By three in the morning, the only accomplishment the men in the building had to show was the consumption of several pots of coffee and the added business to the Chinese restaurant where the agents ordered a late meal. The SAC broke up the late night search party and sent almost everyone home.

"...And I don't expect to see anyone in early tomorrow morning. We will have to live with a few hours delay, none of you will be any good to this investigation tomorrow if you are asleep on your feet," he added as the agents filed out the door. He asked a couple of agents to stay behind and keep an eye on the computers as the search for the owner of the face was running through CODIS, AFIS and all the other acronyms that dealt with facial recognition.

Brand asked the SAC for a copy of the drawing; he wanted to fax the sketch to Brent's offices in Ottawa. When he had confirmation that the fax was transmitted, he left the FBI office and headed back to his hotel room. He desperately wanted to put a name to the face of the terrorist leader, but his body was shutting down from exhaustion.

As he lay exhausted in bed, he racked his brain for other options that could be used to discover the identity of the man with the terrorists. What other options he thought, a room full of agents searching through military databases, facial recognition programs running non-stop. What was he missing, he kept asking himself. His mind methodically ticked off the different approaches that could be employed.

While he ate breakfast the following morning, an idea wormed into his weary mind. Pushing his plate aside, he reached for his phone and placed a call to Brent's office. Checking the time he knew that Sara should already be at work. He needed her help with the search from a different angle.

"Hi. I need you to try something for me?" he asked.

"Sure," she said laughing lightly at his grave tone. "It's pleasant to talk to you, too," she told him and then inquired about Brent.

"I haven't heard from either Brent of the hospital yet. I'll call right after we're finished talking," Brand explained. He switched the conversation back to the task at hand.

"I faxed a description of a suspect late last night. I think this guy orchestrated the attack at the stadium," he clarified. "The local FBI are running his features through every available database right now.

But as I was eating breakfast an idea occurred to me. Remember the Imam friend of mine, the one who called me with the mercenary killings in Afghanistan? The Afghani that escaped said the mercs were working with the Taliban, right? And the Imam told me that the group left the massacre and drove to an airport in Peshawar, Pakistan." Brand realized he was talking very quickly in his excitement. He paused, took a long breath then continued at a less hurried pace,

"What I need you to do is hack into the Pakistani air authority and run and search the airport logs? See if you can find any passengers who closely resemble our drawing?" he continued with his train of thought. He asked Sara to check it out because the FBI would have to go through diplomatic channels but maybe she could skirt the system.

She thought about his request and then teasingly replied, "What. Just illegally hack into another country's secure databases? I could go to jail!" she mocked him.

Distractedly he replied, "No. I don't think so." Then catching on to her light tone he added. "…Don't worry; I'll come and visit you in prison if you get extradited. Maybe bake you a cake," he joked before turning serious again. "If you do run into any troubles call me immediately. I know someone who may be able to smooth the path for you."

After talking to Sara, Brand made a call to the hospital asking about Brent's condition. Brent told him he was to be released later in the day, and he wanted to know where the two could meet.

"The FBI offices, unless some new development came up since I left," Brand stated matter-of-factly and then told Brent about the sketch that the FBI now had of the man he thought led the attack and how they had not made any progress last he had checked. Promising to keep him posted with any changes the two agreed to meet up at the FBI building after Brent's release.

The mood at the FBI field office when Brand walked in reeked of dogged determination. Several agents had returned to the blast site to sift through the debris searching for evidence; others sat glued to their computers looking through the endless faces of the American military from all the sources they had available, conventional or not.

Brand declined an offer to join the men at the ballpark. No, he told them, he'd seen all he needed to see yesterday while the attack was happening. He wandered around the office for a while checking on the progress made by the other agents and listening in about directions to take the investigation. Biding his time he found an unoccupied workstation where he went back to looking through military mug shots. He was disappointed to learn that none of the facial recognition programs had turned up anything either, Interpol included.

His mind drifted as he looked at picture after picture, he was presuming that the man he saw had been or was employed by the military. He could be totally wrong and have all the agents wasting time on a wild goose chase. Well, he considered, nobody had found any better leads at the moment.

Silent Crusade

Chapter 52

By early afternoon Brand was wrapped up in his search through the facial archives, the hum of activity around the office was blocked from his mind as he focused. A shadow fell across the desk where he sat and remained unnoticed by him for several minutes. The sound of a throat clearing caused him to look up. Brent had patiently waited, watching him scroll from face to face,

A look of relief crossed Brand's face as he considered his friend's appearance. Brent still looked like he had gone three rounds with an angry bull. His face was a series of small cuts; black circles underlined his eyes and the sling supporting his left arm practically glowed against his dark shirt.

"The hospital got tired of having you faking an injury and sent you packing I see," Brand said. Relieved at seeing his friend up and about he stood up and shook Brent's good hand.

"I think that they were afraid that you might show up again and scare the staff with that ugly mug of yours," Brent answered. The two long-time friends stood and chatted forgetting for a few minutes the tension that had filled their days as of late. Brent looked past Brand at the computer screen filled with mug shots and bios.

"Any luck?" He pointed inquisitively at the screen.

Brand frowned. "No. Not yet. The guys are checking every available database," he said referring to the FBI. Back on the subject Brand quickly gave Brent a run down on the investigation.

"Very little has changed since yesterday," he confessed. "I made a call to Sara this morning." Brand led Brent away from the room of agents and found a private spot in the hallway.

Talking quietly he explained the task he had requested of Sara. The perhaps illegal hacking of airport manifests from Pakistan.

"I haven't heard back from her yet," he confided in Brent. "If she runs into any problems I may need you to talk to Senator Meadows and smooth the path for her." Knowing that Brent would take care of that now that he back in

211

the field took a weight off his shoulders. "My eyes are crossing from staring at this computer screen, what say we find a restaurant and grab a drink and something to eat?"

The two left the FBI building. The Special Agent In Charge had called a meeting for the four o'clock until then there wasn't much to do other than staring at more faces on the computer, the proverbial needle in the haystack. A lot of times investigations consisted of hundreds of hours of sorting through evidence or in this case mug shots hoping for a break in the case.

The men exited the building onto the busy Chicago sidewalks opting to take a stroll and enjoy the sunshine before stopping for lunch. Walking on the crowded sidewalks, they talked about the investigation and the small amount of evidence involving the attack at the ballpark trading ideas and expanding on theories. The sun beat down on them from a cloudless blue sky, the temperature reaching into the high twenties Celsius. They decided on a restaurant a few blocks from the FBI building and entered into the cool air-conditioned interior, happy for the respite from the mid-afternoon heat. A waiter delivered coffees and left with their lunch order. Brand's phone rang. He glanced at the call display. Sara was calling from Brent's company office.

Sara rushed through a greeting and with excitement told Brand about the search for the airport security cameras from Pakistan. Success, or so she believed, captured on a video was a man closely resembling the sketch Brand had faxed. The image she found was on security footage from the Bacha Khan International Airport in Peshawar, Pakistan. She guiltily admitted that she had commandeered the rest of the office staff and had everyone sorting through video feeds from the airport.

"When you see Brent, don't tell him what I did," she sheepishly added. Brand snickered and gazed across the table not having the heart to tell her that he was sitting with her boss in a restaurant.

Sara continued, "We located his image on a camera overlooking a ticket counter. Once we had this footage, the next step was to stream video from all the airlines that were scheduled to board around that time. We scanned the video until finally discovering which airline he had boarded. Once we knew the carrier, all we had to do was check the passenger manifest for that flight."

Sara fell silent long enough to regain her breath, "To make a long story short there were only a few Americanized male names that stood out from the list," Sara read the information off her computer screen. Brand slid a napkin from across the table scribbling down the names. Several times he interrupted and asked her to spell the names so he could be sure he copied them down correctly.

"Anything else?" he asked her. Brent caught his attention and flashed a thumb up. "Brent says, good job,"

"Oh!" Sara exclaimed, "I have had several people in the office helping me do background checks on names. I can fax the results back to the FBI office for you."

Thanking Sara for the information, he and hung up the phone. Emptying his coffee cup he told Brent that he was going to forget about lunch and rush back to the FBI office.

"This could be the break we need," Brand said as he rushed out of the restaurant leaving Brent stuck with the bill.

At the FBI office, Brand walked straight to the fax machine checking for the information. It would have been easier to have Sara email it, but Brand didn't have a clue what the email address for the office was, so the fax would have to suffice. The fax machine hummed and squealed. Brand skimmed over each sheet. The list included four names.

Two names Brand set aside, the bios and background combined with the physical descriptions were nowhere near what he was looking for. The last ones he scrutinized closer, one was a businessman who could fit the profile but the last one he found interesting. Michael Johnson. No information was attached to this name, no background details, nothing, only a picture and a name. Brand knew what this meant. No matter who you were or where in the world you lived chances were very good that there was information of some kind to identify you. Unless. The only exception was when someone consciously had the information removed or hidden. And that rarely happened except for people involved in the intelligence or black ops world. Brand showed this to Brent when he joined him. Brent nodded and retrieved his phone calling Sara back at his office.

"How are you doing? She blurted when she heard his voice, "I am so relieved you weren't seriously hurt. You are lucky you didn't sustain worse injuries." She rushed out the words before he could say anything.

"I've had worse... Nothing but a flesh wound," Brent quipped trying to make light of his situation, he changed the subject, "this fourth man," he said to her, "Concentrate on him. There will be records of him somewhere, find them. Get every hacker in the office working on this, the quicker we can get a handle on this guy, the better."

She promised to keep him updated. "We'll find them," she reassured.

Brand carried the papers into the SAC's office and explained his theory to the agent. The Special Agent in Charge weighed the possibilities of Brand's info, agreed that the picture and the name matched Brand's earlier description and jumped into action. He put a call out to all the agents in the area to meet. He would throw a lot of resources on this lead.

"There's a lot to do to coordinate a large-scale manhunt and time was wasting," the SAC commented.

The FBI Special Agent in Charge reached out to a contact of his within the Department of Defense. He wanted to have the picture and the name confirmed as being the same person. His source told him that yes, the man in the picture was indeed Michael Johnson, but that was all he could confirm. Nothing more. The SAC smiled. The fact that his contact did not supply any other details about the man in question was more than enough information. Obviously, this man was or had been involved in service for his government. The face and name matched, now the hunt could start in earnest, finally a substantial lead.

*****

FBI agents packed the conference room. The two Canadians stood in the back and listened to the Special Agent in Charge as he spoke. He had started the meeting by passing around copies with the picture of the alleged terrorist leader. Assignments were divided up and handed out. The first order included an APB circulated to all the law enforcement agencies in the Eastern States. Airport authorities were to be issued the name and picture and put on high alert. Train stations and the port authorities were next in line to be informed.

214

Richard Cozicar

As the SAC assigned agents their specific tasks they left the room and went straight to work. If the terrorist leader were still anywhere in the vicinity they would have to act quickly to draw a net around the area to trap the man before he completely disappeared.

Brand's phone chimed. He looked at the screen and read a text. Sara had made another possible discovery. She asked Brand for an email address at the office that she could forward another set of pictures that she pulled from the cameras at Peshawar. Brand checked with an agent sitting beside him for the offices e-mail and texted her back.

The officer led Brand quietly from the conference room and sat down at one of the computers in the outer office. The message was waiting by the time the two men sat down at the terminal. The agent opened the email account and left Brand to read it. Sara had forwarded several other pictures of men she thought might be helpful. Brand studied the face of each man as he scrolled through the photos. One of the faces he was certain he recognized. Included with the photos, Sara had added a name, George Williams. The man Brand saw ushering the suicide bombers toward the stadium.

Printing off the picture, he walked back into the conference room and checked the name among the many casualties from the bombing. None of the agents involved in the investigation recognized the picture. Brand passed the photo to the SAC along with the name. Another piece of the puzzle had fallen into place.

"You might want to add this name to the APB," Brand suggested. The SAC nodded

"What are the chances of finding either man?" Brand asked. The question was rhetorical; he was well aware chances were slim but he asked anyway.

"If the men have gone into hiding or have fled the area it will be nearly impossible. If we don't catch them trying to board a plane or any crossing, they would have to be extremely careless for us to find them. It would be more luck than anything else we could do on our part. These are trained military operatives," the SAC pointed out. "They are not likely to slip up and give themselves away, not after what had happened.

We were lucky to get the tip about the flights they were on, or they would have all made it into the country undetected and the results could have been so much worse. I can't see them being that careless again," the SAC conceded. "Within the hour we will have every agency in the country looking for them, but that's a lot of ground to cover, and there are millions of places to hide. That is if they haven't already fled for somewhere safer."

"Do you think the President will hold off the bombs until you have a chance to prove that these men aren't part of any known terrorist factions?" Brand asked.

"What makes you think that these guys weren't associated? From the way this group operated when they attacked Wrigley, the bombings are no different than other terrorist activity," the SAC questioned.

"I think you're wrong. I firmly believe that someone else is pulling the strings. It's not impossible, but highly improbable that this group is terrorist affiliated. A lone wolf, sure that's plausible, but not this many men," Brand once again voiced his doubts and tried to persuade the SAC to trust him. Brand knew that he alone would not be able to convince the American President to abort.

The Special Agent in Charge Macalester stared at Brand. "Unless you have hard evidence to support your theory I'm afraid that I can't back you. We'll do everything possible to get to the truth but for now, this attack will be treated as the act of war it was! As it stands now, the Islamists have claimed responsibility for these horrific acts."

"But you are making a terrible mistake, one that will cost thousands of innocent lives!" Brand added his frustration levels were rising.

"Mr. Coldstream, I am most grateful for your help and certainly for the information that you have provided but don't attempt to tell me how to do my job. You are a visitor in my country; I would advise you to remember that!" the SAC stated and abruptly turned away ending the conversation.

Well, that didn't go so well Brand thought. He motioned to Brent as he left the conference room and headed for the elevators. He needed some way to prove that his hunch was right before the whole world was wrapped up in this mess.

Chapter 53

The two men walked in silence back to their hotel. Brand used the time to run through a few likely scenarios he could use to locate the men behind this attack. There must be a way to prove that the bombing was not what everyone thought. In his mind, the facts were indisputable. But why, why would someone go through all this trouble to frame the terrorists…unless, unless the idea was to provoke the Western leaders to resort to nuclear warfare in the Middle East. The bombings would set that whole cluster of countries back to medieval times decimating the Muslims.

An idea had started to take root in his mind during the short walk to their room. Both men entered and sat in the chairs that flanked the small table in the corner. Neither spoke, the silence was almost deafening.

"I may have an idea on how we can get Johnson to show himself." Brand outlined the basics, filling in the gaps as the plan built while he talked.

"Have you lost your marbles?" Brent looked at him as if he had two heads. "What you are suggesting will break several laws and probably just end up with us doing jail time in some high-security American prison."

"What choice do we have?" Brand defended. "We can't just sit on the sidelines and watch the bombs drop, and thousands of innocent people get fried."

Brent stared off into space as he thought of the implications. He shrugged, made some suggestions here and there as he began to see the benefits of Brand's strategy. Brent dug his phone out of his pocket and started to dial.

"What are you doing?" Brand asked.

"If we are going to pull this shit off we may want some backup. I need to explain to Senator Meadows what we are about to do. If we're lucky, she won't call the FBI and have us arrested."

"Here, pass me the phone. It's my idea; I might as well try to sell it to her," Brand dialed and waited for the Senator's phone to be answered. Brand identified himself and tentatively explained to Senator Meadows his hastily thought out proposal. The Senator listened in silence, waiting until Brand had finished before expressing her concerns.

"Mr. Coldstream, you realize that I cannot authorize a scheme like you've laid out. The ramifications could irrevocably damage the trust between the two countries," she rebuked him.

Undeterred, Brand forged ahead, "Senator Meadows, would you rather thousands of people be killed and the Middle East turned into a nuclear wasteland," he paused letting his words settle on the Senator. "Give us a chance to see if we are right or wrong."

Silence filled the line as the Senator carefully balanced the consequences of Brand's scheme and his reasoning.

"You do understand I cannot offer you any help. When this is over, assuming it is successful, I may be able to smooth things over with the American authorities. But until then you would be on your own. The chances of pulling this off are not good; I have every belief that you will end up being hunted by the American authorities as well."

"Fair enough," Brand agreed and told her that she would be kept in the loop as the operation unfolded. He spent the next few hours in the room refining the details. Brent placed a called his office and had Sara, along with some other employees book flights for Chicago. Brent's instructions for them were to rent a car and meet at the hotel.

"Bring all the information you have on these men," he added, "We're going to need it."

By ten that evening, Sara and two others checked into the hotel. The new arrivals dropped their luggage at rooms Brent reserved then everyone met in Brand's room. After a few polite pleasantries, Brand outlined the plan that he and Brent had mapped out. Brent explained the expectations he had for the newcomers. The late hour meant little would happen tonight, but Brand wanted everyone onboard and prepared when morning dawned.

The group took a few minutes and talked over drinks while Brand reviewed the information on Michael Johnson. He was looking for some leverage that could be used to flush the man out. Johnson's parents lived in Minnesota, a day's drive from Chicago. Tomorrow the group would leave Chicago and head east.

Richard Cozicar

*****

At dawn, they checked out of their rooms and began the trip east on I-ninety for a six and a half hour drive to Minneapolis, the city where Michael Johnson's parents lived. Along with his parents, Johnson had other siblings living in Minnesota area; his family was about to become major players in the plan to force the mercenary out of hiding.

Brand drove while Sara and the other worked furiously on their computers, checking information and tweaking the details for the operation. First off they had to find a hotel to use as a base of operations. Next, line up the equipment that they would need to pull this off.

"As ill-conceived as your plan seems, I understand your thinking," Sara said to Brand as the car rolled down the road. "But, do you think the man will be flushed out?"

"Hard to say really." Brand replied. "We don't need him to find us. We only need him to reveal where he's hiding. If we can create enough anxiety maybe he will get careless, react on his emotions before he realizes what he's doing."

By the time Minneapolis was on the horizon the guts of the plan had changed numerous times and a workable version was mapped out. Everyone would check into their rooms and meet in the hotel restaurant. There once again they would refine the details before putting the operation into action the next day.

*****

The morning sky was still dark as Brand and Brent left the hotel and drove to the quiet neighborhood where Johnson's parents lived. The idea was to arrive before the couple had a chance to leave for work. Brent parked the rental car across the

219

street from the house and turned off the engine. He sipped a coffee and watched the home.

At six, lights started appearing in the house, one or both of the residents were preparing for the day ahead. The two men waited in the dark car outside and rehearsed the events that they would put into action once their targets left the house.

At seven, Johnson's parents walked out to a brown car parked in their driveway, backed onto the street and pulled away from the residence. Brent started the rental and followed at a safe distance. The next part of the plan involved more improvisation than actual planning. Sara had told the men where the two worked, what she didn't know was the route they would take to get there. Brent followed a few car lengths back, not worried about being spotted. If people weren't aware of being followed the chance of them discovering a tail were very slim.

On a deserted stretch of road Brent sped up and pulled beside the brown car forcing the couple to the curb. Before the parents could recover from the sudden stop, Brand jumped out and ran to the driver's door his gun leveled at Johnson's father.

"Open the door," he yelled threateningly.

Brand grabbed the older man by the coat and pulled him from the vehicle. Next, he ordered Johnson's mother to climb out of the vehicle and join them. Brand kept his gun pointed at the father's head as he walked the two back to the rental. He placed the mother in the front seat and climbed into the back after the father.

Brent put the car in drive and rapidly left the scene. Brand collected the couple's cell phones, which he tossed from the moving car. The father started to protest, Brand pointed his gun at the man and told him to remain quiet.

"Close your eyes. Both of you!" he ordered, "And leave them closed until you are told to do otherwise."

Leaving the quiet residential area, Brent merged with the morning traffic and pointed the car northeast. The direction would take them out of the city. He followed a route that connected with the highway and in less than of an hour brought them to a cabin that Sara had booked north of the city in the White Bear Lake area.

Forty-five minutes later, Brent in front of a cabin. Another car sat in front of the cabin. Sara and the others had rented a separate vehicle and drove out to the cabin earlier with the equipment they purchased in the city.

Brand pulled a couple of blindfolds and gags out of his jacket and bound the man and his wife. He had waited to put them on until now, they couldn't risk someone seeing them during the drive and reporting them. He and Brent climbed out of the car escorting the couple into the cabin.

Brand let his eyes roam over inside of the cabin as he entered. It wasn't large, but it would suffice for what they needed. They left their captives standing in the front room where a video camera on a tripod had recently been set up. Leaving the two, Brand stepped aside while the tech's that had accompanied Sara attended to the father.

"He's all yours," They called out when they finished.

Brand pulled the father over in front of the recorder and forced the man onto his knees, his face toward the camera lens then he repeated the process with the mother. One of the techs moved behind the camera and guided Brand as he lined the parents in the camera's view. Satisfied that the couple knelt in the right position he turned to the cameraman and signaled him to begin recording. Brand quickly glanced at Brent. Action!

Brand fingered his gun and turned to face the camera.

"Michael Johnson." He stared into the camera. "I'm going to make this short and to the point," the camera panned past Brand and focused on Johnson's parents bound and gagged on the floor. "We know who you are and what part you have played in the ballpark attack." Brand paused, his eyes narrowed as he glared into the camera. "Surrender to the nearest authorities," he instructed then turned his back to the camera and pointed his gun at Johnson's father.

The camera angle widened. Brand stood in front of the couple; his finger tightened on the trigger. The bark of the gun followed by a puff of smoke. The body of the Johnson's father jerked and toppled to the floor; blood sprayed on the wall behind. Muffled cries rose from the throat of Johnson's mother, the gunshot in the small room, the terror of the unknown driving her to scream hysterically.

"Mr. Johnson. You seem to have no regard for the scores of innocent people you've killed for your cause. Well." The camera zoomed back into focus on Brand's face. "Game on. Your mother will suffer the same fate as your father. I don't intend to wait very long for you to comply." The camera followed Brand again as he made a point of looking at a clock on a table beside him, a brochure of White Bear Lake barely visible beneath the clock on the table.

"I don't know which rock you're hiding under so I will allow you time to make a decision. If I don't hear from the authorities that you've turned yourself in by this time tomorrow then by all means…look to God and pray for your mother." The camera's view was expanded to show the floor behind Brand. He nodded to have the camera turned off.

"Okay everybody you know what to do. Let's get this video ready to upload to the Internet. Brent, calm this woman down and take her into one of the other rooms," he shouted, his anger apparent.

"What do we do now?" Sara asked from across the cabin.

"Now we wait," Brand replied.

Chapter 54

Michael Johnson, George Williams, and the remaining members from the attack at Wrigley Field drove to a house northwest of Chicago. The location set up in well in advance for their seclusion after the assault. The men sat in the living room, their attention fixed on the television, their only distraction from the endless monotony of waiting. They dared not go outside and risk the chance of somebody recognizing them.

Johnson was not paying attention to the game show the others were so raptly watching, God how he hated daytime television. He was lost in his thoughts when one of the others tapped him and drew his attention to the TV.

The game show was interrupted by a BREAKING NEWS story. The announcer gave a brief lead into the story about a video that had surfaced on the Internet earlier in the day. The video was causing quite a stir; going viral he explained and then quickly warned of its graphic content. The news anchor reported that the authorities were trying to verify the authenticity of the video and searching for the people who made it.

Johnson's attention focused on the TV. The face of the anchorman faded out and in his place was a headshot of another man. The man was speaking to the camera. The first word out of the man's mouth was Johnson's name. That caught his attention as he and the other men sat transfixed watching the video play out. Johnson's jaw dropped as he saw his parents behind this man. He could not believe his eyes as he watched the man turn and shoot his father. What the HELL he thought, this wasn't backwoods terrorist Ville, this was the united friggin States of America, and people didn't get executed like this. The news anchor came back on the screen; he rambled on adding very few details.

Johnson sat motionless, his eyes staring at the screen. Everyone in the room shocked with disbelief. Not one man amongst them remembered ever witnessing this type of thing in the good old USA. They had no idea how to wrap their brains around the shooting on the video. No one had seen this coming.

George Williams broke the silence.

"What are you going to do, you can't be thinking about turning yourself in?" he asked the leader. Johnson ignored him at first. His eyes and his thoughts locked onto the TV screen. The man, sitting on the couch beside Johnson, gave him a nudge breaking the trance that gripped Johnson.

Michael Johnson looked around the room at the others, his mind racing, trying to cope with what he had witnessed. His father bound and gagged and shot, it couldn't be. He pulled a burner phone out of his pocket and started to dial when one of the others stopped him.

"You think that's a good idea," the man asked.

"This phone is untraceable; nobody has the number. And even if they did, it's impossible to trace it back to me," he replied sternly. The last thing he needed right now was bullshit from the other guys. Johnson left the couch and stormed into the kitchen with the intention to call one of his siblings and have them check on his parents. The video had to a fake, he rationalized.

Before phoning his brothers, he punched the number for his mother's house. The phone rang several times before the answering machine picked up. He hung up when the animated voice answered. The next calls went first to one brother and then the other. Neither had seen the video and placated him with the same reassurances that their folks were at work, not at home at this hour but promised to check on their parents. They told him he was paranoid; their parents were okay and not to worry. Then he placed a call to his sister; maybe she knew more but didn't seem concerned either. He didn't leave a call back number with any of them; he would call back later he assured them.

Johnson stormed back into the living room. He grabbed a laptop and returned to his seat on the couch and immediately went to a video-streaming site in search of the video shown on the news. He played the video over and over while the other men in the house gathered around him. As a collection, they studied the video trying to determine its authenticity. Deciding there was no way for them to know for certain they remained watching it searching for clues. One of the men pointed out the brochure that sat by the clock as the man in the video turned to check the time.

White Bear Lake. That was just a short distance from his parent's house in Minneapolis. Johnson's parents had taken him, his brothers and sister there numerous times over the years. That man in the video had fucked up big time Johnson swore to the others. He had made a grave mistake that Johnson would gladly exploit and make the person suffer if harm came to his parents. For the moment, he would wait to hear back from his family; the update would determine which way he would precede.

His crew kept their distance from him. The tension in the house was off the charts; every man was taken aback and appalled at what they had witnessed, angry that a blatant execution could happen on American soil. The irony of their indignant attitudes over one death after the mass destruction and loss of life they were responsible for just hours before totally lost on them.

Once Michael Johnson calmed down, he gathered his men. If the execution of his father was proven to be real, he wanted a plan for retribution in place. The small bunch of mercenaries huddled together to work out the details for a possible trip to Minnesota. Every one of them had served their country in a military fashion so formulating a strike force against an enemy was something they were trained to do.

Surely the man in the video would be cautious and undoubtedly prepared for a retaliatory attack. He would be if he were smart enough. The fact that the brochure was left lying on the table and that the camera had accidentally picked it up gave Johnson and his men hope.

It didn't matter to Johnson. He and his men would prepare for the worse. A siege against a cabin in Minnesota needed a lot less preparation than the attacks they had plotted against foreign enemies hiding in caves and mountains.

While the group took a break, George Williams snuck outside and unknown to the others he made a call to his parent's house. What if his identity had also been discovered along with Johnson's? Would that mean that this same crazed vigilante would be targeting them as well?

Williams's call ended at the answering machine at his parent's house. A tough decision now confronted him. He was aware that his parents were probably still at work, but now came the burning question. Should he risk calling their cell phones or was that pushing his luck? He didn't carry a disposable phone like Johnson, but he doubted that if he made a couple of quick calls, his phone would be traced.

Silent Crusade

Chapter 55

With the help of other techs, Sara had edited the video than with a few keystrokes uploaded the finished product to the net. The three worked furiously distributing the short production to every television station surrounding the Chicago area. Before long the video took on its a life of its own. The major cable networks interrupted their daytime programming to air the video. Then came the cable news stations. Online the execution-style production was posted and reposted.

The group at the cabin had watched as the video went viral. Comments on social media rolled in fast and furious with a huge uproar following, people outraged, condemning the execution shooting of an American citizen. The group at the cabin monitored the news, the video spreading across the country, gaining the public's attention and creating the desired effect they had hoped.

The minute the video hit the air; Sara put in play a program to monitor the phones of Michael Johnson's parents and siblings. Any calls made to those numbers would show up on her screen. One of the other techs mirrored Sara's program monitoring all incoming calls to the family of George Williams. As he was an only child, this task was much simpler. The techs sat glued to the open laptops in front of them. The crucial time to pick up any phone activity was during the early minutes after the release of the video.

Brand's theory proved right. Within moments of the video's release the TV stations picked it up and rebroadcast it nationally. The one problem with his plan was the uncertainty of whether Johnson or Williams were still in the States or had already fled the country. It was a chance he was willing to take. Brand figured he would know the answer within hours until then as others he would just have to wait.

Brand walked outside and settled in a chair. Lighting up a cigarette he raised his feet, resting them on the wooden rail surrounding the deck, he leaned his head back and closed his eyes taking advantage of the peace and fresh air. Through the afternoon, the cabin door would open at random intervals as one of the techs stuck their head out and updated him on the circulation of the shooting. From local stations, it spread to neighbouring states than it went national; from there it went international.

Not long after the video made the national news, Sara poked her head out the door called to him. He rushed into the kitchen behind her. The small room had been transformed to resemble a computer lab. The table littered with laptops and cables running to the various machines spread across the table. Brand watched his step, careful to avoid tripping on the array of wires as stood behind her.

"What ya got?" he asked her, placing his arm around her shoulders peering at the screen before him.

"We've picked up several different calls to the parents house, but only one of those numbers contacted the other family members," Sara showed Brand on her computer screen.

"Can you get a bead on the number and trace it back to its source?"

"I'm on that already. As long as the phone remains active, I can locate a location or at least the general vicinity near it," she explained.

"Perfect." The video had served its purpose. They didn't need Johnson to do anything now but panic and break phone silence.

Another tech piped up. "I think we might have a second phone to trace; a call to William's house. It only happened once, but maybe Williams was worried by the video and decided to check on them."

"Well, get a lock on that number and see how it plays out. Is the phone still powered? Can you trace it along with the phone Sara's tracking?" Brand asked. He watched as the techs monitoring the computers typed away in the search for the terrorists' location. He was amazed at how the three scrolled through command after command on their laptops. He wasn't computer savvy enough to follow along but these were three of the best technological operatives in the country. He had faith in their talents.

Sara shifted to get his attention, pointing at the screen of her computer to a satellite map with a flashing beacon. Brand tried to read the coordinates over her shoulder. He gave up and asked her to write the information down.

"How positive are you about the location?" he asked as she handed him the paper with the coordinates.

"It should be within a couple of blocks," she assured him.

"Good enough for me," he said and turned to Brent, who had been leaning against a counter in the kitchen out of everyone's way.

"You're on!" Brand said as he passed the paper to Brent.

"Jimmy," Brand spoke to a one of the techs, "Can you reroute Brent's phone while he makes this call. The FBI is almost as good at running phone traces as you are."

When Jimmy signaled that he was ready, Brent punched the number into his cell and called the FBI's SAC back in Chicago. Brent spoke briefly; sharing the coordinates of the phone Sara had tracked. The SAC wanted to know how he had acquired this information trying to prolong the conversation for obvious reasons. Brent ended the call and smiled. He had to give the FBI points for effort.

Brand paced the kitchen occasionally turning to watch the computer screens.

"Keep a lock on those phones; I want to know if they move. I don't think this little charade is over yet."

The first number they were monitoring went silent. The second number remained on for a while longer before it too was disappeared off the screens. Sara and the other two stayed at their monitors vigilantly tracking the activity on the computers. Brand walked out the back door of the cabin and sat down on the deck chair. Pulling his pack of cigarettes out he lit up and thought through the rest of the operation as it was unfolding. He had asked Brent to try to secure another cabin close to the one they were at in case a change of venue was needed. His group had thought out several contingencies while planning for this event; their consensus was that the man they were pursuing was not an idiot, underestimating him could have grave consequences.

Brand was crushing out his cigarette when Sara bolted through the door.

"They're on the move," she exclaimed, not sure if the excitement of her discovery or the sudden dash outside had caused her to gasp for breath. Brand told her to relax and led the way back into the kitchen.

"Show me," he said. Sara sat back down in front of her laptop and quickly explained the program she had been running. Brand interrupted her occasionally with questions while he tried to follow her. The screen on the computer showed a green dot pulsating on a map, and that dot was moving! What direction were they moving he asked her? She showed him a cursor that indicated north.

"If I'm reading that correctly, I think that the phone is moving in our direction. Is that right?"

Sara nodded. Bingo, Brand thought. Part two of the plan was now under way.

"You don't think that we screwed up and left something in the video that would give away our location?" he commented facetiously and grinned. The group had had a discussion about the brochure with the resort's name sitting beside the clock Brand looked at during the video and whether the clue was too obvious. Either way, the man they were hunting was now headed in their direction. Whether the cabin was his destination or not remained to be seen.

The one small unavoidable glitch in their plan was the FBI. They too would have viewed the video, and there was no doubt that they would be searching for the house where the recorded execution took place. The FBI had offices across the States and the manpower to conduct a massive search of their own. The race was on to see which of the two parties found the cabin first.

Brent joined the group in the kitchen.

"The cabin a couple doors down appears to be vacant. I didn't call about renting it, but I figured that we could use it; we are only going to be there overnight at the most," Brent volunteered. "It's buried among thick trees so we should go unnoticed. Hopefully, the owners don't show up and give everyone a surprise!"

"Sure. Why not?" Brand quipped. "We've broken enough laws today. One more sure as Hell won't hurt. All right everybody let's grab our stuff and move it next door. Once we get it set up, I can come back and get this place ready in case this Johnson fellow is as bright as we think he is."

Chapter 56

Michael Johnson grew impatient. The waiting to hear back about his parents combined with his paranoia latched onto his brain, his anxiety growing worse with each passing minute. The rational part of his mind screamed fake, but then why bother to post that type of video if it were not real, a clever ploy to smoke him out of hiding?

His emotional side prayed for it to be a fake.

Tired of waiting he ordered his men to grab their things. He would be leaving shortly for Minnesota. One of the men questioned him about the wisdom of leaving the safe house. If the law was hunting them, then any movement could potentially compound their troubles.

Johnson glared at the man. In his opinion, he was still perfectly rational in spite of the personal attack, real or implied, to his family. He had gotten his men away safely the first time, and he said he could do it again. The group had dumped the cargo vans for once they fled the city; the vehicles exchanged for passenger vans, untraceable as far as Johnson was concerned. If they traveled inconspicuously, then the chances of being discovered were minimal.

He told the men that he wanted to be on the road soon. One of the men in the house tried to reason with Johnson. When his attempts failed, he flatly stated that he wasn't going on this wild goose chase.

"Anybody else?" Johnson challenged the others. A second of the group decided that he too would be staying behind. Johnson looked to the remaining pair. The third man was in, and George Williams agreed to go.

Johnson grabbed his things and thundered out to the van. Williams excused himself walking to his bedroom to collect his belongings. When he was out of sight, he pulled out his phone and checked it praying for a message from his parents. The phone would be powered off during the trip if a call weren't received from either of them soon. In his mind, his imagination reeled with flashes of his parents suffering horrible ordeals. Stuffing a few items into a bag he willed his phone to ring before leaving the house to join the other two.

Michael Johnson sat behind the wheel, the third member of the party firmly ensconced in the back leaving the passenger seat open. Reluctantly Williams climbed into the van.

The trip to White Bear from their location was a relatively short five hours. The man in the video had provided a twenty-four window. Johnson did the math; he had more than enough time to find the cabin. He was very familiar with the White Bear Lake area. If he allowed time for a search of the area for the cabin in question, he would still have plenty of time left to plan and execute the extraction of his mother.

*****

Three hours after Johnson and the others left their safe house, the FBI, with the help of the local police had begun to reduce their search area and tighten the net on the properties in the vicinity. One after another property was surrounded, cautiously approached and then cleared, narrowing the search area. The combined police task force moved apprehensively to each new location. Consideration factored in for the firepower the group had shown at the stadium. The size of the search force increased as more law enforcement arrived to aid in the assault.

One more hour passed as the legion of law officers zeroed in on the property where the safe house sat. Like all the other properties they had cleared before, the group coordinated and approached the house from all sides. Stealth with this many people was impossible. As the agents moved closer to the house in a shot was fired from inside the house.

The two remaining men trapped in the house watched the approaching wave of officers and knew that surrendering was not an option either of them would choose. The death penalty them if they were found guilty. That was a given. The men fired haphazardly, killing these officers was not something they relished. Both men were torn between being taken alive and having to shoot their way to freedom.

While their minds waffled between the two options, the growing group of law enforcement agents viewed the gunfight differently. Everyone was already on edge from the attack on the stadium; they were not going to take any chances of the culprits killing any more of their members.

In the coordinated siege, the large advancing force sought better positions of cover before returning fire with semi-automatic rifles and standard issue handguns sending a fusillade of bullets ripping into the building. Some shells sank into the exterior of the house while others shredded the windows and doors. The sounds of the various weapons blending into one continuous roar.

The two men hiding inside ran out of options. The bullets entering the house found their bodies. The men jerked like marionettes on strings as bullets gouged and tore. By the time an order to stand down sounded and the officers eased on the triggers, the mercenaries had been virtually cut to pieces from the volley of bullets.

The ranks of police waited and then slowly approached the house. A senior officer approached the door and waited as he called into the house. When he received no reply, he waved a couple of his men forward and prepared to breach the door that hung precariously from its hinges; bullet holes riddled the surface.

The lead officer moved toward the opening and guardedly nudged the door open with his foot. From where he stood, he could see two men, their bodies torn apart by bullets, lying at awkward angles on the floor. He waved his men forward and sent them to check the rest of the house.

The FBI and local police took hours to confirm the body's identities. The faces of the deceased shredded by the multitude of bullets that had assaulted the house. The verified results showed that the man who had led the attack on the stadium was not among the dead. Evidence was found proving that Johnson had been at the house, but somehow he had eluded the raid. Had he known that the police were coming or where he had gone was anybody's guess? The investigation was back to square one when it came to finding the Terrorist leader.

Silent Crusade

Chapter 57

The hour was late; almost midnight Brand noted as he glanced at the time highlighted on his phone. He yawned and turned his attention back to the evening news. The coordinates of the area for the suspected safe house that Brent had furnished to the FBI had paid off. The newscast showed an acreage overrun by emergency vehicles. Flashing lights threw an eerie cast over the scene of police and medics on the property. The FBI had yet to release a statement on the raid, but a news camera crew on the property followed paramedics as they wheeled two gurneys out the front door of the house. Early reports from the scene told of only two bodies inside the building.

Brand had no idea how many men Johnson may have had with him, so the count was irrelevant. It would be nice to know the names of the occupants. If Johnson had been one of them, this charade would end. By the time, the FBI forensic teams identified the bodies the names of the men would no longer matter.

Brand watched the news as it repeated. He turned his attention back to the problem that was heading in his direction. Sara kept him updated on the phone signal as it moved west along the highway. The original signal had stopped abruptly but the second phone remained on allowing Sara to track it. The men driving toward the cabin must be confident that their phones were unknown. Having a cell phone activated while trying to hide was not a wise tactical move.

Brand's cell phone vibrated interrupting his thoughts. He looked at the screen. Sara was confirming that the phone signal was still moving in their direction. Brand continued waiting; his mind focused. He mentally checked items off a list in his mind ensuring that all the preparations were in place.

Earlier in the day, Brand with the help of the two techs installed motion-activated cameras around the property. What they lacked in manpower they made up for with technology. The feed from the cameras was monitored by on the computers then relayed his phone allowing him to follow the feeds in real time. He felt confident that at least two people were in the vehicle they tracked, the different cell signals showed that. How many were on the drive was still a mystery.

Without knowledge of the exact number of individuals, his plan had to allow for different scenarios. He and Brent would be the only line of defense and Brent's damaged arm might be a slight liability, so Brand made his plans accordingly. He would have to move quickly and unnoticed to even the odds.

Only one dim light remained on in a back room of the house. The faint glow from the television lit the front room, the volume loud enough to hear but not loud enough to signal a trap. He had walked the interior of the house several times, double and triple checking the doors and windows, making sure they were locked, all but the back door which led into the cabin from the deck. He had left that one unlocked intentionally. Brand closed all the blinds and curtains obstructing the view of the house's interior from the world outside.

His phone vibrated again. The signal was close to the property and had stopped. From here on in Brand and the others would remain silent. He left the cabin by the back door and got into position. From here on in he would have to rely solely on the cameras as his eyes to track the incoming assailants.

Brent watched the same feed on his phone. The two men had encountered enough of these situations that any further contact was unnecessary. They each knew their part of the plan.

A camera covering a trail in the bush at the back of the house flashed onto Brand's screen. The trees were almost a hundred feet from the back of the house at the far end an expansive backyard barren except for a few randomly planted shrubs, the only hiding places between the edge of the bush and the backdoor. With an eye on his phone, Brand watched as three men approached the end of the backwoods in a crouch.

The clouds blanketed the night sky allowing only the odd slivers of moonlight into the yard. The dim light masked the features of the men crouching in the darkness; only their silhouettes appeared on the phone screen. The three crouched hidden among the bushes talking before two separated and inched their way toward the house. Brand split the screen on his phone to add the feed from a camera mounted near the back door. The remaining man stood on the path keeping watch as the others moved to flank the house.

Brand saw the two disappear around the house to the front then the sentry started to advance from the trail into the yard. Stuffing the phone into his pocket, Brand slipped his shoes off and took a deep breath. Showtime!

Brand let the man walk a few steps further into the yard before he eased out of the bush with a stealth learned from years of experience. Moving in his stocking feet he felt the dampness of the grass on his feet as he closed in on his prey.

The last of the trio to leave the trail was only a few yards in front of him. Brand crept closer, his gun raised like a club. The man must have sensed a presence behind because he started to turn. The swinging metal in Brand's hand caught the side of the intruder's head sending the man crashing onto the grass.

The momentum forced Brand into an awkward tumble, so he tucked his head and hit the lawn in a somersault. Coming out of the roll he gained his footing and turned back to face his opponent. The intruder was dazed and slower to get to his feet. Brand dove and with the force of his body drove the man backward into the ground. Rising in the air, Brand dropped on his assailant crushing the man into the grass, the breath fleeing from the man. Brand raised his gun again, swung and delivered a blow to the winded man's head knocking him unconscious. With an ease of repetition, Brand pulled plastic zip ties out of his rear pocket, rolled his captive over and secured the man's hands behind his back.

He rolled the body back over, quickly jumped to his feet and ran across the yard springing up the rear deck bee lining for the back entrance. At the door he paused and listened, not a single sound interrupted the silence of the interior. Brand turned the doorknob and silently slipped into the house.

This group might have some signal to alert each other, one that he certainly didn't know. He crouched out of sight beside the back door and gave some thought to the type of sign they could use. To hell with it, he quickly decided and let his hand snake up the wall to the light switch. Here goes nothing. He quickly flashed the ceiling light in the back room twice before turning it off and changing his location.

Within seconds, the front door burst in and the other two rushed into the house. As they were crossing the threshold, the door slammed back into them. Brent had been waiting in the closet at the front entrance. The men were knocked off balance, stumbling into the house. The first fell hard, crashing into the television and knocking it to the floor as he dropped. The second man stumbled further into the room, tripping over a blanketed prone body left from the video shoot and landed beside it.

Brent, his movements restricted by his bandaged arm dropped both his knees onto the back of the closest man delivering a crushing blow to the man's chest. With his good arm, he smashed his gun down several times against the man's head.

The second assailant let out an agonizing cry realizing what he had stumbled over. He struggled to his feet and was half standing over the body when Brand came running from the back of the house and dove. Brand's momentum straightened the third person and sent the two men across a coffee table and into a couch against the far wall.

Michael Johnson recovered first after the impact and swung at his assailant. Brand's arm blocked the blow sending it flying past his ear. Driven by unspeakable agony, Johnson twisted his body and pushed Brand beneath him. Wrapping his fingers around Brand's throat, he raised his fist and smashed it into Brand's face.

Spots of light danced before Brand's eyes as his opponent landed blows to his head. Moving his head to the side as the fist shot toward his face a third time, Brand stretched out his arm, his hand sweeping frantically for any object he could use as a weapon. His fingers touched a thin bar, the base of a lamp.

Brent found his attention drawn toward the men fighting across the room. In a brief lapse, he eased up on the man he had pinned with his knees. The intruder sensed his foes distraction and rose on all fours, sending Brent flying backward. His back hit the floor, but he managed to raise his gun and fire two shots into the form rising in front of him. The man stopped standing up and fell back to the floor.

Johnson turned his head toward the shots, unsure who had fired. Brand closed his hand around the lamp and swung with desperation at his opponent's head, the force knocking Johnson back on his heels. Brand rolled off the couch and surged to his feet. He pressed on, fists swinging, the man crouching before him with raised arms attempting to block Brand's advancing blows.

Johnson lowered his head trying to avoid Brand's fists. As his head went down, Brand raised his knee and connected with Johnson's nose. The nose crumpled under the force of the impact propelling Johnson upward. Johnson's eyes glazed as he swayed and then sank onto the couch. Brand grabbed his gun and flipped the safety. Johnson attempted to rise, so Brand lowered the firearm and shot the mercenary in the thigh indicating the fight was over.

Backing up, Brand bent over and tried to catch his breath, his eyes remaining fixed on the bleeding man, his gun unwavering.

Brent rose, walked over to a switch by the front door and flipped it on, lighting up the front room.

Brand straightened up and stared down at the man on the couch. He had studied this man's face and knew it well. Michael Johnson.

"Man," Brand spoke to Johnson as he fought to calm his breathing. "I have to admit; I thought you would be a hell of a lot tougher."

Johnson glared at Brand then he through misted eyes glanced down at the blanket covered body from the video. Johnson's eyes filled with rage. His father's death was real! The hopes he had held onto, that this was all an elaborate hoax, lay dead on the floor. If he had a chance, he would kill the man in front of him he thought as the reality sank in of his father lying dead.

"Stand up," Brand demanded. Michael Johnson struggled through the pain in his leg and was directed into the dimly lit back room. His eyes filled with alarm as he glimpsed another figure tied to a chair in the corner of the room. The room was a shade lighter than dark, but he had to presume that his mother was the one tied to the chair with a sack over her head.

Brand led Johnson to a spot near the door and told him to kneel. Johnson hesitated, so Brand kicked the mercs feet out from under and forced him onto his knees facing the body in the chair.

"Start talking!" Brand ordered. Brent moved into the room and stood beside the chair. He pulled his phone out and punched a couple of commands into it.

"Go straight to hell," Johnson answered in a voice filled with venom. Brand turned the barrel of his gun toward the chair and fired.

Johnson bellowed like a caged animal and started to rise to his feet. Brand swung the pistol around and shot Johnson in the other leg.

"The next shot will be much higher," Brand promised. Michael Johnson eyed Brand and then he lowered his head onto his chest.

"Alright, just leave her alone. What do you want?" he conceded.

"Who is behind the bombings? I sure as hell know that they were not carried out by Muslim extremists like we have been led to believe."

Johnson looked around the room. Then in a tone of defeat, he told Brand about the Christian Crusades that he and countless other true Christian soldiers had served. The bombings were an elaborate scheme to frame the Muslims community. Create enough death and destruction that the western countries would have no choice but to retaliate. The goal was to turn the Middle East into miles of nuclear wasteland ending the Muslim religion once and for all before it consumed the world.

As Johnson finished his confession, Brand turned toward the door and flicked on the overhead light. He nodded to Brent who pulled the bag off of the figure in the chair. The look on Johnson's face turned from fear to disbelief.

"You have got to be fucking kidding me!" Johnson uttered as he stared at a mannequin strapped to the chair. He looked up at Brand, his emotions struggling between solace and disbelief.

"And the body in the other room?" he asked. Brand shook his head.

"Another dummy. We're not blind Christians like your fraternity; we don't kill innocent people." Brand nodded at his friend. Brent raised his phone to his ear.

"Sara. Did you get all that?" he asked.

"Every word! Loud and clear," Sara replied. Brent sighed then issued instructions for her to gather the equipment and leave with the other techs.

240

"We'll catch up with you guys later, but you better hurry," he added and ended the call.

Brand stared down at Johnson with a look of disgust. He was turning to leave the back room when the house lit up and swarms of FBI agents rushed into the house.

The small room quickly filled with FBI agents, wearing stamped vests, pointing guns and hollering. Brand and Brent dropped their firearms and raised their hands. The FBI moved behind the two men, twisted their arms behind their backs and slapped them in cuffs. Brent cursed the men while they pulled his damaged arm from its sling. Special Agent in Charge, Glen Macalester of the Chicago Office, walked in the front door.

Silent Crusade

Chapter 58

Sara had her coworkers disconnect the computer and surveillance equipment and load it into the rental car. On her laptop, she separated the recording of Johnson's confession and bundled it together to e-mail the FBI office in Chicago. With her finger, Sara pressed the send button then passed her computer off to one of the techs instructing him to go to the car.

She pulled a knife off the counter and left the kitchen walking into the back bedroom of the appropriated cabin. Sara checked the couple's blindfolds and adjusted the straps on their wrists then cut the plastic straps that bound the feet of Johnson's parent's. Without a word she walked out of the house and climbed into the waiting car. A couple of properties away from the cabin flooded with police cars, the techs backed slowly out of the driveway and drove away.

*****

Macalester had his men lead the two Canadians out of the house.

"Do you think there is any chance I'll get my security deposit back for this cabin?" Brent quipped as they were out of the cabin.

Brand watched the swarm of agents roaming the property. Like a colony of ants, the men efficiently went about their jobs. Through a screen of trees, Brand watched the lights flash from a pair of ambulances. Johnson was strapped to a gurney and escorted to the back of the closest rig. FBI agents followed the stretcher into the back of the ambulance before it sped off to the hospital. A non-descript sedan carrying more officers followed closely behind the ambulance. The man Brand had knocked unconscious in the back yard sat in the back of an FBI car, the door open while a paramedic examined his head. The last member of the trio that attacked the house, the one that Brent had shot, lay on the floor covered by a tarp.

When things quieted down, SAC Macalester walked out of the house and stood beside the car next to Brand. Brent sat in the backseat of the car, his feet hanging out through the open door. The SAC looked at them and shook his head.

"I'm sure you fellows have a fascinating story to tell me," he said.

Brand interrupted, "Before we start, you might want to check with your office. There will be an email waiting there; it may explain a lot." Brand continued, "Don't ignore it, I think your President will be indebted to you after he sees the message."

The Special Agent in Charge called one his men over to drive the car.

"Watch your head," he said motioning for Brand to climb in the car. "We'll have this discussion over at the FBI field office in Minneapolis," Macalester replied before slamming the door behind them. The SAC walked around the car and climbed into the front seat telling his driver to leave.

The two Canadians spent the night in separate interrogation rooms of the Minneapolis building as a stream of FBI took statements and filled reports. Over and over they were asked to retell the events that had transpired at the cabin in the woods. When the FBI had finished questioning them, they were led to the basement of the building and locked in separate cells. The two were read their rights and informed of the numerous charges filed against them.

The two remained in lockup in Minneapolis for the better part of a week before transfer to the Chicago FBI headquarters. Escorted into the building in handcuffs, SAC Glen Macalester's met them at his office door. He pointed to the chairs in front of his desk.

"The President has asked me to convey his sincerest thanks. The recording and evidence you provided averted a nuclear catastrophe." Macalester cleared his throat, "Michael Johnson is confessed to masterminding the bombings in France, Britain and your country. He signed a confession and gave up the names of his accomplices, most who I might add are now dead." The FBI agent hesitated, "The one thing he won't share with us is who was funding his operation. Eventually, I am certain; we will get the names from him." Macalester looked Brand in the face, "Mr. Johnson will probably spend the rest of his days in a wheelchair thanks to your special interrogation techniques."

"Shit happens I guess," Brand shrugged. "Some people just need a bit more encouragement than others."

"There is still the matter of the kidnapping charges," the SAC continued. "For now, we are going to allow you two to return to Canada but sometime shortly you both will be subpoenaed and will very likely have to come back to face an inquiry.

It appears that you two have a very tenacious Senator from your country who has been relentless in fighting for your release, and the President informed me that your Prime Minister has discussed these matters with him on your behalf," the agent smiled.

"I have a man waiting for you. He has collected your belongings along with your guns. You can change in one of our offices if you like. Then the agent will give you a ride to the airport when you are ready." The Special Agent in Charge stood up and waited for Brand and Brent to rise. "I want to thank the two of you personally for your help," he told them as he shook their hands. "Let's not do this again anytime soon." He smiled and gestured toward his office door.

Chapter 59

Brand remained in Ottawa two weeks after he and Brent were released by the American authorities and allowed to return to Canada. He had met with Senator Meadows several times over that span; numerous diplomatic problems had to be cleared up in regards to his involvement with the events in the States.

He was relaxing in his hotel room late one night. He had taken Sara out for an evening on the town, and the two had just recently returned to their room when the hotel phone rang. Sara answered it; listened for a short time and then carried the phone over to Brand.

"It's for you I think." She looked at him quizzically. "Some gentleman asking to speak to the Boogieman?"

Brand raised the phone to his ear.

"Boogieman. Nelson Bakker. I was wondering if you would be so kind to meet me at my office at your earliest convenience?"

"I'm in Ottawa; your office is in Toronto?" Brand stated.

"I know where you are," Bakker said. "There will be a ticket waiting for you at the airport tomorrow."

"What is this about?" Brand asked. "Can't you tell me what you want over the phone?"

"What I need to talk to you about is not anything I would like to discuss over the phone," the old man replied. "I will have a car waiting for you at the airport."

Brand accepted and told Bakker he would be on a plane in the morning. When he hung up, he explained to Sara that he had to fly to Toronto in the morning. How long he would be there, he wasn't sure.

Brand had little time to think on the short flight to Toronto. True to his word Bakker had a driver meet him at the terminal and drive Brand to the businessman's downtown office. The driver escorted Brand up to the thirty-fifth floor. The whole floor occupied by Nelson Bakker's Energy conglomerate.

At the door to Bakker's personal office, the driver stopped Brand and asked him to surrender his cell phone. He could reclaim the phone once the meeting was over before he showed Brand into the office. Bakker sat behind an enormous desk. Hell, Brand thought, the room was bigger than the entire hotel suite Brand was currently residing at in Ottawa.

Bakker rose acknowledging his guest as Brand crossed the office floor toward the desk.

"I'm glad you could make it," Bakker greeted him. "Can I offer you a drink?" he asked.

The hour was still early, but Brand accepted, a drink would be appropriate.

"Sure," he answered, "Rye and Pepsi if you have."

The old businessman turned in his chair and gestured at a man standing beside a bar in the corner of the office. The two men waited until Brand had his drink served.

Bakker picked up a glass on his desk and raised it in a toast.

"To a job well done," he toasted Brand. Brand's face clouded in confusion. Whatever the old man was talking about, Brand had no idea. Then Bakker, noting the confused look, explained what he implied with his toast.

"I have heard that you were very busy Stateside," Nelson Bakker replied. He told Brand that he was aware of the terrorist plot Brand helped the American's end.

"Let me tell you a bit about the group that was behind the whole conspiracy. For starters, as I am sure you have figured out, I once counted myself among the crusaders." Bakker delved into the background and the long history that surrounded the Christian resurgence.

"Unfortunately, Mr. Coldstream, you dealt quite a blow to our or rather, their plans. I have come to realize the pain and death we have caused with our crusade so consider my talking to you as my repentance, my last shot at redemption." Bakker's speech started to slur as he talked. Brand watched as the man's eyelids started drooping.

"Are you alright?" Brand asked.

"Yes. I'm fine, thank you. The doctors have diagnosed an inoperable tumour on my brain. My time on earth is very short," the confided. He reached for his glass and took a drink. Brand waited patiently for the reason of this meeting.

Bakker closed his eyes for a minute. His breathing was shallow. Brand watched the man curiously. Then the old businessman began talking again. He introduced Brand to the man standing by the bar. Kirk Remmings, remember that name Bakker said.

"One day Mr. Remmings may prove to be an invaluable asset to you."

Finally, Bakker got around for the reason he wanted to meet with Brand.

"I hope that the moniker 'the Boogieman' holds true for you," he said as he stared at Brand. "The crusade is run by a group of very affluent and individuals, men who will not take kindly to your interference, Mr. Coldstream. You may have disrupted their plans, but they will regroup. You certainly have caught their attention with your intrusion of their fight against the Muslims. But, I am afraid though that all you have accomplished is to piss these men off and these are not men who will accept that. I feel obligated to warn you. I believe they will be coming after you with all the power they command."

Nelson Bakker raised his glass to his lips. "After your visit to my house I realized the error of my ways, these men will not. You have to understand that in their minds they still walk the righteous road. I could give you their names, but that won't do you much good. Neither you or the government will be able to prove any of the charges against them."

Nelson Bakker wrote on a piece of paper and slid the paper across his desk toward Brand. "I will not furnish you with anymore more information than this; I still count the Crusaders as my brethren even if I have changed my views." Bakker took another sip from his glass, "Once I am gone, you may need someone for your corner when they come after you. Mr. Remmings has been instructed to provide help in any way he can. This favour is my way of thanking you for opening my eyes and steering me back from evil." Bakker started to cough. He slumped in his chair. From behind weary eyes, the old man bid Brand farewell. Bakker released a rattling breath and collapsed onto his desk.

Brand reached to help the old man glancing toward Bakker's assistant, "What's the matter with him?" he asked. "Call a doctor."

Kirk Remmings stopped him.

"This is the way he wanted to leave this earth," Remmings told Brand. Brand threw an inquisitive look at the man.

"Poison, in his glass," Bakker's assistant said by way of explanation, "He mixed poison with his scotch. He knew the brain tumour was about to take him. His doctors told him he only had days, maybe a week remaining so he wanted to come clean and clear his conscious. He decided to fight the devil on his terms."

Chapter 60

August Jackson remained secluded in his mansion since the failed attack at the ball stadium in Chicago. With agony, he watched while the Cabal's carefully laid plans crumbled. The news stations kept rebroadcasting the attack and then when his soldiers were later killed or arrested, the news ran with the stories.

The biggest blow against the crusade came when he watched Michael Johnson carried out of a cabin in Minnesota surrounded by police.

In his mind, he kept replaying the demise of the Cabal's years of meticulous planning. As he fixated on the ruined crusade, he started having very un-Christian thoughts. Especially about the two Canadian interlopers the news now referred to as heroes. As he kept vigil behind his desk he stared blankly at the streaming news broadcasts he felt his anger building.

In a fit of rage, he snatched his phone off his desk and dialed the number for one of his contacts in Washington.

"I want those two Canadians to pay with their lives." He uttered when the call connected.

"I will make certain of it." The United States Attorney General replied.

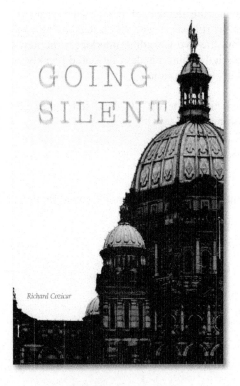

Richard Cozicar

Ice Racer Trilogy

Part One

Global warming is a thing of the past. Long past. In the 23rd century the remaining inhabitants of earth exist beneath the ice covered surface of the planet. Small groups who have survived the freezing of the planet live in ice domed cities far below the treacherous surface with no contact from the outside world.

Mike Ryan, a young Ice Racer, is one of the very few brave enough to venture to the surface in search of life sustaining supplies for his home, the city of New Capital.

Separated from the crew of his ice sled and fighting against certain death on the planet surface he falls into a world he would never have imagined existed and becomes trapped in a city ruled by Climate Prophets who will do anything to keep their city secret.

EBook Coming Soon

Sneak Preview

The Wolves of Satan

A Brand Coldstream Novel

On a wet summer night Brand and his colleagues are idling their time between fly tying and beers. A burst of gunfire interrupts their evening sending one friend to the hospital and the other to the morgue.

The police suspect a drug connection with Brand on their radar. In a search for the gunmen responsible for his friend's shootings, Brand gets caught up in the middle of a turf war between rival biker gangs.

Turning to a long time acquaintance for help, Brand must avoid both the police and the bikers in his quest for answers. The streets of Calgary turn into a battle zone as rival groups ramp up their fight for control of the drug trade.

With his friend's daughter under his protection, his world spins out of control as he battles against a rising drug cartel and betrayal.

Coming fall of 2016

Richard Cozicar

The Ice Racer Part 2:

The Climate Wars

Before the planet froze, before Mother Earth fought back, came the Climate Wars.

A University dropout angered by his oil rich father finds a means to get even with his parents on the steps of city hall. The chance meeting at an environmental protest sets him on the path to become the biggest threat to the industrial world.

From dropout to Prophet, Lucas Pensworth 3rd turns his spite against his father to declare war on a world faltering between fossil fuels and the environment. The consequences are more than the people of earth are prepared for.

An online exclusive featuring a new chapter every week at Richardcozicar.com/blog.

Silent Crusade

Richard Cozicar

Silent Crusade

CPSIA information can be obtained
at www.ICGtesting.com
Printed in the USA
LVOW04*0348170516
488567LV00001B/1/P

9 780995 094628